DEMANDING MOB BOSS

by Lucy Monroe

1st Printing September 2023

COPYRIGHT © 2023 LUCY MONROE

ALL RIGHTS RESERVED

DEMANDING MOB BOSS

LUCY MONROE

DEDICATION

F or my grandsons Ozzi & Archie. You bring so much joy into our family and I am so proud of both of you for being who you are and living the life you are meant to live. Elliott is for you.

A NOTE FROM LUCY

*D*ear Reader,

Neurodiversity is just that. Diverse. And it is my privilege, as someone who is neurodiverse herself, to share such characters with my readers.

If you have Autism Spectrum Disorder, you already know this, but for readers who do not:

1. Not everyone with ASD wants, or is able to get, a diagnosis.

2. ASD manifests differently in each person's life.

Please do not presume that because you have read a book, or watched a show, or a documentary, or even know someone who has ASD, that you know what that looks like for everyone.

Like many of you (whether you are aware, or not) I have several people in my life with ASD and they are all unique. Each of them has their own way of relating to the world and the other people in it.

Like Anna, who wormed her way into my heart from the moment I "met" her in my brain. I saw her first and her reaction to Cian before I even knew his name, or that he was a mob boss.

Cian is a self-admitted sociopath. Which can present at times as overly aggressive and angry, or an emotionless disregard for the feelings and rights of others. We never see ourselves entirely as we are, and this demanding mob boss is no exception.

I hope you'll give them both a chance to find their way into your hearts too.

Hugs and happy reading!

Lucy

IRISH MOB HIERARCHY*

Chicago Irish Mob

Irish families engaged in organized crime in this book are Doyle & Byrne, Murphy & Walsh.

Doyle & Byrne mob

Boss

Cian Doyle

Underboss

Lachlan Farrar

Captain

Ronan Byrne

Specialists

Enforcers

Connor Doyle

(Cian's Cousin)

Arlo, Eoin, Tommy, Gulliver, Sully, Finn, & Malone

Sniper

Oscar (aka Scáth)

GREEK MAFIA HIERARCHY*

Godfather of the Night
Leandros Drakos
(Considered the top boss for the Midwest. Oversees a broad territory that includes several Greek mafia families in the Midwest United States and central Canada.)
2nd in Command
Xander Christakos
Chicago Greek Mafia*
Boss
Stavros
(Head of Greek mafia family in Doyle Byrne territory.)
Jeweler
Yiorgos
*While the mob/mafia (criminal families) found in this book are loosely based on known hierarchies within Irish mob & Greek mafia organizations, they are fictional. They do not represent any actual mob/mafia family. Nor are their hierarchies meant to be an exact replica, but rather inspired by research.

CHAPTER 1

ANNA

I really need this job. Only I don't know how long I can sit here. There's so much movement, so much noise.

Stay calm. You can breathe. Inhale. Exhale.

One, two, look at my shoe.

My feet are aligned under my chair, no scuffs on my leather flats. Should I have worn heels? I have a pair, but they feel unsteady.

Three, four, find the door.

It took nine steps to come into the room and meet the HR person who checked me in. It was six more to reach the chair where I sit. If I went directly from the chair to the door, that would be twelve steps, I think.

Five, six, click, click, clicks.

I tap my thumbnail and my middle fingernail together three times, the familiar sound soothing me.

Seven, eight, release the weight.

Breath out slowly. One. Two. Three. Four. Five. Six. My lungs are empty. I do not breathe in or out for seven and eight.

Nine, ten, inhale the Zen.

I inhale counting to ten.

Now start again.

The rhyme is something I made up with my mom and it still gives me comfort when my anxiety spikes.

Mrs. Bantry is in the doorway.

She gives us all that big fake smile. But her eyes...they are not friendly. They're smug. She will decide which one of us gets the job, and she likes knowing that. She looks around at all of us, like she's measuring our worth.

The other people in the room sit up straight and smile at her, hoping they will be the next one called in. The longer it takes for her to call our names, the more chance the position will be filled before she gets to us. It's simple math.

Her gaze skips right over the two men in the room, like it has each time she's come out of her office. I do not know why. Men can be receptionists as easily as women. I do not understand most people's prejudices. They confuse me because they make no sense to me.

She points at a brunette sitting across the room from me. The woman grips her purse tightly but smiles brightly and follows Mrs. Bantry into the office. The door closes behind them. The noise and the movement start all over again, only worse, because she has been in here. People talk and speculate. They shift and adjust their clothing.

I want to leave. I can't. Ini is relying on me to pay my half of the rent and everything else. I only have two friends. Her and Mrs. Hart. I met Ini in elementary school right after I moved in with my aunt and uncle. Ini had just been placed with a new foster family.

When she found out my parents were dead like hers, she said we would be best friends. And we have been, ever since.

I can't let Ini down. Not again.

Keeping a job is as hard for me as getting one. After a certain point, they all become too much. Too many sounds. Too many people. Things get too bright. Too chaotic. I say my rhyme so often, I lose track of what I'm supposed to be doing on the job itself. Either I leave and can't go back, or I get fired. It's inevitable, but I have to work.

I force myself into stillness, not even letting myself say my rhyme again. Though I cannot control the chaos around me, I try to control the anxiety within.

Suddenly, everyone goes quiet. No one even moves. The stillness is delicious. I look up and I see a man standing in the doorway to the hall. He's big. Well over six feet tall. His shoulders are broad; power exudes from him. *He* caused the stillness.

I want to thank him.

The door to Mrs. Bantry's office opens again. The broad smile and smug expression fall off her face when she sees the man. Shock widens her eyes. Her mouth opens, but I count five seconds before she speaks.

Five seconds of peace.

"Mr. Doyle, I did not expect you today. Can I do something for you?" She sounds obsequious.

He does not look at her. There is an air about him, like he is taking everything in with his blue gaze, assessing, cataloguing.

No one looks at him. They don't want his attention to land on them. I wonder why. We are all here to apply for a receptionist position in the main lobby for Doyle Construction.

I don't know what his role in the company is, but he must be either one of the owners or related to them. All morning, everyone in this room has done their best to catch Mrs. Bantry's eye. Yet no one wants to catch his.

He fascinates me. The effect he has on the room is amazing. I revel in the calm.

His eyes land on me. Although I cannot tell him thank you because he probably would not understand why, I smile for the first time this morning.

Something flashes in his eyes. "Who are you?"

"She's nobody. She is just here to apply for the job downstairs." Mrs. Bantry dismisses me with a wave of her hand.

I'll take self-important petty tyrants for five hundred, Alex.

Mr. Doyle's eyes do not leave mine. "I was not talking to you."

Mrs. Bantry gasps. "I am sorry Mr. Doyle. I did not mean to overstep."

I wonder if he can tell she is lying like I can. I do not have to see her to know. I can hear the insincerity in her voice.

"My name is Anna Lake," I tell him.

"You want to be our receptionist?"

I do not know how to answer. It feels wrong to lie to him. "I need the job."

He nods, like he hears the subtext of my words when almost no one else ever does. "I need someone to work with my personal assistant, doing the grunt work."

I am not sure what he wants me to say. I like his bluntness. He does not try to dress up the job. Not like Mrs. Bantry, who gave us all a peptalk this morning about how being a receptionist here is a great opportunity, with potential to go far.

I did not believe her. I wonder if anyone else did.

"Oh, so that's why you were down here. I'll get right on that for you Mr. Doyle," Mrs. Bantry gushes.

Mr. Doyle looks over his shoulder at someone behind him. "She is what we have in charge of our human resources?"

"Apparently." I can't see the speaker, but there is an Irish lilt to his voice.

"Tell Uncle Jimmy to get someone else. She annoys me." Though Mr. Doyle's name is Irish, his accent is pure Chicago.

Mrs. Bantry makes a squawking noise and I look at her. She's furious, her mouth set in a flat line, the fake smile completely gone. "You can't just fire me."

"You don't think so?" There is a quality to Mr. Doyle's voice, like he's daring her to disagree with him.

Mrs. Bantry flinches and remains silent.

CIAN

What the fuck is happening? I feel like I took a shot to the chest with my vest on.

It aches. Looking at the blonde beauty with the gorgeous tits sitting so primly in that boring office chair is doing something to me.

I fucking want her.

My cock is surging like she dropped to her knees and offered that pretty mouth. Violet eyes trap my gaze and I cannot look away.

I felt something like this. Once. A long time ago. But it wasn't this strong.

My world exists in shades of grey. Right now, a kaleidoscope of colors surrounds Anna Lake like a damn aura. I don't believe in that shit.

But I can't look away from her. From the color. From the *feelings* bombarding my insides. Feelings I would have told you ten minutes ago I don't have the capacity to experience.

It is only my iron control that stops me grabbing the little beauty, throwing her over my shoulder and carrying her up to my penthouse. How much Lachlan will bitch if I kidnap a woman in front of witnesses from our own HR department helps me keep my urges under control too.

But I want to take her and keep her until I figure whatever this is out.

I can see myself doing it. Picking her up. Ignoring her shocked scream. Holding her kicking legs so she doesn't fall off my shoulder. My muscles bunch with anticipation.

Anna blinks. Innocence shining out at me from her eyes. She looks at me like she's happy I'm here.

People are rarely happy to see me.

My sister sure as hell isn't. Shea is glaring.

But this sweet little morsel watches me like I'm all that and a new, fully loaded gun.

Women play their roles in my life. Mother. Sisters. Soldiers. Employees. I do not have lovers. I do not date.

I don't do relationships. Hell, I don't do sleepovers.

I do not feel whatever it is that makes men want to keep women in their bed. Once I get my rocks off, I'm done. I prefer getting blown because there are fewer complications. Less talking that way too.

But the thought of never seeing Anna Lake again fills me with a killing rage. It does not matter that we haven't spoken more than a dozen words. Or that we met only moments ago.

An atavistic certainty that this woman is mine settles low in my gut. I'm about to complicate the hell out of her life. She caught the attention of the apex predator and I always take down my prey.

I almost feel sorry for the sweet thing, but that's too much like regret. An emotion I don't experience.

ANNA

I can't look away from Mr. Doyle. I *enjoy* looking at him. He is handsome and I like the red gold of his hair. It's so different from my boring blonde.

There's an odd expression in his blue eyes though. Like he's hungry and I'm his next meal. I don't always read emotions right in other people, so I'm sure I'm wrong.

But if I am right? I don't mind. And that is really strange because I don't like being noticed. I don't like being the center of attention either, but I want this man's attention.

I want it a lot.

"Anna, you have been here all morning?" he asks me.

I force a single word past my suddenly tight throat. "Yes."

"Who do you think would make a good receptionist?"

Taking his question seriously, I consider everything I have seen and heard this morning.

Then I point to an older woman, who has been here since 7:30 AM just like me. "Her."

"Why?" He asked me.

Do I have enough words right now to explain? I've been psyching myself up for the interview, but if I use my words up with him, I won't have any left for that. I need this job, but I *have to* answer Mr. Doyle. Even if there are no words left to talk to Mrs. Bantry.

Only Mrs. Bantry won't be interviewing anyone else, will she?

Relieved that I can use up my words without worrying about later, I say, "She's kind. She answers questions but does not pretend to know more than she does."

I haven't spoken to the woman, but I've observed every interaction since I arrived. She looks at me now with surprise and gratitude. I do not know why. I am only speaking the truth. I have no influence on who will get hired. I am simply answering a question.

Mr. Doyle looks at the woman and asks, "Do you want the job?"

"Yes, very much."

He looks back over his shoulder again and says, "Tell Uncle Jimmy to get her on-boarded and the other one out of my building."

His focus turns to me, and it is absolute. Like there is no one else in the room. I wish I could do that. Only, when I'm looking at him, I can. It's odd.

"Anna, you come with me." He shifts his gaze to someone else and I miss the intensity, the ability to block out the rest of the room that locking our eyes gave me.

"Shea, go up to Uncle Jimmy's office. If you want to work for the company this badly, he'll find you something to do."

"I don't want a *found* job," says a woman who looks a little younger than my twenty years. "I want to get a job and live my own life."

Mr. Doyle moves out of the doorway. Toward me. My heart does this funny skip thing in my chest.

He says, "Lachlan."

The other man steps around Mr. Doyle and into the room. He is a couple of inches shorter than his boss, though he is also over six feet tall. His hair is brown though, not nearly as pretty as the reddish gold of Mr. Doyle's and the woman he called Shea. Are they related?

Mr. Farrar goes straight to Shea and takes her by the arm. "Come on, Trouble. Jimmy is expecting you and you need to call your mammy to let her know you aren't dead in a ditch."

"As if, with all you goons looking over my shoulder." She stands, yanks her arm from Mr. Farrar's hold and flounces out of the room. Smirking, he follows her.

Mr. Doyle puts his hand out to me. "Come."

Usually, I avoid touching other people, but I place my hand in his without hesitating. Weird. His big fingers curl around mine, warm and safe.

This man, who can bring stillness, makes me feel safe. And he's going to be my boss. I have a job! Ini is going to be so happy.

With Mr. Doyle as my boss, this job might even last longer than the others.

CIAN

"What the hell is going on?" Lachlan takes a drink of his whiskey, his eyes on me and not the raised dais with three of our best dancers on the poles.

"We're checking on the clubs like we do every week." The Doyle clan owns three clubs in Chicago. Two are strip clubs and one is a nightclub.

Just like the construction business, clubs, because they do a lot of cash business, are a great way to launder money. This one is my favorite. There is always a dancer or staff member eager to suck off the boss. They think it will earn them special privileges. It won't.

But I'm not interested in getting my rocks off tonight and I'm paying no more attention to the dancers than Lachlan is.

"We weren't at HR this morning to hire an assistant for Connor." Lachlan frowns at me, like he expects me to say something.

But he already knows why we were there. To track down my errant sister. I'm not sure how to handle Shea. She's unpredictable and emotional. Both things I am not. I'm not known for my tolerance in dealing with those traits either. Even in my family. But because Shea is my youngest sister, I try with her. Tolerance doesn't make it any easier to understand her.

"Why the hell was Shea applying for that job?" I ask Lachlan.

He's a stone-cold killer, just like me, but he has a wider range of emotions.

"She said she wanted to take the summer to explore her options before starting at DePaul in the fall. Maybe getting a job is part of that."

"She can't work in reception. It's not safe." We have too many enemies for her to be that exposed.

"You heard her as well as I did." Lachlan's gaze wanders to the dancers. He sees something he likes and watches in silence for several seconds before turning to me, his gaze intent. "She wants to forge her own path."

"She can forge it working for Uncle Jimmy."

Lachlan shrugs. His attention moves back to the middle dancer. She's tall with big tits, brown eyes, and long brown hair she uses to tease the customers.

I turn away and back to my drink. Big tits still do it for me, but I've got a new preference for tiny blondes with pretty, heart shaped faces.

"Why did you hire an assistant for your assistant?" Lachlan asks. "The boy can do his job."

"Connor bitches about doing the mundane shit. So, I got him someone to do it for him."

"He's been bitching since he started working for you a year ago. Why now?"

What he means is why did I hire Anna Lake. "I like Anna's smile." I like her name too. Just saying it settles something inside me.

Lachlan chokes on his whiskey. "Did you just say you like her smile? Since when do you like anything about a woman except how tight her pussy is?"

"You're the one who likes to audition pussy." When I'm looking to blow a load, I want a woman on her knees in front of me. When her mouth is busy, she can't talk.

Most people talking annoys the shit out of me.

Right now, Lachlan is no exception.

"So, you made up a job for her in your office because you like her smile."

"It's real." Anna's smile is even more genuine than the job. I probably wouldn't have given into my cousin's moaning about how much time he wastes filing and other shit like that. "There's no fear in her eyes when she looks at me."

I like looking at her, whether she is smiling or scrunching her nose in that cute way she has when she's trying to figure something out. She spent a lot of time today trying to figure out the office machines, the computer and how our filing system works.

"That will change once she finds out who you are. With her working in your office that's going to happen sooner than later, or did you forget that you run both the mob business and the construction company from there?"

"Uncle Jimmy runs the construction side of the business." His office is on the same floor as mine, and his title is project supervisor, but he makes all the major decisions for that side of our business. Those in Chicago who need to know, do.

"My point exactly. She's in your office, Cian, helping Connor. She's an outsider."

I say the one thing I know to be true, but that she has no clue about yet. "She's mine."

"Bloody fecking hell."

CHAPTER 2

ANNA

I like working for Cian Doyle, though I guess, technically, I work for his personal assistant, Connor.

The job pays more than the receptionist position would have. Which is nice. There are only a handful of people I see most days. Mr. Doyle, who comes out of his office three or four times a day to say something to Connor. He always greets me and asks how I'm doing. It's nice. He told me to call him Cian. I do, but it makes me blush every time I say his name. It's a nice name though.

I see Connor, of course, who I have learned is one of Cian's cousins, Jimmy Doyle, who seems to be in charge of all the construction projects and I think is Connor's dad, and Lachlan Farrar. I'm not sure what Mr. Farrar does, but he's almost always with our boss. He doesn't ask me to call him Lachlan.

It turns out that Cian is the CEO of the entire conglomerate, of which Doyle Construction is only one business. He seems young to be in charge of such a big company, but he's got the boss vibe down. It's kind of thrilling. Everyone, even Jimmy, who is old enough to be his dad, defers to him.

And best of all, whenever Cian is in the room, he brings tranquility with him. Which makes this the best job I've ever had. When his attention is on me, *everything* inside me quiets. It's amazing.

Ini is happy for me, and I can tell she's relieved because it looks like I'll stick with this job. We're both thankful we can afford groceries *and* rent now. We haven't had to get a free meal at a shelter since I got my first paycheck.

CIAN

I come into the office early, before anyone else. I have something I need to do. Having Anna working here is good, but I need to see more of her.

It's an itch in my brain that I can't scratch without laying eyes on her. And it's only getting worse as the days go by. I made up an excuse to go into Connor's office six times yesterday. I can't afford this kind of distraction. So, I'm installing a couple of cameras in my cousin's office. They are tiny and I know my shit. No one else is going to notice them.

It takes me about fifteen minutes, all told. When I'm done the feeling of wrongness that has been nagging at me since she left to go home yesterday is silenced. For now.

I think I'm going to have to put a couple of cameras in her apartment too. I'll need to find out her roommate's work schedule, but once I do, picking the lock on their door and getting the cameras in place will be easy. It's the kind of stuff I've been doing since I was a boy, training under my dad to take over the Doyle clan one day.

Maybe I can get it done today. That would be good.

ANNA

Cian has a meeting with a bunch of men in his office. They've been arriving for the past thirty minutes. Connor doesn't introduce any of them and I don't mind. I don't like meeting new people and these men are all like Mr. Farrar, with an air of repressed violence around them. I keep my head down and focus on my work, so no one talks to me.

"Aren't you a sight for sore eyes," someone says from in front of my desk.

I force myself to look up. The man standing there is almost as tall as Cian, but he's not as broad. His hair is brown, and his eyes are dark too. He's wearing an expensive suit and his smile makes me think of a shark.

I don't say anything, waiting to see what he wants.

He comes around and leans against the side of my desk. "When did you start working for Cian?"

Pushing my chair back, I stand up. "I need to do some filing." He's in my personal space and I don't want him there.

"Murphy," Cian barks from the open door to his office. "Get your ass in here."

"Give me a minute, I want to get to know this sweet little employee of yours a little better." He sounds like he expects Cian to go back into his office.

My muscles tense and I look at my boss, hoping the man called Murphy is wrong.

Cian moves with the stealth and the speed of a panther across the office and grabs Mr. Murphy. "Get the fuck away from her."

He tosses the other man like he weighs nothing. Mr. Murphy lands against the wall by Cian's office door with a thud. I'm sure this show of physical dominance should upset me. Ini wouldn't like it. But I find it way less stressful than having Mr. Murphy in my personal space.

He stumbles, but he stays upright. "It's like that, is it?"

"My employees, like my clan, are off limits. You want to talk to one of them, you fucking show respect and ask."

Mr. Murphy doesn't seem offended. He smiles and this time, he seems genuinely amused. "Hey, Cian, I want to ask your receptionist here out. That okay by you?"

I don't give my boss a chance to answer. "I'm not a receptionist and I'm not interested," I say, feeling like my heart is going to beat out of my chest.

Cian nods to me then glares at Mr. Murphy. "You heard her. Stop pestering my employee, and get into the meeting. We're done waiting on you."

The way he says *my employee* sends a frisson of confusing delight through me. He's just a really possessive guy. I get that, but it sounds personal. In my heart of hearts, where I don't let anyone see, I wish it *was* personal.

Mr. Murphy winks at me. "Maybe another time."

The air around Cian charges with menace.

"All right, all right, I'm going." Mr. Murphy puts his hands up like he's surrendering, but nothing else about him gives the impression he's giving in.

I don't want to be here when the men come out of Cian's office. Maybe I can time my lunch hour to coincide with the end of the meeting.

Though I don't know how I'm supposed to know when that will be. Connor is attending the meeting as well. The phone on my desk rings and I know I have to answer it since Connor forwarded calls to my line while he's in the meeting.

"Doyle & Byrne," I answer.

So far, I haven't met any Byrnes but the parent company must have been started by one, along with one of Cian's ancestors.

"It's Jimmy, lass. I could use some help with my filing. Will you come to my office?"

I don't know what to do. I want to be out of here when the meeting ends, but I don't want to do something that will upset Connor or our boss.

"Cian approved it," Jimmy adds.

I let out the breath I am holding, relief making me sag into my desk. "I'll be right there."

CIAN

I text Uncle Jimmy and tell him to get Anna into his office and keep her there until I give the all-clear. Fucking Quinn Murphy. He's distant family. My mom was a Murphy before she married a Doyle, but I'll end him if he doesn't leave my Anna alone.

Thinking he can ask her out. She said she wasn't interested though. My Anna doesn't say much, but she said that, didn't she?

Once I know she's safe in my uncle's office, I get down to business. We've got a gang trying to move in on our territory to sell their low-quality shit that's put more than one user into the hospital already. Since the

Kicks Bandidos are doing the same thing in the Murphy and Walsh clans' territories too, it's a matter for all of us.

We argue over how to handle it for a while, until I'm sick of the bickering back and forth. Éamon Walsh doesn't like that both the Murphy and Doyle clans are now headed up by men young enough to be his sons. He thinks his age makes him the de facto big boss. Neither Quinn nor I agree.

"Enough," I say, cutting off a shouting match between him and Quinn. "Walsh, if you want to negotiate with the fucking Kicks Bandidos for the right to deal in your territory, I'm not going to stop you."

I don't say I can't stop him, because we both know that if I chose to become his enemy rather than his ally, I would crush him. My clan is three times the size of his. But we've got family ties through the Byrnes with the Walshes. That's how we became allies seventy-five years ago.

"We're kicking them out of Doyle territory," I bark. "I'm not letting that cut-rate shit bring the heat down on us."

"Same," Quinn says.

Most days I appreciate his succinct use of words. His clan is almost the same size as the Doyles and he's a good ally. But today, I want to cut out his tongue for talking to Anna. Maybe cut off his hands so he won't even think about trying to touch her.

"Do you want to coordinate attacks?" Lachlan asks him when I just sit and stare at the man as I picture his demise in my mind.

"I think it would be more effective," his underboss replies to Lachlan. "Right Quinn?"

Quinn is busy staring back at me. There's no expression on his face. Some might find that intimidating. I don't. I will fucking cut him and bathe in his blood if he comes near Anna again. We stare at each other in silence until the other men in the room start to move restlessly, but no one speaks.

Finally, Quinn asks, "That what you want, Cian?"

"So long as you remember what's yours and what's mine," I say.

He jerks his head in agreement. "I'll let Paddy work out the details with Lachlan."

We both trust our men so I have no problem with that.

~ ~ ~

After the meeting I text Jimmy.

Me: **Send Anna back**.

Jimmy: **She just left for lunch with Shea**.

I pull up the app that monitors my mother and sisters' phone trackers and see that Shea and Anna are at a Greek deli a couple of blocks from our offices. "Let's get some Greek food," I say to Lachlan.

"Sounds good. I thought you were going to make me work through lunch figuring out these logistics with the Murphys."

"You can meet with Paddy away from the offices later today."

"Away from Anna you mean."

I don't reply.

~ ~ ~

The deli is crowded. It usually is, which is what makes it such a good front for the Greek mafia's less than legal endeavors. They've been our allies sharing territory for three generations. They cover smuggling, illegal prescription drug sales, and weapons. We have the protection racket, illegal drugs and gambling. We both hire our soldiers out for hits and do our own money laundering. Anything not covered in our blood oath agreement is fair game for both families.

Stavros, head of his family, comes rushing up to us, his usually affable manner a front for a total sociopath. I relate. Except for the affability part.

I let Lachlan greet him while I scan the tables for Anna and Shea. They're sitting in a booth against the back wall. Heading toward them, I notice that Anna looks tense. She's smiling at Shea, but it's not her usual smile. It's forced. Her hands are in her lap, her fingers twisting together.

A couple of jerks wearing identical button ups and chinos are standing beside their table. They're saying something and Shea is laughing, nodding. Anna looks like she wants to bolt.

CHAPTER 3

ANNA

Working with Shea this morning was fun, so I forced myself to agree to go to lunch with her. I usually eat a sandwich in the copy room where it's quiet. But I didn't know if it was safe to go back to Cian's office suite and I was hungry. Now, I'm wishing I'd gotten a bag of chips from the vending machine and found a corner to hole up in until after lunch.

There are so many people here. It's noisy and there are too many competing smells. The food, perfume, body odor...we're too close to the bathrooms.

I'm trying to carry on a conversation with Shea, but all I want to do is jump up and leave.

One, two, look at your shoe.

I can't see my shoes under the table. Unable to continue the rhyme, I start tapping my nails together. Click, click, click... How many steps to the front door? Too many bodies to navigate. Three people touched me on the way to the booth. I want to go. Click, click, click...

"Is anyone joining you?" a man's voice asks.

I look to my left. There are two men standing by the booth. One of them is blocking my exit. It makes me nervous. Okay, I'm already agitated, but not having an escape route makes it so much worse.

Shea is laughing and chatting with the men.

"Can we share your table?" the man closest to Shea asks. "It's crowded in here."

I want to blurt out, "No," but I can't get my voice to work.

"Sure," Shea says with a big smile. "It's the only socially responsible thing to do."

She slides closer to the wall, making room for one of the men to join her. Doesn't she know how dangerous that is? Once he sits down, he'll have her trapped and her only way out will be under the table. I'm desperate to get out of here now, but I can't leave her. I can only hope these men are as harmless as they are trying to appear. I'm not going to sit by the wall though.

I scoot toward the man who is blocking my way and hope he'll take the hint and move. He doesn't.

"Excuse me," I force words from my tight throat.

"Don't you want me to sit by you, sweetheart?"

"No, she fucking doesn't."

My head jerks up and I look into furious blue eyes. They scan over me as if checking to see if I'm alright before they're turned on the now frowning man.

"Leave." Cian's tone is harsh, his expression deadly.

I feel a jolt in my core. He's so dominant. Powerful.

"For cripe's sake, Cian. Go away. We're having lunch."

"Where is Sully?" Cian demands.

Shea rolls her eyes. "He doesn't follow me to work."

Who is Sully?

The man next to Shea turns toward her and says, "Is this guy an ex? You want me to get rid of him?"

Shea's eyes widen and she sends Cian a pleading look. "He didn't mean anything."

The guy sees the look and makes his own interpretation. He puts a hand on Shea's shoulder and turns and glares up at Cian. "Look buddy, whoever you are, the lady isn't interested."

"I'm not your buddy and if you don't take your hand off my sister, I'll break every finger before I knock you out and leave you in the alley for the rats to find."

The man's eyes widen and then narrow, his chin juts out. "Your threats don't scare me."

"Are you an idiot?" Shea demands. "Get out while the getting is good." She's pushing against the guy, fear washing over her face. "Cian, let him go. We were just talking."

She wasn't worried about letting a stranger sit beside her, but she's scared of what her brother will do?

Cian isn't holding onto the man. He's not even blocking his exit from the booth. I don't understand what has his sister so worried. She's showing all the anxiety I was feeling moments ago. Only now that Cian is here, my heart is beating slower and it's easier to breathe.

I could start my rhyme over again and look at his shoe instead of mine, but I don't need to. I already feel a lot calmer.

"I'm not afraid of your brother." The man is lying and his still jutting chin is false bravado. I can smell the sweat of his fear and see the other telltale signs of anxiety I am so intimately familiar with.

"You should be." Mr. Farrar is now standing to the left and behind Cian. He's looking at the man sitting beside Shea like he wants to punch him.

"What the fuck, dude? Come on Devon, there's an empty table over there. Let's take it." The man near me finally moves, stepping back a couple of paces.

I look up at Cian, letting his blue gaze further calm me amidst all the chaos of this crowded restaurant. "Would you like to join us?"

Shea makes a disbelieving sound. Mr. Farrar barks out a laugh, but Cian nods.

And I smile.

The deadly fury in Cian's blue gaze disappears. I scoot toward the wall, hoping he'll sit beside me and not his sister.

He does.

"I need that seat, mate." Mr. Farrar grabs the man still stubbornly sitting next to Shea and yanks him from the booth, tossing him away.

I hear a thump and cursing, but I ignore it.

Cian's hand is in my lap untwisting my fingers. "You're all right."

He's not asking, he's telling me. And I believe him. His big fingers brush against my thigh and my anxiety is pushed out completely by sexual awareness. I hope he doesn't notice.

Unlike almost everyone else, his body being so close to mine does not agitate me.

Mr. Farrar is now sitting beside Shea. He's looking at me like a bug under a microscope. It's weird but not stressful.

Shea stares at me, then at her brother, like she's trying to figure something out. "I thought you were going to kill him."

Cian's arm brushes mine when he shrugs. "I was thinking about it."

"But you didn't even break his hand," Mr. Farrar says, like that's some kind of feat and a surprising one.

Shea turns to glare at Mr. Farrar. "You didn't have to manhandle him like that. You're such a bully."

"He should have left when your brother told him to."

"Not everyone in this town does what my brother says."

"Those who don't learn to regret their mistake." Mr. Farrar grins and rubs his belly. "What did you order? I'm starving."

"I'm not sharing my food with you."

"Will you share your food with me, Anna?" Cian asks.

I nod.

"She only ordered a side salad," Shea says. "I was going to give her half of my gyro."

I give the younger woman a grateful look. "Thank you." Even if Mr. Farrar will be eating that now, it was a nice thought. "You can eat my salad," I tell Cian. "I have a sandwich in my desk back at the office."

"It must be peanut butter and jelly if you leave it in your desk drawer and not the fridge," Shea says.

I shrug. That's all I can afford for lunches. Ini and I can buy groceries, but we have to be frugal, especially since we share our dinner with Mrs. Hart every night. She gets her Meals On Wheels at lunchtime and has a piece of toast for breakfast. She needs to eat more, but she won't take anything from us except dinner, and only when we eat together.

Even after everything she's done for us.

Ini used to volunteer with Meals On Wheels. One of her foster moms was really into acts of service and that's how she met Mrs. Hart.

When we both had to leave our homes at eighteen, Ini because she aged out of foster care and me because my family didn't want me anymore, Mrs. Hart let us stay with her until we got our own one-bedroom two stories up. We took turns sleeping on the sofa and the floor.

She said she liked having the company. I only know I felt safer on her floor than I had in my big bedroom at my aunt and uncle's place. It took me and Ini longer to find a place than it would have otherwise because we didn't want to move out of Mrs. Hart's building.

Cian jerks his head at Mr. Farrar, bringing me out of my reverie. The other man jumps up and heads toward the counter where we ordered our food.

"What are you doing here?" Shea demands of Cian. "Are you tracking me again?"

"You assume I ever stopped."

"That's such an invasion of privacy."

"Your safety is my responsibility."

"You're a Neanderthal."

Cian shrugs. He's not offended, which shows that he knows more than most people do about the Neanderthals. They're usually depicted as lacking in human intelligence, without understanding of social norms. Only modern archaeologists say that picture isn't the right one.

People often look at those they don't understand through a lens clouded by their own biases.

"Seriously." Shea looks appealingly at me. "I hope your family doesn't smother you like mine does me, Anna. It's the pits."

"I don't have any family." None that want to know me anyway. My aunt and uncle took me in after my parents died when I was ten. When I turned 18, they told me I was an adult, and their duty was done.

Shea's face contorts with sympathy. "I'm sorry." Then she frowns fero-
ciously at her brother. "But sometimes I wish I was an only child."

"It's good to have people watching out for you," I tell her.

Mr. Farrar returns with two trays laden with food. There are four gyros,
two baskets of round fries that look delicious and four bottles of water. "I
cancelled your order. There's a lot of veg on the gyro so I didn't think you'd
want the salad, Anna, but I can grab one for you if you do."

I shake my head. "Oh, no, thank you. I..." I can't afford to pay for a gyro
though.

"My treat," Mr. Farrar says, like he's reading my mind. "A thank you for
sharing your table."

Cian makes a sound of displeasure and Mr. Farrar says, "You can pay for
lunch, boss. I guess that makes this Cian's treat."

I turn so I can see Cian's face. He's looking at me, his blue gaze intent.

Feeling relaxed and happy, I smile. "Thank you."

"You're welcome."

CHAPTER 4

CIAN

The day after our shared lunch at the Greek deli, I tell Anna she's to start ordering lunch instead of Connor. I instruct her to get something for herself. She doesn't. The next day I add an extra meal to the order I send her and then when she brings it in, I give it to her.

She blushes and thanks me. And she smiles.

Choosing her lunch for her every day is strangely satisfying even if it does make Lachlan laugh his ass off. I consider killing him, but he's one of the few people I trust, so I ignore his misplaced humor.

Connor thinks he's the shit because he's not doing all the grunt work anymore. He asks again about becoming an enforcer, so I tell Lachlan to loop him in on the move we're making against the Kicks Bandidos.

That's going down tonight. We're taking out every street dealer we've identified in our territory. We'll bash and grab and then interrogate before sending them back to their gang beat up, and every fucking one of them will lose a finger tonight. Maybe more than one if they piss me off.

It will send a message the Kicks Bandidos had better listen to. The only payment for encroaching on my territory is pain and loss.

The Murphys are doing the same. We've agreed to share intel. Quinn Murphy will offer whatever information doesn't compromise his own clan. I don't blame him. I'll do the same.

Even allies don't show all their cards to each other.

In between answering Lachlan's texts and answering emails from the men who run our mob-owned businesses, I watch Anna on the camera I installed near her desk. Seeing her sitting there, her delicate brow wrinkled in thought while she works sooths me. She's so damn innocent.

The angle of the camera lets me see her face, but it's far enough away that I can see her body too. She has nice, big tits, which I want to see without the clothes hiding them from my eyes. My fingers itch with the need to touch. Are her nipples the same pretty pink as her lips? Anna doesn't wear makeup, not even lip gloss. I never realized how much I prefer that.

She likes working here and smiles often, but when she smiles at me, something happens to her eyes. The violet orbs calm, and she'll stand staring at me until someone interrupts her. I nearly strangled Connor this morning for being the one to do that.

When Anna realizes she's been staring at me, she blushes and turns away. I don't want her turning away. I want her attention on me.

I told Connor never to do that shit again. I said it holding him against the wall with one hand and my knife to his throat with the other. I think he knows I'm serious.

Her desk is still in my cousin's office and that irritates me. I want her in here with me.

I told Lachlan this.

His reply: "Get your shit together or you are going to scare her into quitting."

I don't want her to quit, so I haven't moved her desk. Yet.

I have installed the cameras in her apartment though. I didn't tell my underboss about that, and he doesn't know about the camera feed I'm watching now. He doesn't need to know.

Anna is mine.

I wonder how she'd react if she knew about the cameras. Maybe they'd make her feel safe. They should. I'm watching over her. Unlike her fucking useless family. Anna lost her parents when she was just a kid and the aunt and uncle that raised her after that kicked her out as soon as she turned 18.

I'm thinking about what I'm going to do about that. Anna deserved better.

The only places Anna goes besides work and her apartment are to the bookstore, grocery store and to visit an old woman who lives two floors down. The old woman never leaves her place so installing cameras there is going to be tricky. I've already tapped into the grocer's and bookstore's security feed.

ANNA

Ini is off today because she switched shifts with another one of the cashiers at the pet store who wanted my friend's usual dayshift instead of her own evening one. It means Ini can come by for lunch and I'm excited, but I'm nervous too. She's never been to my work.

Will she notice the crush I've developed on my boss?

She already teases me that I talk about him all the time. I don't. Do I? Maybe. But I talk about Shea too. I really like her. Her family is protective, and she's sheltered, but she thinks she knows all about the world. I'm glad she doesn't. It's not a kind place sometimes.

Anyway, I also talk about Lachlan. Cian told me not to call him Mr. Farrar. Lachlan didn't say anything, so I try not to use his name at all, but I think of him as Lachlan in my mind now. Because Cian told me to. He's the big boss after all. I talk about Connor and Jimmy too, though not as much.

Lachlan gives me a lot of weird looks. Especially when Cian is around. I think he's noticed my crush, but he hasn't said anything. And I'm grateful for that.

"Hey, girl, this place is the bomb." Ini's confident voice interrupts my thoughts.

I jump up from my desk to give her a quick hug before stepping back. "You were supposed to call me from the lobby. How did you get up here?"

Security is pretty tight in the building and it takes an elevator pass card to access this floor.

"Mr. Hotty McHotterson brought me up when I told him I was coming to have lunch with you."

"Cian brought you up?" I ask, a little jealous she's remarking on his hotness.

Which I shouldn't be. I don't own him and I know that's just Ini. It's not like she wants to date him. Does she?

"I think I'm the hottie she's talking about," Lachlan says with a smirk.

Oh. Relief floods me, though I don't know why. "Thanks for bringing her up."

"Any time." Lachlan winks at Ini. "It was my pleasure."

Ini tosses her braids and gives him a flirty smile.

Wishing I had half her confidence, I show my roommate around the office, and introduce her to Connor. "No wonder you like working here. You've got plenty of eye candy."

I laugh, but I never think of Connor or Lachlan as being all that good looking. Ini is practically drooling though. She wants to know if Lachlan and Connor are single. I have to admit I've never asked.

My boss isn't married, or dating, according to his sister, but I've got no clue about the other men at the company.

Cian comes out of his office as I'm confirming with Connor that he doesn't mind getting the lunch order today.

"Nah, I got this. You girls have fun."

"Join us for lunch," Cian says. It sounds like an order, though I know he meant it to be an invitation. "We're going to the pub on the corner."

"We are?" Connor asks, then coughs. "Uh, yeah we are. Their cook is my mam's friend and she makes a wicked Shepherd's Pie."

"I thought you Irish liked your corned beef and cabbage," Ini teases.

"Hers is pretty good, but it's not a patch on my mam's. Ma brines her own beef."

"Sounds yummy," Ini says doubtfully. I don't think either of us has ever brined anything. She looks at me like it's my decision whether we join my boss and coworkers for lunch.

We've ordered food from the pub before, but I haven't been there. I don't know how crowded it usually is. I was hoping to get something from a food truck and take it to eat at the park. But if Cian's going, I don't think even a crowded pub will bother me. I enjoyed lunch at the Greek deli after he showed up and sat down next to me.

When he's close to me, the only thing I smell is him. The only body that registers with my senses is his.

"Lachlan, you coming?" Cian yells.

Lachlan comes out of Cian's office, talking on his cell phone. He clicks off. "Shea'll be here in a minute."

I smile up at Cian. "It looks like we're all going."

He nods. His gaze drops to my chest. Something warm sparks in his eyes. He does that a lot, but no more often than he looks at my face. He seems to like when I smile. I like smiling at him, so it works. I smile now.

Lachlan shoves Cian toward the elevator. "Let's go."

We're walking toward the pub, when Ini sidles up close to me and whispers, "Your boss was checking out your rack back there. And you didn't seem to mind. You smiled at him, Anna."

I shrug. When other men look at my body, it feels creepy, but not Cian. When he stares at my chest it makes me feel warm and tingly. I want to know if he likes what he sees, but I'll never have the nerve to ask. When he's looking, his expression shows nothing but blank calm.

He's good at that.

"Do you have a thing for him? Because if you do, I think the feeling is mutual."

I don't know how to answer that. Do I have a thing for Cian? I feel things for him I've never felt before, but I don't know if I could be intimate with him like a man would expect from his girlfriend. And why am I even thinking like that?

Even if he likes looking at me, that doesn't mean he wants to date me.

The pub owner greets Cian effusively and insists on seating us himself. People tend to treat Cian with respect. I like it.

"You weren't kidding when you said being around your boss turns the volume down for you." Ini bumps my shoulder with hers. "I've never seen you so calm around so many people."

"Shh..." I say, embarrassed, hoping no one overheard her.

We are in the pub, sitting in a U-shaped booth. Ini sits on one side of me, and Cian is on the other. He's on the outside. Shea is sitting next to Ini with Connor beside her. Lachlan is across from Cian, seated next to the opening on the other side of the table.

Once again it doesn't bother me to have Cian blocking my easiest exit. I feel safe, like he'll make sure nothing bad can get to me. I don't know why I feel that way, I just do. I'm glad the Greek deli wasn't a fluke. Having Cian nearby allows me to focus on him instead of everything else playing like the fractals of a kaleidoscope in my brain.

It's too bad he's my boss and not my boyfriend, or even a friend really. I think I'd like to be his friend. Considering how few people I place in that category, I'm a little surprised at myself.

CHAPTER 5

CIAN

Ma insists I come for dinner. I can tell by her tone that she's worried about something. When I ask, she says she just wants to see me.

When I arrive at the house I grew up in, I find out that Shea is out with friends tonight. Usually, my mom would invite my driver and bodyguard to share dinner with us in the kitchen, but she's set the table in the dining room for just me and her.

"There's plenty of stew and potato bread, boys. Help yerselves," she tells Finn and Malone as she bustles around the warm kitchen. "Sully is trailing after Shea tonight."

"Where's Gulliver?" I ask.

"It's his night off."

And he left my mother alone? "Did he know Sully would be leaving with Shea?"

"No. You know your sister. She made plans at the last minute."

"Where's your temporary guard then?" When both Sully and Gulliver are gone, my mom is supposed to call Connor so he can send someone over to watch her.

"Och, don't be worrying yer head boyo. I knew you were coming over. And I don't need protecting every minute of every day. I'm no longer the boss's wife."

"But you are my mother. Next time you will call Connor."

"Don't you take that tone with me, boyo. You're still my son, even if you are a mob boss."

Finn tries to hide his grin behind his hand, but Malone frowns. "I'll clear the house," he says.

I nod, approving his vigilance. Who knows how long Ma has been here alone? I don't feel softer emotions, not even for my mom and sisters, but I need them to be safe. Always.

"I will assign additional soldiers to you and the girls." I send a text to Lachlan, since this will be a permanent assignment.

"They consider themselves women, son, and don't you forget it." She shakes her spoon at me. "Or you'll be hearing an earful. Especially from Shea."

After Malone has cleared the house and Ma has made sure he and Finn have plenty to eat, she shoos me into the dining room. I always find it odd the way my mother treats me. Like I'm just another man. She acts like she's got no idea that I torture and kill men when I need to. That my bodyguard is for appearance's sake, not because I need one.

The most hardened criminals in Chicago fear me, but not this tiny woman.

Anna is not afraid of me either. I don't find that odd though. I find it necessary.

"You made my favorite dinner," I observe. No one makes Irish stew like my mother.

"We don't see you often enough for dinner," she says, but she's got a nervous look about her.

"You know I don't do subtly," I can usually read emotions in others because I've studied them so carefully, but what causes those emotions often eludes me. "If you've got something to say, say it."

She puts her spoon down and sighs. "Lachlan told me you've got a young lady working for you."

"There are several employees that could be described that way."

"He said you *made* a job for her. In your office."

"Technically it is in Connor's office." For now.

"Why did you hire her?"

I don't know how to answer that. Not without worrying my mother. Though she already seems concerned.

Still, I shrug.

"Oh, boyo. Tell me this isn't like Helen."

Helen was a girl I went to school with. She had a nice smile, not as nice as Anna's, but it sparked something inside me. Just a tiny ember of pleasant emotion. Since that was more than I felt around anyone else, it was something I needed time with her to understand. My attention freaked her out and my father paid for her family to relocate. He refused to tell me where.

"Anna likes me staring at her."

My mother's eyes widen. They're the same blue as mine, but where mine reflect nothing but the cold-hearted killer I am, hers are always filled with emotion. Right now they are shining with worry.

Before she can voice her concerns, I add, "She stares at me too."

"A woman looking at you doesn't mean she's experiencing the same level of..." Ma lets her voice trail off.

But I know what she's going to say. Obsession.

Her and my father thought I was obsessed with Helen. I wasn't. I was determined to understand what made her different. I didn't get the chance before she was gone.

Obsession might be the right word for Anna though. She sparks a hell of a lot more than an ember of feeling. Being around her is like having a whole fucking inferno inside. I need to know where she is. All the time.

I need to see her, to know she's safe, even when she's in the same building as me, but especially when she's not.

I'm a sociopath, not a fool, so I don't say any of this to Ma.

I tell my mom the one thing I can say I know won't worry her. "Anna will stand for ten minutes, or longer, just looking at me if no one interrupts her."

"She does?" Ma asks, sounding uncertain, but looking hopeful.

Normally I wouldn't bother to try to convince someone, not even my mom, but that hope pulls at something inside me. "Ask Connor, Ma. He'll tell you." But he'd better not tell her that I pulled a knife on him the last time he was the one to interrupt Anna.

Done with the conversation, I go back to eating my favorite dinner.

Anna is mine and I will claim her. No one is going to stand in the way of that, not my men and not my family.

I leave Malone with Ma when I go to meet Lachlan and the rest of the crew assigned to tonight's operation.

Finn drives into the underground parking garage below our apartment safehouse. This parking level is off limits to anyone but me and my men, sealed off from the rest of the garage with a soundproof steel gate. There are no security cameras on this level or pointed toward the entrance to it.

The apartment safehouse above is fully soundproofed with a dumbwaiter that goes to the furnace room in the basement. We've got an incinerator there that takes care of evidence. The other apartments that used to have access to the dumbwaiter have been renovated and the access bricked up. We own the building and only mob members have apartments, but even so, we're cautious.

When I get out of the car, Lachlan and the soldiers are already waiting. Good. He assigns the team leads we agreed on.

"I want them alive," I tell my men. "I can't get information out of a dead dealer."

"We can rough 'em up, though, right boss?" one of the soldiers asks.

"You're not inviting them to a fucking tea party. Yes, you take them with force."

"You get all of their product too," Lachlan says, my underboss's tone steel hard. "And their money."

"No witnesses. Be smart." My men know the cost of fucking up, so I don't remind them, but I let them see it in my eyes.

More than a couple swallow and take a step back. I scare the shit out of most of my men. Even Lachlan can get wary around me. They should fear me. I am loyal to them all, but I have no pity. If they betray that loyalty, they die. Painfully.

Normally, I would wait in the apartment safehouse to begin the interrogations when the first dealer gets nabbed and brought in. Not tonight. I'm hitting the dealer that thought he could peddle his shit three blocks from Ma's house. No one sells in this neighborhood. Not us. Not the Greeks.

I take Connor and Finn with me. The dealer is leaning against the wall of a closed hardware store. Right under a fucking streetlight.

What the hell good is the extra cop presence I pay for in this neighborhood? How is this asshole flying under their radar? Yes, we are on the edge of the business district, but this street is in the designated area for the additional patrols. I might be a mob boss, but that doesn't mean I want criminal activity in my mom and sisters' proximity.

However, tonight, there will be no cops in any of the locations we're doing our snatch and grabs. This part of the city is under my control and tomorrow the Kicks Bandidos will know it.

Connor approaches the dealer from his right, looking like a college kid out looking to score something to party with. He's doing a good job of looking around and back over his shoulder like he's nervous about being seen. I'm walking up to the jerkoff doing business on my streets without my permission from his left.

My feet make no sound on the sidewalk. I'm a predator moving in on my prey and he's too damn oblivious to sense the danger stalking him.

He calls a greeting out to Connor, casual as shit. Not even a little worried to be selling his product on *my* street. Rage turns my vision red and I'm jogging before I realize it. He looks toward me. Finally. But it's too late.

I punch him in the side of the head, sending his body crashing back against the cement wall of the building. He falls to the ground like a client I'm done with after I release the chains holding him upright.

"Aww, damn it, boss. Couldn't you have left a little of him for me?" Connor whines.

"You'll get to work on your interrogation techniques tonight."

Connor takes a step back before realizing he's done it and moving forward again. "That's not usually my job."

"You want to be an enforcer?"

"Yeah."

"Then you learn."

My younger cousin nods, but I'm not sure this is a good path for him. We'll see in a couple of hours. Connor has too much humanity left in him. He's a lot like his old man. Uncle Jimmy does good running the legit side of the business. Pops always said it would have ruined a good businessman putting him in charge of mob affairs.

Connor is a made man, but he doesn't have a specialist designation. My cousin says he wants to be an enforcer, but I don't believe him. Why does he claim he wants to do something he's not wired for? I'll give him a chance tonight. If he chokes, we'll talk.

We head back to the apartment safehouse.

Now the fun begins.

CHAPTER 6

CIAN

Within the next three hours, all the Kicks Bandidos dealers in our territory are swept up and the cops resume their normal patrols. A text from Murphy tells me it's the same in his territory.

Naked from the waist up, my torso and face are splattered with blood from the men I've already questioned. I'm not happy with the intel so far. These dealers don't know shit. They swagger like badasses until the first kidney punch. All but one of them starts crying soon after. It's pathetic.

They all say the same thing. Some claim they didn't know they were in our territory. Others say they thought their gang had an agreement with us. Eventually, they all admit they knew and were sent to our territory on purpose. They were told that the mob is made up of weak old men.

I would never send my people into someone else's territory without warning them what to expect. I sure as hell wouldn't lie to them. Loyalty goes both ways.

Do the leaders of Kicks Bandidos have bad intel on our clans?

I coach Connor through interrogating one of them. "Use the brass knuckles and hit his jaw. It'll break bone and he'll be eating through a straw for a few weeks, but it won't kill him."

I want them alive to send back to their gang with a message. Stay the fuck out of my territory, or the next time it won't be a finger you lose. It will be your life.

Connor does okay with the beatings, but he has to grit his teeth to cut off the fingers. Lachlan has finished the men he and his crew have been torturing by the time my cousin cuts off the first finger.

He turns green, but he leaves the room before he vomits. Almost everybody throws up the first time. Some never stop. As long as they don't show weakness in front of the enemy, I don't care how fucking fragile their stomachs are.

It's not Connor's fault, but the guy he's questioning with his fists doesn't know who else deals in the city. Just like all the others, he's only ever been assigned to one spot. They all get product and instructions from the same guy. I got his name from the first dealer I strung up.

They all say the same thing. None of them think he's very high up in the gang hierarchy though. Another thing that pisses me off is that these dealers don't know jack about their gang's plans or even the leadership structure. How the hell do the dealers not know who they're working for?

They're members of Kicks Bandidos and all wear the same high end brand running shoes to prove it, but their only point of contact after induction is their supplier.

I did learn that the head of the gang goes by the name *El Fantasma*. I'm Irish and my Spanish is basic, but I know that means *ghost*. Is the guy trying to be clever, or does he have a reason for keeping his real identity a secret?

The FEDs might not know for sure that I'm the Doyle & Byrne mob boss, but my men sure as hell do. And the FEDs suspect. They'd have a file on me an inch thick, if I didn't have someone on the inside of the FBI that makes sure reports get deleted and paper trails disappear.

My people are good at covering our tracks, especially mine, in the criminal underworld, but the Doyle & Byrne mob has been in Chicago for more than a century. They know someone is the boss, just not who.

We'll know *El Fantasma*'s real name soon enough. No matter how good his people are, mine are better.

I send Lachlan and his team out after the supplier. If we don't take him tonight, Quinn's people might get to him first. I want the information before anyone else gets it.

I'm competitive that way. Information is power.

ANNA

Ini and I are having dinner with Mrs. Hart.

I made spaghetti. It's an easy meal to stretch and the leftovers are good. I know Mrs. Hart will have enough for the next day. I made extra garlic bread too and the family size can of green beans. They only cost a little more than a single can and there's enough for all of us and leftovers. Because I'm making more money than I ever have, I even splurged on real bacon bits to flavor the green beans.

"You two are too good to me." Mrs. Hart pats Ini's cheek and smiles at me, knowing I don't like to be touched.

We're all eating at the tiny table in our friend's apartment. It's hard to believe she made room for me and Ini to live here. Even with two of us trading nights on the sofa and the floor, three women was a lot of people for such a tiny space.

"You should see all the eye candy Anna gets to enjoy everyday, Mrs. Hart." Ini grins around a bite of garlic toast. "Her boss even bought us lunch."

"Where did you say you're working now, dear?" Mrs. Hart asks me. "You do seem much more settled than you have been with your previous places of employment."

When I told her I got the job, she didn't ask much about it. I think she figured I'd be leaving it soon enough, no reason to learn about a place I wasn't staying. But I've been there a few weeks now. Even I think I'll be staying.

"I thought I was applying for a receptionist job at Doyle Construction, but it turns out I ended up working for Doyle & Byrne, the parent company."

Mrs. Hart's wrinkled face turns worried. "Did you say Doyle & Byrne?"

"Yes. I work in the president's office for his assistant, Connor Doyle."

"You're working for one of the Doyle's?" Mrs. Hart asks faintly.

Ini is starting to look concerned too, but I just nod.

"The *president* of the company? Cian Doyle?"

"You know who he is?" That makes sense. He's kind of a big deal in the business world, especially in Chicago.

"Oh, yes, but I don't think you do."

"What do you mean?" Ini asks, putting her fork down and staring at Mrs. Hart intently.

"He's the boss for one of the biggest factions of the Irish mob in Chicago. The only mob near the same size are the Murphys."

"How do you know that?" Ini asks.

"Young lady, when you have lived in Chicago for as many decades as I have, you learn a thing or two. When I was young, one of my friends cleaned house for the Doyles. Cian's father was in charge then. When he died two years ago, Cian took over, even though he was only in his mid-twenties."

Mob is organized crime, isn't it? I haven't seen any evidence of criminal activity, but that doesn't mean much. I'm not sure I'd recognize it if I did see it. I've never known a criminal. Neither Ini or I smoked pot, or shoplifted like a lot of kids. We knew we couldn't afford to get into trouble. We didn't want to get kicked out of our homes any earlier than we had to.

"I met Quinn Murphy," I say with a frown. "I didn't like him much. He got in my personal space."

Cian didn't like him asking me out. Because he's a mob boss too? Cian doesn't seem to be worried about having me around him and his company.

"You need to watch yourself around those men, dear. They are dangerous."

Cian and Lachlan wear power like their suits. Like it's tailored to fit them. Dangerous? I can see it. It just doesn't feel real that they are dangerous *to me*. Not even Lachlan.

"Cian makes me feel safe."

Ini shakes her head. "You need to find another job. We can go back to ramen noodles and tuna fish, Anna. I don't want you getting mixed up with the mob."

"I'm not quitting my job." I say it more forcefully than I usually speak.

Both Ini and Mrs. Hart look at me with surprise.

"I like working there. It's the only place I've ever worked that I didn't dread going to every day. Not being a criminal doesn't make someone a good person, or even safe."

My aunt and uncle never broke a law that I know about, but they never made me feel safe and they couldn't wait to get rid of me. Ini's foster parents didn't break the law, but they kept kids so they got the payment from the state. They never loved Ini or took care of her like parents should.

Cian's not my family, but he takes care of me. He came to the Greek restaurant and made sure I was okay along with his sister. He asks how I'm doing and he listens to me. He gets me lunch every day and he forced Quinn Murphy out of my personal space. He watches over me.

Maybe he is a criminal, but he's not a bad man.

"Nobody I work with thinks I'm weird. They don't judge me. They don't tease me." I never have to use my rhyme to control anxiety when I'm at work.

And I have a massive crush on my boss. I've been having sexy dreams about him, and I enjoy them.

"But, Anna—"

"No," I cut Ini off. "I'm not quitting. It's a good job and they're good people, even if they are mobsters." Was that the right term?

I've never even watched The Godfather. Maybe I should. I bet I could find books at the library about the Irish mob in Chicago. I'll check this weekend.

"Ever since my parents died, my only friends have been you two. Now I have Cian, Shea, Connor, Jimmy and even Lachlan."

Ini has that stubborn look on her face. "You can make other friends. Ones that aren't criminals."

"No. *You* can make friends." She has lots. I'm lucky to be her best friend because everyone likes Ini. "You can work and take college classes at the same time. You can juggle life!" I don't know why I'm shouting. Only I need her to hear me. "I can't. Before I started working for Cian, I thought my life was going to be an unending and *miserable* cycle of looking for jobs, getting one finally, and only keeping it until I couldn't stand it anymore, or I got fired."

"They're crooks," she says stubbornly.

I don't care. "Maybe criminals are my kind of people. "

"You're not the criminal type." Ini laughs, like that's funny. "You're too sweet."

"I *fit* there. I belong." I start to cry. I never cry, but I can't help it.

Ini's face changes and she grabs my hand, gives it a quick squeeze and lets go. "You belong here."

"I don't want to leave," I repeat. Please hear me, friend, please. "Working there makes me happy."

"You call Mr. Doyle by his first name?" Mrs. Hart asks.

"Uh huh. It's such a pretty name." I feel the smile that always comes when I see him break over my face. "He's so kind."

Mrs. Hart stares at me like I've got spaghetti sauce all over my face. "You think Cian Doyle is *kind*?"

"To be fair, he sort of dotes on her," Ini says grudgingly.

I wipe at my face with my napkin even though I'm pretty sure it's clean. It is.

One, two, look at my shoe.

I shift in my dinette chair so I can see my feet. I'm wearing tennis shoes. Good for running.

Three, four, find the door.

It's eight steps to the door to the hall.

Five, six, click, click, clicks.

I tap my fingernails together three times and then three more.

"Oh, honey, no. You don't need the rhyme with Mrs. Hart and me. We love you."

But she wants me to leave Doyle & Byrne.

Seven, eight, release the weight.

Exhale. One. Two. Three. Four. Five. Six. Seven. Eight.

Nine, ten, inhale the Zen.

Inhale. One. Two. Three. Four. Five. Six. Seven. Eight. Nine. Ten.

Ini is frowning. Mrs. Hart looks sad.

Now start again.

CHAPTER 7

CIAN

Lachlan and his team don't find the supplier. He's gone to ground. It was an inevitable risk. Picking up all the dealers at once sent up red flags.

It also sent a message. So did sending all those dealers home beat up and missing a finger. I know Quinn doesn't have the supplier either, because I've got eyes inside the other Irish mob clans.

I call my best tracker and get him looking for *El Fantasma*. Then I send a text to my information specialist telling her to research *El Fantasma* and his gang. Do they have their own cook for the drugs they're selling, or are they getting them from an outside source?

I want to know why the dealers don't interact with each other. There's something off about this gang. It's more like a syndicate that sources out the low level jobs. The dealers think they are members, but they're really just employees.

Too many markers indicate *El Fantasma* and his lieutenants aren't loyal to their foot soldiers. Either that, or their dealers aren't considered members, no matter what they've been told.

How many of the dealers we picked up and interrogated last night will ghost the ghost?

My men would lose more than a finger for the Doyle & Byrne Clan and remain loyal. They know that breaking their vow will result in death, but they know I'd never leave them hanging either. I wouldn't send them into enemy territory with some fairytale about weakened old men that will look the other way.

~ ~ ~

Regardless of the Kicks Bandidos problem, I'm talking to Connor when Anna arrives, like every other morning. She looks troubled. I only checked in on her feeds last night to make sure she was safe. Did something happen?

She gives me a wan smile and heads to her desk.

I follow her. "Are you alright?"

She turns to face me, her face filled with misery. What the hell is going on?

"Anna, tell me who hurt you and I'll take care of it."

"I don't want to stop working here," she says.

"You won't." I can't watch over her like she needs if she's somewhere else all day long.

"Before I came to work here, I only had two friends."

I nod. I know this. "You have more now."

"I..." She looks down at her shoes and I know what she's doing. I've seen the ritual she goes through to calm herself.

Though after the first couple of days, she never did it in the office again. Grasping her shoulders, I look down at her. I need to know what is triggering this anxiety in her.

She looks up at me, her violet eyes swirling with emotion. Emotion I feel.

"I don't like to be touched."

"I know."

"But when you touch me, it's okay. It turns down the noise."

I don't know what she means. "Is that good?"

"Yes."

"Good."

"I know you're just my boss," she says and then stops, like she isn't sure where to go from there.

"I'm your friend. Not just your boss."

"That's what I told them."

"Who?"

"Ini and Mrs. Hart."

"Do they think you shouldn't be friends with your employer?" Too bad. I'm going to be a whole lot more in Anna's life than a friend, but not before she's ready.

"They think I shouldn't work for you."

What did her friends say to Anna?

I don't have sound on the feeds. It wouldn't be right to listen in on her private conversations. The cameras are so I can make sure she's safe, but maybe I need to rethink that decision.

"Why?" Ini hadn't given off any quit-your-job vibes when she visited Anna the other day.

"Mrs. Hart told us you're a mob boss."

Things go still inside me. "Does that bother you?"

"I think it's supposed to."

"That's not what I asked."

"No, it doesn't bother me. I like working here. I like you." She blushes.

I want to kiss her, but she's not ready. She just learned I'm not a nice man. I'm not a good man. Fuck.

"I like everyone that I work with here. That never happens."

"We all like you too."

"You do? They do? I mean, I thought so, but sometimes I don't read people right."

"My sister thinks you're sweet. Connor is thrilled you're here so he doesn't have to do the grunt work. Lachlan thinks you're good for me." My underboss didn't say those words, but he told me to get my act together so Anna won't quit. That's as good as a notarized endorsement. "Uncle Jimmy wishes you worked in his office."

I had to set my uncle straight. Ma called me after and read me the riot act for threatening my uncle. I did not care.

Anna is not leaving me.

"You are not quitting," I tell her.

"Uh...boss, maybe dial back the intensity. You're going to scare her," Connor says from behind me.

I turn my head and bare my teeth at him.

He backs up.

"Cian doesn't scare me. He makes me feel safe," Anna says.

My head whips back around. "I make you feel safe?"

She nods. "You turn down the noise."

"What does that mean exactly?" This is the second time she's said it. It must be important to her.

"Usually when I'm around other people, outside of my own room where I keep things like I need them, I get overwhelmed by all the noise. People talking, the sounds of them doing things. Colors get too bright. I can feel people being too close even if they don't touch me."

She's talking about overstimulation.

"And being around me calms things down?"

"Yes, exactly." She smiles for the first time this morning, her pretty eyes shining with approval that I get it.

"Did you tell your friends that?"

"Yes, but they're still worried about me."

"Do you want me to talk to them?"

"You would?"

"For you, Anna."

"Oh." Her eyes fill with tears.

I want to hit something.

But her smile doesn't dim. "I told them you are kind."

Connor coughs. The little shit is still listening. I turn to growl at him over my shoulder but when I see how he's focused on Anna, worry etched on his face, I decide not to knock him into next week. He's watching out for her.

"I am not a good man," I acknowledge. "Most of the city is scared of me."

"I'm not."

"And you never have to be."

"Maybe if you told Ini and Mrs. Hart that, they would stop trying to get me to quit."

Threats are easier, but for my Anna, I will try diplomacy.

"Cancel my morning shit," I tell Connor.

"You're going now?" he asks, shocked.

"Yes." I'm not risking them convincing Anna she has to quit and me having to take more serious measures to make sure that doesn't happen. I don't want Anna upset.

"But Lachlan will be in any minute. He's got intel from the Murphys."

"He can wait."

~ ~ ~

Leaving my bodyguards stationed outside the building, I knock on Mrs. Hart's door. I have to knock a second time before I hear an old lady's voice asking, "Who is it?" through the door.

"Cian Doyle."

Silence. Then, "Go away."

I sigh. She's afraid.

"I am not going to hurt you."

"I'm calling the cops."

Sighing again, I kick the door and it breaks open despite the extra deadbolt.

The old lady screams. Being careful not to hurt her, that would upset Anna, I grab her and put my hand over her mouth. "Calm down, Mrs. Hart. I'm here at Anna's request."

She bites my hand. It hurts, but I smile. No wonder she's friends with Anna. She's got spunk.

"Anna's not afraid of me either."

Mrs. Hart glares up at me.

"I'm going to pull my hand away. Don't scream." Thinking of my ma, I say, "Please."

The old lady's eyes widen on the word and then she nods. I think maybe I should have started with the please and not the door kicking. It's a piece of crap door though. I'll get her a new one, something that will keep her safe. Anna will like that.

I pull my hand away. "Can you give me a second?" I ask her.

I've got to get the door on its way because I'm not leaving her alone with a door that doesn't shut, much less lock anymore.

"I'll make some tea." I think it's more for her nerves than because she's being polite.

I call Uncle Jimmy as she fills a kettle with water in her tiny kitchen. "I need a team to install a steel door in an apartment. Make that two apartments. I also want the team to check out the wiring and any other source of possible threat from the building for the occupants' safety."

"Text me the address." Uncle Jimmy doesn't ask why which is one of the reasons he's so good at heading up the construction side of our business. He knows when to keep his nose out of things.

"You're replacing my door?" Mrs. Hart asks. "And having my apartment inspected?"

"And any repairs necessary made." She needs to be prepared for the team being in her apartment a good part of the day.

"That's the landlord's job."

I shrug. Keeping Anna safe is my job. She spends time here as well as the apartment she shares with her friend, Ini.

Mrs. Hart looks at me like she's trying to get a read on me. I should tell her not to bother. Right now, I have no emotions to read.

"You told that man two apartments," she says leadingly.

I don't mind telling her my plans. She'll find out soon enough. "Yours and Anna's."

"You realize if you have steel doors installed, you won't be able to kick them in?" She gives me a mocking look.

I like this lady. She's got courage.

I shrug. "Neither will anyone else."

The kettle whistles and Mrs. Hart goes back to the kitchen. She sets a wooden tray, dinged and the flowers painted in the center faded by years of use, on the counter. Like she's done it a thousand times before, she places the tea things on the tray.

I grab it and carry it to the small table before she can. There are two mugs and I hope that means she's ready to listen.

I wait to be invited to sit down like Ma taught me.

Mrs. Hart looks at me curiously. "You don't mind breaking down my door, but you wait to be invited to sit at my table?"

I don't bother answering. Kicking the door in was expedient and she needs a new one anyway.

She indicates one of the small dinette chairs. "Join me for tea, Mr. Doyle."

I settle my big body on one of the small chairs and she pours tea into both mugs before placing one in front of me.

"Anna is safe with me." I take a sip of my tea. No milk. No sugar.

"How can you say that?"

I could tell her it is because Anna works for my legit business, but that's only part of it and not the important part. "Because I will always protect her."

Mrs. Hart does not look comforted. If anything, she looks horrified. "You want her."

"She's safe with me," I repeat.

"But is she safe from you?"

I think about that. Anna is mine, but I will give her all the time she needs to come to understand that. "I will never do anything she does not want."

"How can I believe you?" She sounds genuinely worried. This woman cares about my Anna.

I'm glad. So, I decide to reassure her. "If you know my reputation, you also know I keep my word."

"And you're giving me your word that you won't let harm come to her? That you won't push her for a relationship she doesn't want?"

"Yes."

"Why are you here?"

"Anna is upset."

"And you don't want her to quit."

"She won't quit." That is not going to happen. "But if you keep pushing her to, it will hurt her."

"And you will protect her, even from her friends."

"Yes." In any way I have to, though I don't say that.

Mrs. Hart is scared of me as it is. She doesn't need to know that I've got no compunction about getting rid of obstacles, whatever and whoever they are, in whatever way I need to. She can probably guess though. She is the one that told Anna that I'm a mob boss.

"Are you planning to have one of these little chats with Ini?" Mrs. Hart sips her tea and watches me over the rim of the mug.

"Yes."

"Does Anna know you are here?"

"Yes." I already told her that. Maybe she didn't believe me. "Would you like to call her and confirm that?"

"I would."

I just wait. And she realizes I'm not going to stop her making the call, so she does. I only hear Mrs. Hart's side of the conversation.

"Mr. Doyle is here."

Anna speaks.

"No apologies necessary, dear. Ini and I should have realized how important it is to you that you found a place to work where you are comfortable."

Anna says something else, and the old woman laughs.

"Plenty of people work for the mob that aren't criminals, dear. Don't you let it bother you." She gives me a long look and then says, "I think your boss is sweet on you. Are you comfortable with that?"

I don't know what Anna says, but Mrs. Hart's expression turns pained. "You're a very special girl, Anna. Loving and sweet. Any man would be lucky if you returned his interest." She gives me a glare. "And any man worth having you will wait until you're ready."

They hang up.

"Don't you hurt her, Mr. Doyle. She deserves to be happy and as much as it pains me to say, working for you seems to make her that way."

I've already told the woman that I will not hurt Anna, so I don't reply. We drink our tea in silence until the construction team shows up.

I leave them with Mrs. Hart after giving instructions to replace the door on Anna and Ini's apartment as well. "Leave the keys with Mrs. Hart."

"You're not keeping one of the keys for yourself?" she asks with surprise.

"No." I've installed the camera I wanted to here in Mrs. Hart's kitchen already, while she was talking to my men about the new door. They let her pick the color. "But I suggest you give each other keys in case of an emergency."

"You don't mind not having one in that case?" she asks.

"If Anna is in danger, a steel door won't stop me." The walls around the door are made of wood and plaster.

"Why does her safety matter so much to you?"

I don't have an answer for her, so I don't bother replying.

My conversation with her roommate goes pretty much the same, except I don't have to kick down any doors at the pet store where she works.

It's a good thing that Anna's happiness and safety are both her friends' main concerns. Ini didn't like that Anna reverted to her rhyme at home. When I told her she doesn't do it in the office, that cinched it for the other woman.

CHAPTER 8

ANNA

It takes Cian two hours and twenty-seven minutes to get back after he leaves to talk to Ini and Mrs. Hart. Both of my friends called me while he was there to confirm I knew he planned to talk to them. It was weird.

Why on earth would a president of a multinational company show up if he hadn't been asked to? I mean, I'm not sure why he's so willing to make things better for me, but I'm glad he is. Mrs. Hart thinks Cian is sweet on me.

I want it to be true so badly I cannot allow myself to believe it because I will be devastated if it's not true. Better not to hope than to hope and hurt. I learned that when my parents died. Neither died at the site of the crash; both passed in the hospital.

My babysitter told me there had been an accident when they didn't come home. She said they were both taken to the hospital and we had to hope they would be okay. I hoped so hard all night and the next day, right up until my aunt showed up to tell me they were gone.

Gone and never coming back.

I hated hope after that.

So, I'm not going to hope for Cian to crush on me like I'm crushing on him.

But I'm not quitting my job either and my friends both promised to stop harassing me about it. They also both told me to be careful.

I look around the office where I work. There is nothing that can hurt me here. I'm in more danger going to and from work every day than the time I spend in this building. If it wasn't safe Cian wouldn't let his sister work here. He's very protective of Shea.

I've never met the other sister, Máire. She's the same age as me, but she's attending university abroad. In Ireland. They still have family there. What would it be like to have family in another country? I never knew any of my dad's family. My aunt is my mom's sister and she never talked about where their family came from.

"You look lost in thought," Cian says. "Are you still worried what your friends think about you working for me?"

"No." I smile, glad he was able to convince them when I couldn't. "I was thinking about family. You know where yours comes from. I don't even know if my dad had siblings."

"Why not?"

"My dad wasn't on speaking terms with his family and none of them came to the funeral, but when I asked my aunt if my grandparents were all dead, she said no. That my dad's parents were both still living. And they didn't want me."

"She told you they didn't want you?"

"Yes. It had to be the truth, because if anyone in my father's family had wanted me, she and my uncle would have been relieved to be able to send me away."

His hands fisting at his sides, Cian makes a strange sound, but his expression doesn't change.

Connor curses.

My brows furrow. "What's the matter, Connor?"

"Uh..."

"Nothing," Cian says. "Right, Connor?"

"Right." Connor doesn't look convincing, but I'm not one to pry, so I don't ask again.

"Thank you for talking to Ini and Mrs. Hart," I say to Cian. "That was really kind of you."

Cian shrugs. "It had to be done. You're not quitting."

His forcefulness might bother someone else, but it makes me feel safe. I've never responded to the world like other people.

Lachlan comes into the office suite, his gaze taking in everyone standing around my desk. "You ready, boss?"

"Yes." Cian's less than revealing expression shutters completely. "Connor, I want you in this meeting too. Anna, you are on the phones."

I take them their lunch when it arrives. Tension thrums in the air and they don't say anything when I'm in the room.

Shea joins me for mine. "I love that you're here, Anna. I miss Máire and it's like having another sister around."

I don't let people in. I don't get close to people, but these Doyles, it's like they've always been there, inside the wall I put between me and the world.

"I hope I get to meet her someday," I say.

"I'm sure you will. Ma wants to meet you."

"Your mother? I wonder why."

"I talk about you. That's not so shocking. But Cian does too and that's got Ma in a tizzy."

"Your brother talks about me?"

"Yep."

I want to ask what he says, but that would seem like I'm spying on him.

"Did he really go talk to your friends so they'd stop bugging you to quit?" Shea asks.

"It was really nice of him. I like working here but I hate upsetting my friends." I slept very little last night because I was so anxious over the situation.

"Connor said you know that Cian is mob now."

So, that is who told her. I don't mind. It wasn't like Cian and I were having a private conversation in his office. We were in mine and Connors. And we weren't whispering. I kind of like how up in each other's business this family is.

"Yes."

"And it doesn't bother you?"

"No."

"Wow. I was born into this family and sometimes I wish I hadn't been."

"Why?"

"Do you know what a mob boss does?" Shea asks me instead of answering.

I shrug. "I don't work for the mob side of the business." Though I'm not sure it would bother me if I did.

Maybe my bother meter is broken.

"The mob handles stuff outside the law."

"So do lots of politicians." This is Chicago. "So do the police sometimes."

I don't think Ini is the only reason I care that so many Black people have died unlawfully in police custody, but she brought the problem to my attention. She was crying one day, and I wanted to know why. A young Black woman had been killed during a no-knock raid on her apartment.

They weren't even looking for her, but somebody else.

Ini said it could have been her. I didn't see how, because she's never dated anyone more than a few weeks, much less lived with them. But after that, I paid closer attention to the news and saw it was a widespread problem. I've noticed that even with my idiosyncrasies, some people treat me more respectfully than they do Ini. She's smart and personable, but all they see is the color of her skin.

It makes me so angry. So, I research candidates before I vote for them. And that's how I learned so many politicians seem to think the law is for everybody else.

"But my family don't even pretend to be law abiding. At least not with each other." Shea frowns.

"Do you think it's better to pretend to respect the law, but break it anyway?" I prefer straightforward honesty, but some people like to be able to lie to themselves.

Shea looks at me funny. I'm used to that. Only Shea doesn't seem to be judging me, just not sure how to take what I said.

"You think everybody breaks the law?"

"No, but I think that a lot of people who pretend to be good aren't and I know some people think your brother is bad, but he's good to you. He's good to me."

"He takes care of the family, even if he doesn't love us."

"You don't think he loves you?"

"Anna..." Shea trails off, looking conflicted. "Listen, my brother, he doesn't feel things like normal people."

I hate that term. *Normal people.* My aunt and uncle were always telling me to act like a normal person when all I could do was act like myself. What they meant though, was to act the way they did. Only, I didn't really like them, so why would I want to be the same as them?

"Some people think I don't have the same emotions as so-called normal people either."

"But you do. I know you do."

I nod. "I know I do too. They don't express the same way with me though."

"And you don't mind working for a man who kills people."

"Does he? Is that what it means to be a mob boss?" I ask curiously.

"He has. You can't be a made man without killing and you can't be the boss unless you are a member of the mob."

"Can women be made men?"

"Depends on the organization, but my brother has women that work for him."

"I know. I'm a woman."

"I mean on the mob side. Máire has four bodyguards with her in Ireland. Two of them are women. They scare the crap out of me, but I'm glad they're keeping her safe. My brother might not be touchy feely, but he's also not a misogynist or a bigot. So, he's got that going for him."

I think he has a lot going for him, but if I say that, Shea will know I have a crush on her brother.

"I never had a brother, but I have cousins and they're both of those things."

"Did you grow up with them?"

"I lived with them from when I was ten until I turned eighteen."

"You had to get away from them, huh?"

"Their parents kicked me out. They said their duty was done."

"That's awful."

Was it? I don't have a lot of experience with family dynamics. "It was scary. If Mrs. Hart hadn't let me and Ini sleep in her living room, we would have ended up in a shelter."

Shea stares at me like she can't believe what I'm saying.

I like her innocence, but I wish she appreciated her brother more. "Neither of my cousins are in the mob, but they wouldn't cross the street to give me a sandwich if I was starving either."

"You're saying I'm lucky to have my bossy older brother."

I'll take Finally Listening for the win, Alex.

CHAPTER 9

CIAN

"The supplier is still in the wind." Lachlan frowns. "The Murphy clan is looking too, but they haven't found him."

"We need the names of the people in the gang's inner circle to dismantle it." I won't let a threat like this remain in my city. "Does Walsh have information for us?"

Lachlan shakes his head. "He wouldn't tell us who he's meeting with to negotiate the dealers staying in his territory. Walsh is pissed about how we handled the dealers in ours."

"We warned him." What the hell was the man's problem? Did he really think he could negotiate with a gang that hadn't approached him in the first place to deal in his territory?

"Our contacts in the Walsh mob are looking into it."

Maybe it's time to absorb Walsh's territory into ours. Quinn will want a piece of the action since the Walsh clan runs the area between our two mobs.

"The Kicks Bandidos are running girls too," Connor says. "Ronan called while you were gone."

"What did he say?" I ask.

"His people picked up three whores working the street outside the Lucky Charm."

On paper, the Lucky Charm is an escort service. One of three we run. The men and women who work for us get medical, dental and vacations. The services offered that are not listed on the websites are lucrative for us and them.

Ronan's team makes sure the johns don't break our rules or push for anything not agreed to up front. Our people set their own limits, and some are straight up escorts with no extra bennies offered. There's plenty of rich old men who like to have arm candy.

They don't solicit on the streets. Safer for them and it keeps the cops out of our business. No sweeps and mass arrests. No leverage for law enforcement.

Not all the clans handle things the way we do, but the others know that our streets aren't their playground. When Ronan runs across someone tricking on their own, he assesses. If they're of age, sometimes, he recruits for one of our places, or he moves them on. He's got a soft spot for vulnerable teens and has a shelter he works with to help them. If there's a pimp involved, then they learn to respect our boundaries.

Ronan is damn good at dealing the pain necessary to make sure those lessons stick. If the pimp is running underage whores, Ronan is also damn good at disposing of bodies.

"He questioned them."

It's not a question, but Connor nods. "They didn't want to talk at first, but admitted they're working for the gang after some persuasion."

"Where are they now?"

"Ronan has them in a room at the Lucky Charm. He wants to talk to you."

"I'll go over there when we're done here. Let him know."

Connor pulls his phone out and sends a text.

"Do you want me to come?" Lachlan asks.

"No. You stay on the search for that fucking supplier. I want him found. And put some pressure on our informants in the Walsh mob. If the problem is bigger than him being an ass about giving us contact information for the gang, we need to know now."

If Walsh has decided to ally with the gang, that puts a new spin on the dealers and sex workers showing up in Doyle & Byrne and Murphy territory.

~ ~ ~

Ronan is waiting in the hidden basement of the Lucky Charm. The entrance is in the back of the storage cellar, behind a shelving unit that slides to the side. It doesn't rest on the floor so there are no tell-tale marks from the shifting of the shelves.

There are cells down here where we keep people on ice and an interrogation room like we have in the apartment safe house.

His grey eyes empty, Ronan nods in greeting when I enter his office. He has an office upstairs, but this is where he keeps the real records and the computer that cannot end up in the hands of the FEDs.

"Where are the girls."

"Cells 1, 2 and 3."

"You kept them separate. Good."

"The woman in Cell 3 is tough, but I think she's the one with the intel."

I doubt sex workers sent to ply their trade on my streets are going to have any more information than the dealers, but Ronan has good instincts.

"You questioned her?" I ask.

"Yes, but without persuasion."

Without torture, he means. I don't like torturing women, but having ovaries doesn't make a person weak or exempt when they come against me and mine.

"The other two?"

"They know the name of their handler, but that's it. They were told where to go and how much they had to earn before going back."

"Going back where?"

Ronan lists off an address. "My team checked it out last night. No one was there. We've got eyes on it in case anyone returns."

"Nab anyone who shows up." I think and then add. "If a cop shows, get his information without letting him know we're watching."

Ronan inclines his head. "Those are the instructions I gave my men."

Ronan Byrne is four years older than me and when my father died, he could have started a civil war. He had as much right to be Boss as I did. Merciless and intelligent, he would have been good at the job.

He didn't want it.

I never asked why. I don't care. He's good at running this side of the business and I'm glad I didn't have to kill him or any of his men. They're strong fighters and they don't make trouble within the organization.

We head toward Cell 3. A quick check of the camera feed from the room on his phone and then Ronan opens the door with a code.

A woman sits on the narrow cot, her knees up, her back against the wall. Her skirt would barely cover her ass if she was standing up. In her current position, it doesn't hide her thong covered waxed pussy. Her top is snug and short. The four-inch heels she'd been wearing are lying carelessly on the floor by the cot.

She's older than I expected. Mid thirties maybe. There's a cunning glint in her dark eyes.

"Did you wand her for tracking devices?" I ask Ronan.

"Don't need to. There's no signal getting out, or coming in here."

He doesn't say *down* here. Ronan would have had the women blindfolded when he brought them in. The Cells have no windows. The walls are finished with sheet rock. There's no way to know they are in a basement.

Something flickers in the woman's eyes.

"Where are their things?"

"My tech guys have them."

"Good." Maybe we'll get lucky, and they'll find something useful. The gang members sure as hell haven't been so far.

"What is your name?" I ask the woman.

"Carmen. What's yours?"

"Boss. You were tricking in my territory, Carmen. Who sent you?"

She looks at Ronan, her expression mocking. "And here I thought it was your territory, tough guy. Didn't you tell your boss the name of our handler? I'm sure one of the other girls gave it to you."

"Why didn't you?" I ask, knowing Ronan isn't going to answer her.

She shrugs. "Why should I?"

"Because then we wouldn't know that you're the one with any real information."

"The only real information I have is how much I charge. Interested?"

I give Ronan a signal and he has a hood over her head and her wrists in restraints in seconds. Leading the way to the interrogation room, I consider our options. We need information and we need it fast. This whole situation with the Kicks Bandidos feels hinky.

There's something going on that I don't know about. What I don't know could hurt my clan. It could hurt my family. Or Anna.

I nod my head toward the bench near a drain we use for water boarding. Ronan secures Carmen to the bench and then grabs the hood and yanks it off. Some of her hair comes with it.

She doesn't squeal but gives Ronan a sultry look instead. "You like it rough, tough guy?"

Ignoring her, he grabs one of the porous cloths we keep for this and covers her nose and mouth with it, connecting it around the back of her head with the straps for that purpose.

"You think you'll hold out," I say to her in a conversational tone. "You think you'd rather die than talk."

Her expression tells me that's exactly what she believes.

"The problem for you is that we aren't going to let you die, but we will get you to talk."

The defiance in her gaze lasts through the first two rounds with the water splashing over her airways. This makes her gag and feel like she's drowning. The cloth remaining on her face makes it harder for her to catch her breath between sessions with the water. It feels like the water is still being poured as every breath in she takes is heavy with the water dripping from the cloth.

I know because my father taught me by example.

Ronan was trained the same way. He's an expert at this technique and Carmen is at no risk of dying. Her expression and body language says she wants to by round three.

Ronan doesn't pause. He doesn't bother to start questioning until he's warmed up the client.

Her eyes have leached of all defiance by the time he removes the cloth from her face.

"What is your name?" he asks. Then leans down and speaks with his mouth only an inch from hers. "Your full name."

"Valeria Carmen Vega-Martinez." It's a whisper. She's got very little voice left and none of her confidence.

"No one is coming to rescue you, Valeria Carmen Vega."

That sparks a last glimmer of defiance in her dark eyes.

Ronan shakes his head and puts the fabric back over her face.

"No," she says.

He takes her through another session. She's limp, her head lolling back off the bench when he's done.

"Who do you work for?" I ask.

"Kicks Bandidos." She barely gets the words out.

Ronan goes to put the cloth back over her face. She tries to turn her head. "*El Fantasma.*"

"I don't need a ghost," I say, pissed she's still fighting. "I need a name."

Ronan taps her face. He doesn't slap her. He never uses more force than necessary, but he'll cut a throat without hesitation when it's needed.

"Martina," she says.

El Fantasma is a fucking woman. Now we're getting somewhere. "Martina who?"

"Vega."

Fuck me.

"Cousin, sister? Aunt, mother?" Ronan asks.

"Cousin."

Ronan refills his jug of water. "Your cousin has you tricking on the street?"

Carmen's gaze slides to the now full jug.

The truth is obvious. She wasn't tricking. Martina Vega wanted her caught. Which means she's a plant. To what end? They already know where the Lucky Charm is or they wouldn't have been tricking so close by.

Ronan's waiting for her answer. Not because we need it but because every truth she gives us makes her less able to hold back when it matters most.

"*El Fantasma* wants intel."

"And she thinks you can get it?" I ask. Cousins, or not, this woman's boss does not value her life. There were too many risks inherent in the plan.

The fact she is where she is and that her people have no way of tracking her here is proof of that.

"Is *El Fantasma* trying to get rid of you?" Ronan asks.

Yeah, he sees the same things I do.

"No. She trusts me to get the job done."

That's a lot of words strung in a row. Our captive must be feeling better.

"What's the plan? Why drop her people on our streets?" I ask.

Ronan has to put the cloth back on her face twice more before Carmen tells us everything she knows. *El Fantasma's* plan is to keep us busy with the dealers and the sex workers while she launches an attack against our legitimate businesses. Carmen doesn't know what that attack will be.

I'm not worried. This shit is irritating, but it's not going to distract me from running my organization. Which tells me that Martina didn't tell her cousin the truth about her plan. Could all of this have been an elaborate way to get rid of Carmen?

The woman can't even tell us where her cousin is. Only where she has been. *El Fantasma* moves around a lot, never staying in the same location more than a couple of nights. Sometimes, she's in Chicago, but she leaves the city too. Carmen is supposed to oversee activities in Chicago while her cousin is gone.

"She knew you would be taken. She had to guess whatever spyware she has on your person or in your bag was going to be neutralized." Ronan unstraps Carmen from the bench. He strips off her wet top and pulls a generic white t-shirt over her head. It falls down past the hemline of her skirt.

"It was a good plan." Carmen insists, but her eyes tell a different story.

She's starting to doubt her cousin.

"Her actions say she wants to get rid of you. Why? You're her rival," Ronan answers his own question. "Is it professional or personal?"

That strikes a chord with Carmen, and she winces.

"Personal then. What is it?"

"She wants my husband."

She's married. Neither Ronan nor I respond with shock at that news.

"Does your husband know the kind of assignment you signed up for?" I ask. Before Anna, this question would not have occurred to me.

The idea of Anna dressing like Carmen, even if she turned down every wanna be john has me wanting to kill someone. Martina Vega would be a good target.

Now we just have to find her.

"He approved it."

"So, he's part of your organization too?" Ronan asks.

She nods.

"And he wants your cousin too."

"Probably."

"Why?" I ask.

"Isn't it obvious?"

"No."

"They're in love."

"Doubtful." Ronan is cleaning up the area, but clearly still listening.

"Her father has more power than mine in Colombia." Carmen's dusky complexion takes on a green cast. She hadn't meant to say that.

Colombia. Whoever is backing the Kicks Bandidos is based in South America and I doubt *El Fantasma* is ultimately calling the shots. They're here on the orders of someone else.

Carmen has more questions to answer, but they'll wait. Interrogation is as much about mental manipulation as physical torture. Ronan will feed her and let her stew before taking another crack at her. Eventually she's going to realize that it isn't just her cousin that sees her as expendable. Whoever sent her here doesn't care if they get her back, either.

If she doesn't draw that conclusion, Ronan will point it out to her. For her sake, I hope that's enough to flip her loyalties. Waterboarding isn't fun, but neither are the other torture techniques Ronan can use without doing permanent damage. And unless he plans to kill her, he'll stick to them. Still, while fingernails grow back, it hurts like a bitch getting them pulled.

CHAPTER 10

ANNA

Ini and Mrs. Hart like the steel doors the Doyle Construction crew installed in our apartments. I really like having water pressure in the shower. They fixed that too. And the lights have stopped flickering in Mrs. Hart's place.

I don't know why Cian had his people put in the new doors, or fix the problems in our apartment, but it makes me feel taken care of. Like someone is watching out for me. I haven't had that sense of security since my parents died.

I know that Ini will always be there for me, just like she can count on me. And Mrs. Hart too. But none of us has the resources to truly protect the others. We do our best though.

Which is why my friends were worried about me. I'm glad Cian convinced them I am safe working at Doyle & Byrne.

They both ask a lot more questions about my day now. It means more talking than I'm used to, but I'll deal. As long as neither of them tries to make me quit my job, I can put up with the extra interest.

~ ~ ~

A few days after I find out Cian is a mob boss, I'm working in Jimmy's office again with Shea. Things have been tense in Cian's office with a lot of men coming and going. I don't mind being away from that, but I miss seeing Cian.

"What are you doing tonight?" Shea asks me when we're working on a project.

"I'm going to the bookstore after dinner." I go once a week. The people who run the bookstore aren't nosy. They don't try to talk to me, or get me to buy books. I like to browse and sometimes, when I've saved enough I get to buy a book.

I have enough money to get the new book in one of my favorite series tonight. I'm looking forward to it.

"Do you want to go to a party with me?" Shea asks.

My entire body goes rigid in horror at the idea. "No."

Shea laughs. "Wow, okay. Not your thing, huh?"

"I don't like people."

"You like us. You really like Cian," she says teasingly.

"There are lots of people at parties. They bump into you. They touch you." Memories of my aunt and uncle's holiday parties make me nauseated. As a member of the family, I had no choice but to go.

Unfortunately, no matter how hard I tried to hide in a corner and stay out of the way, something always happened with me that embarrassed my aunt or infuriated my uncle.

"I hate parties."

Shea pats my arm. "It's okay. I guess you're a better match for my brother than anyone thinks because he doesn't like them either."

"You talk to people about me and your brother dating?"

"Are you kidding me? The way you two are with each other, it's the talk of the office and the family."

"Oh." I don't know if I like that. I go hot at the idea of people I don't know talking about me.

"I think you and Cian are great together."

"But other people don't?" I torture myself by asking.

"Well, you can't blame them. He is a mob boss and you are pretty shy."

Feeling sad for no accountable reason, I can only nod. They're all correct. I'm not in Cian's league. I'm pretty sure my friends would be really upset if I started dating a mobster too.

"Cheer up, Romeo and Juliet's families didn't think they were good together either, but they were deeply in love."

"And they both ended up dead."

"Don't be so morbid."

I'm not being morbid. They did end up dead. I sigh, feeling for the first time like I don't fit here and I'm really glad when it's five o'clock and I can go home.

I have a trip to the bookstore to look forward to. Only, the warmth of happiness that thought brought me earlier has been snuffed out.

~ ~ ~

I can hear furniture smashing in Cian's office when I come in to work the next morning. Connor and Lachlan are standing outside his door, but neither are making a move to go in.

"What's wrong?" I ask. "Is Cian all right?"

Lachlan and Connor both turn quickly to face me. Connor looks worried. Lachlan has a speculative gleam in his eye. It would make me nervous, but I'm too concerned about Cian to let it bother me right now.

"He's upset," Lachlan says.

That surprises me. I've seen Cian angry, but never upset. Maybe that's what Lachlan means. Even so, Cian's voice goes all harsh and deadly sometimes, but he doesn't yell. He doesn't stomp. Not even when people make really big mistakes.

"Can I do anything to help?" I ask.

Connor shakes his head vehemently.

"Are you sure you want to?" Lachlan asks.

I nod without hesitation. Even if he can never return my feelings, Cian is special. And he's been really kind to me. If I can help him, I want to.

"No." Connor glares at Lachlan. "She's just a girl."

Indignant, I assure him, "I'm not a child."

Connor shakes his head again, but he's looking at Lachlan. "You cannot do it."

"Last time he took out an entire gang almost single handedly. What do you think he'll do to that fraternity, to find the ones who hurt Shea? No matter how many cops we have in our pocket, he'll go down for it and it will give the FEDs an in to our organization."

I ignore the reference to crooked cops. Everyone knows the construction business in Chicago runs on wheels oiled by paid off politicians. Why not cops too?

His other words make my heart pound though. "Someone hurt Shea?"

Lachlan jerks his head in a nod, banked fury making his gaze hard.

"Last night?" I ask. "At the party?"

"How did you know about the party?" Lachlan demands menacingly.

I step back from him. "She invited me to go."

What if I'd gone? Could I have stopped her getting hurt?

Lachlan glowers at me. "Why didn't you tell someone she was planning to go to a party?"

"Come on, Lach. How was Anna supposed to know that Shea was sneaking out?" Connor moves so he's standing between me and the furious man.

"She snuck out? But isn't she eighteen?"

"She's not allowed to go out without a bodyguard," Connor explains. "It's not safe. She ditched her bodyguard last night to go to the frat party."

"I thought school was out for the summer."

"Classes resume next week."

It is mid-August. Wow. Hard to believe I've already been working here for almost two months.

"I'm so sorry she got hurt."

A crash sounds from Cian's office.

"It's bad, isn't it?" I ask, my heart squeezing with pain. I like Shea.

"They found her this morning," Connor answers.

But that's not what I asked.

Lachlan's expression is grim. "She's in the hospital. And if we don't calm Cian down, he's going to do something he can't come back from."

I don't know what he means, but I hate the thought of Cian being so upset.

"*We* aren't doing anything. You want this innocent colleen to beard the lion in his den." Connor sounds angry.

I'm sure they all are. And he's Cian's cousin, which makes him Shea's cousin as well. He's got to be furious about what happened to her.

"Do ye mind going in there and smiling at him?" Lachlan asks.

Um... "You want me to smile at him?"

Lachlan doesn't look like he's making a joke. His expression is dead serious. "Yes."

"Oh...kay...I mean if you think it will help."

"Lachlan." Connor shakes his head. "If this goes sideways, he'll never forgive you."

"It won't."

It's gone silent in Cian's office. Maybe he ran out of things to break.

"You ready?" Lachlan asks.

I nod, though I'm not sure that I am. I'm just an employee with a massive crush on my boss. I don't see how me trying to comfort him is going to help Cian. They should call his mother, only that's not what my heart wants.

It wants to be the one to calm him down. Everything in me demands that I at least try.

Lachlan opens the door. "Anna's coming in, Cian. Check yerself."

Then he sort of pushes me into the room and the door shuts behind me.

Cian is standing in the middle of the room breathing heavily. The office looks like a tornado hit it, leaving nothing but destruction in its wake.

"What are you doing here?" Cian's eyes are cold, but the rage is right there under the surface.

I've never seen him angry. Even when he threatened that guy at the restaurant, Cian wasn't mad. He was just resolute. The fury burning in his blue eyes makes my mouth go dry with nerves.

What can I do to help him?

He's given me so much peace, I want to give some back, but I don't know how. I think Lachlan is dreaming if he thinks me smiling at our boss is going to help calm that rage, but maybe something else will. I mean it works for other women. I've never tried anything like this before.

But Cian spends almost as much time looking at my breasts as he does looking into my eyes. He must be a boob man? It makes me feel good, so I don't mention it to anyone else. I don't want him to stop looking at me.

Though Ini noticed that one time.

Having Cian's eyes on me is the best feeling ever.

Right now, though, that gaze almost sees through me.

I'm pretty sure I know how to get his attention focused on me, but will it cost me my job? Even if it does, it's worth it if I can help Cian calm down. Help him back to the present and not thinking about whatever happened to Shea.

I'm nervous. No man has ever seen my naked breasts. Can I do this?

His gaze drops to my chest, and I make up my mind. I'm doing this.

I would risk almost anything for the man standing there in so much pain its only outlet is fury.

CHAPTER 11

CIAN

Anna isn't smiling at me like she usually does. Her pretty eyes are filled with concern. For me.

She doesn't need to worry about me. It's the fucking frat boys I'm going to annihilate that should be worried. For every mark on Shea's body, I will leave ten on theirs. A minute ago, I planned to kill them all for guilt by association. I'm more rational now.

It's Anna. Somebody pushed her into my office. Probably Lachlan.

He knows I won't hurt her, but it was still an unacceptable risk. And he'll understand that when I'm done with him. Later.

Inhaling, Anna's beautiful tits push against her top. It looks soft and clings to her curves. I bet her skin in softer. My fingers itch to find out.

She's so damn beautiful.

Anna swallows like she's nervous, but her violet eyes reflect determination. "Do you want to see them?"

For a second, I'm sure my fucking ears are playing tricks on me.

But then her hands go to the hem of her top. "You look at them a lot when you're not looking at my face."

"Your eyes are like violets." I am not a fucking poet. Why did I say that?

"You like my eyes?" she asks.

I nod.

"My family thinks they're weird."

The same people who kicked her out at eighteen and expected her to fend for herself? "They're idiots."

"You always say the right thing." Her hands flirting with the hem of her top, she smiles.

"Your smiles are always beautiful." But she offered something more. Something I want. I growl, "Show me."

Anna's smile gets a little nervous around the edges, but she lifts her top excruciating inch by excruciating inch. She's not trying to tease me. This is what worried her. Thinking about offering to show me her body. I don't know why she does it; I don't care. I want to see.

Her bra comes into view. It's a beige color, made of some kind of soft, stretchy fabric. No lace. It covers her tits completely. Not a garment designed to seduce, but it's the sexiest damn thing I've ever laid eyes on.

I lick my lips. Anna notices, her own parting on a soft sigh.

"Now the bra," I demand.

She reaches behind herself to unhook it. Then she pulls the fabric up, bunching her pink top and plain bra above her gorgeous pink tipped mounds. My mouth salivates to taste her nipples. They *are* the same pretty color as her lips. They stiffen into points under my lust-filled gaze.

"I want to touch."

Her eyes dilate, her gaze becoming hazy. She nods.

I cross the distance separating us with two large steps. I want to squeeze those tits until I leave my fingerprints in bruises, claiming them and her as mine. But I reach out and cup them with a reverence I have never shown a woman's body. I am not a bad lover, but I have sex with women who don't expect foreplay before or sweet words after.

For Anna, I know there will be both. We aren't having sex right now. She's not ready and I'm still too damn pissed.

"Your skin is soft." I gently knead her mounds, reveling in the feel of her silken skin against my fingers.

Her breath comes in shallow pants, and I can see the pulse beating in her neck. I brush my thumbs over her taut nips, circling around the rigid little nubs.

Anna looks drunk, her face slack with pleasure, but there's something else too. Like she's hypnotized by the feel of my hands on her tits.

"Beautiful," I say.

Her lips part on a soft sigh and her body relaxes, every bit of tension draining out of her. It's only in that moment I realize how much she carries usually.

I continue to squeeze gently and her soft, cushiony flesh gives way under my fingers. Everything about this woman is genuine and so damn enticing. I can't believe she offered her tits to me like this. I'll never be able to go another day without craving them.

I lightly pinch both of her nipples at the same time. She gasps, her knees buckling.

I catch her, lift her, and carry her to the couch by the window. I'll never have another business meeting here without thinking of my beautiful Anna, her gorgeous curves bared for me. Sitting down, I arrange her on my lap with her knees on either side of my thighs.

Her body is totally pliable and she lets me settle her exactly how I want her.

She offered herself this way to calm me down. No one told her to do this. Damn Lachlan probably told her to smile at me. And that was enough to downgrade my plans from homicide to maiming. Except the assholes who actually touched Shea. They are going to die. Slowly. After much pain.

Anna's gaze sharpens, her violet eyes focusing on my face. "Are you alright?"

I want the hazy look back and force myself to release my thoughts of revenge for right now. I can't do anything for Shea, but Anna needs something from me. Something only I can give her. And I need her to let me give it to her.

She starts to shift, like she's going to get off my lap.

I lean forward letting our foreheads touch as I caress her delicious tits. "I'm not done touching you." I'll never get enough of her silken skin beneath my roughened hands.

"Oh." After a couple of breaths, she relaxes once more.

Pulling my head back, I see that her eyes have gone hazy again. Good. I kiss her forehead, her temples and both sides of her neck, before I finally press my lips to hers. I don't use my tongue, but it's so damn erotic, I nearly come in my pants.

Fuck.

I want to watch myself playing with her, so I pull my head back. The sight of my hands against her creamy flesh sends blood rushing to my already hard dick. I don't know how long I play with her, but she never asks me to stop, or moves like she's growing bored. And fuck if I'm bored. I could do this for hours.

The blush of arousal turns her skin pink, her nipples now a dark berry red. I want to taste them. So, I do.

So damn sweet.

Her body tenses and I let her nipple go with a final gentle pull to look and see if she's okay.

She looks confused. "Why did you stop?" Then, not waiting for an answer, Anna grabs my head and pulls me back to her tit.

I suck on her pillowy softness, bringing up a hickey to mark her. She moans and I pull her nipple back into my mouth, suckling hard. Anna's hands fall away, letting me do whatever I want.

I slide my hands over her curves, kneading and tweaking the nipple not in my mouth. Her pelvis rocks against my legs and I yank her body forward so her hot sex is right over my rigid cock.

She's making sounds like a mewling kitten.

I switch my mouth to her other tit and play with the now wet nipple with my other hand. Making a sound halfway between a scream and a groan, Anna's body bows. Fuck. She's coming. I arch up toward her grinding her pussy against me. She shudders and jolts like it's too much pleasure for her body.

Then she goes boneless.

I'm still hard as a pike, but I don't care. I release her nipple and place a kiss on the still hard tip before lifting my head so I can see her face again. Anna's pupils are completely blown, like she's done E. Not my girl. She will never touch a fucking drug. But she doesn't need them. My playing with her tits did this.

I feel peace like nothing I've ever known.

I *feel*.

I replace her bra and then tug down her top. I let her slump forward against my chest, wrapping my arms around her.

She nuzzles her face into me and then goes still, her breath steady and even. "Cian," she sighs.

Sometime later, the door opens slowly. Lachlan cautiously enters the destroyed office. His eyes land on us and widen with shock.

"What the fuck do you want?" I whisper the words, not wanting to disturb the treasure in my lap.

"You need to get to the hospital." He looks at Anna. "We should get her home."

He's right. I need to get to the hospital. Uncle Jimmy is there with Ma. I should be too. But if Anna hadn't come in when she did, I wouldn't have gone to the hospital. I would have gone on the hunt and killed every last fucker in that fraternity.

Now, I can go to the hospital. I can tell Ma not to worry. I'll take care of it, and I will do it without killing them all.

"I'll take her home." I can't trust my Anna with anyone else in her blissed out state.

"Her home?" Lachlan has the fucking nerve to ask me after shoving her through that door like a sacrificial lamb.

I cup her cheek and lift her head. "Anna."

"Mmm?"

"Do you want to go to your apartment or my home?" I ask.

Some of the unfocused satiation bleeds from her soft features. And I hate it. I want her to always be completely vulnerable to me. But only to me.

She's thinking. I can tell. Finally, she blinks like she's trying to clear her head. "My apartment."

I don't like that answer, but I will respect it. For now.

When she tries to stand, she is woozy and I lift her into my arms to carry her out to the car. Connor is driving and Lachlan slides into the front seat with him. They'll both want to check on Shea at the hospital. I'm surprised Lachlan hasn't already gone. He's always been protective of my sisters, but especially Shea.

I realize him still being here is my fault. I lost my temper for the second time in my life, and my head with it. He protected me and the mob from what I would have done without Anna's intervention.

"What is the word on Shea?" I should have been at the hospital checking on her, not losing my shit.

"She woke up, but doesn't want to see anyone except your mam."

That explains why Lachlan hasn't left already.

"Did she give names?" The rage coils tightly in my gut, but it's leashed for now.

"Not to the cops," Lachlan says with satisfaction. "But your mam texted me two names just before I came in to get you."

"Take them. Put them on ice at the apartment safehouse."

Needing to feel her skin, I take Anna's hand in mine and brush my thumb back and forth across her palm. I wish she could sit on my lap, but that wouldn't be safe for her in case someone with a death wish ran into our car.

"Don't rough them up too much." Normally, my second wouldn't need the reminder, but he's got a soft spot for Shea. "We'll interrogate them tonight."

Lachlan nods, his jaw like granite.

We're halfway to Anna's apartment and she tugs at my hand. Not like she's trying to get me to let her go, but like she wants my attention.

I look down at her.

Anna's violet eyes are no longer hazy with bliss but are now drenched with concern. For me. "Are you going to see her?"

"Yes."

"Do you want me to come with you? I mean, you probably don't need me to, I just—" She breaks off, blushing.

Fuck. She's offering to stay with me? "Yes."

Anna smiles and some weird warm thing unfurls in my chest.

CHAPTER 12

ANNA

I tuck everything I experienced in Cian's office in the back of my consciousness. He needs a friend right now and I want to be that friend, but if I let myself think about what happened when I showed him my breasts, I will get lost in my head.

Anxiety pushes against the walls I put up in my brain. I will deal with that later too.

When we get to the hospital, there's a man waiting to show us to Shea's floor. "I'm so sorry, Boss. I didn't even know she left the house."

Cian's body goes rigid, fury coming off him in waves, but it's Lachlan who moves.

He punches the other man, knocking him back several feet and onto his butt. "What the fuck, Sully? It's your job to know." He storms forward, but Cian grabs his arm, hard.

Lachlan turns toward Cian, snarling fury in every line of his body. "He deserves to die for this."

"No."

The other man, Sully, stands. "Her tracker showed her at home."

"And you didn't think to check? Not once, all night long?"

"If I did, the boss would gouge out my eyes," Sully says and then mutters, "If you didn't do it first."

I remember how protective of Shea that Lachlan was at the Greek deli. He's always watching over her at the office too. She told me that he's as bad as her brother when it comes to telling her what to do.

Sully is right. If another man were to check in on her at night, Lachlan wouldn't like it. No matter what he's saying now. Neither would Cian.

He yanks his arm away from Cian and glowers. "She needs a tracker embedded."

"Yes," Cian agrees. "I'll put a thermal camera in her bedroom too, with an alarm if the thermal signature goes dark."

I don't think Shea will like any of that. She hates that her brother, and apparently her bodyguards, track her through her phone. While I would love to have Cian checking in on me like that, which undoubtedly makes me as weird as my family has always claimed, Shea will go ballistic when she finds out.

And she will find out. She's too smart and independent not to.

Also, I feel obligated to tell her about Cian's plans when she's feeling better. She's my friend. I'll tell Cian I told her. He's my friend too.

Without any further violence, Sully leads us to the waiting area nearest Shea's room. It's empty except for a couple of men who acknowledge Cian and Lachlan with nods.

"Gulliver is on guard outside her room, Boss," Sully says. "Your mom wants me to let her know when you get here."

Cian inclines his head and Sully takes off. He's back a few minutes later with an older woman. Her hair is the same reddish gold as Cian's, but with strands of grey. Her plump face is lined with worry and exhaustion.

Grabbing her son's arms, she looks imploringly into his face. "Tell me you didn't blow up the frat house, boyo."

Cian's face is impassive when he shakes his head. "Lachlan will nab the men who touched her. We'll deal with them. If any others knew about the attack, we'll deal with them."

Mrs. Doyle's eyes widen, like she's surprised. "Good. That's good."

Then she notices me. Maybe because Cian is still holding my hand and I'm so close, or because I'm a stranger in a private family situation.

"You must be Anna," she says to me.

I nod. Shea said she told her mom about me. I wonder if Mrs. Doyle thinks it's odd her son is holding my hand. It is strange, but I like it and I think he needs it, so I'm not pulling away.

"Anna helped your boy contain his rage," Lachlan says.

Heat climbs into my cheeks when I think of how I did that. I push the thoughts away, not ready to deal with them yet.

Mrs. Doyle looks down at our joined hands and up at her son, her expression anxious. Then she gives me a strained smile. "My son didn't drag you here, did he?"

"No. I offered to come."

"With your boss to the hospital?" Mrs. Doyle's tone is pure disbelief.

I know I'm not like other people, but the rest of her family is okay with that. I hope she will be too. "He's also my friend."

"Is he? That's um...that's nice. Cian is not big on making friends."

"I'm not either," I admit.

"You're shy," Mrs. Doyle says, like she knows. Then she looks at her son. "Shea said she wants to see you, boyo. Promise me you won't lecture her about sneaking out."

"There's nothing to say that she doesn't already know," Cian says.

I'm sure he's right. "Tell her you love her," I instruct him. "She needs to hear that. And that you don't think less of her for what happened to her."

Cian looks down at me. "She should know that."

"We don't always know what other people think we do." Ini taught me that.

She's much more open with her feelings, but when she needs me to reassure her, she tells me. Because she knows a lot happens in my head that never makes it out of my mouth. I love both her and Mrs. Hart, but I never told them until one night when Ini told me that some words have to be said, not just felt.

So, that's what I say now. "Some words have to be spoken."

Cian nods. "Okay." He squeezes my hand and then lets it go before turning and leaving without another word.

"Tell her I want to see her," Lachlan calls to Cian.

Cian puts his hand up in acknowledgment. I watch him until he disappears around a corner in the hall. Then I turn to face Mrs. Doyle and Lachlan. Best case scenario, they are talking to each other, but I can feel their gazes on me.

Sure enough, Mrs. Doyle is looking at me with a bemused expression.

Lachlan is frowning. "Do you want one of the men to take you home while Cian is busy with Shea?"

Not sure why he's offering that, I shake my head. I don't want to leave until I know Cian doesn't need me anymore.

"Are you sure, lass?" Mrs. Doyle asks. "Cian won't fire you if you go home. I'll make sure of it."

"I know." Why would she think I was worried about that?

Mrs. Doyle doesn't look convinced. "He can be a wee intense."

I nod. It's true. Cian is deliciously intense. Especially when his focus is entirely on me. Aargh! I shove that thought down with the others. I cannot think about his sensual intensity right now. His mother is standing right there.

"I'm sorry I shoved you into his office," Lachlan says. "That wasn't fair to you."

"It's fine."

"I was right though, wasn't I? Your smile calmed him right down."

He'd found me cuddled up on my boss's lap, so blissed out I could barely string two words together, and Lachlan thought it was my smile that had calmed Cian? Mrs. Hart is right. Men can be very oblivious.

"You sent her into his office to calm him down?" Mrs. Doyle asked, her tone scolding. "That could have gone very badly."

"He is my friend. I wanted to help." I'm not sure what I should say right now to relieve the tension between Cian's mom and his right-hand man. Truth is pretty much my only option anyway.

Lachlan's phone buzzes and he slips it out of his suit breast pocket. He reads the screen.

"Shea will see me if Cian stays in the room." He curses.

"Aren't you glad she wants to see you?" I ask.

"Yes," he grinds out, like it's hard to say.

I wish I could understand what is upsetting him.

"It's not that she doesn't trust you, boyo. She probably thinks Cian will stop you from yelling at her for sneaking out," Mrs. Doyle says consolingly.

"Of course, she trusts you," I say. He knows that, but maybe it's another one of those things that has to be said out loud.

Lachlan grimaces, but he doesn't reply. He turns and leaves.

I'm pretty much alone with my boss's mother now. There are still three men in the room with us. Sully, and the two that were here when we arrived, but I don't know them and I doubt they will try to talk to me.

Presumably the one called Gulliver is still standing watch outside Shea's room.

"I could use a decent cup of coffee. Will you come with me, Anna?" Mrs. Doyle asks.

I saw a coffee bistro in the main lobby of the hospital on our way in. It shouldn't take us too long to get the other woman what she wants so I nod. I want to be back in the waiting room when Cian comes out of his sister's room though.

Sully follows us to the elevator.

"Do you like working for my son?" Mrs. Doyle asks as we make our slow descent.

"Yes. He's a very good boss."

"And you consider him a friend?" she asks.

Sully makes a strange noise, but when I look at him, his face is impassive.

"Yes."

"Why?"

"He's kind. When my friends wanted me to quit my job, he talked to them for me."

"Cian spoke to your friends on your behalf?" Mrs. Doyle sounds like she's choking on something.

"He did. And he got Mrs. Hart and Ini and me new, safer doors for our apartments." I don't tell her that her son makes everything less overwhelming. She'll think I'm weird like my family does and I want Mrs. Doyle to like me.

"That didn't upset them, these friends of yours, that my son just showed up out of the blue to talk to them?"

"Mrs. Hart said she was scared at first, but they had tea together and she doesn't try to talk me into quitting anymore."

"Why did your friends want you to quit?"

"Because your son is a mob boss."

The elevator doors open and we step out into the lobby.

Mrs. Doyle grabs my arm and I try hard not to jerk away, but it feels like ants are crawling on my skin. "My son told you that?" she demands.

"Mrs. Hart told me." I hurry to get in the line for coffee, pulling my arm from her grip.

"Perhaps we should continue this discussion upstairs," Mrs. Doyle says when she joins me.

I take a step sideways, creating more distance between us. "Okay."

We get her coffee. She offers to get me something, but I decline. I don't drink caffeinated beverages. My stomach growls when we reach the cashier though and she insists on getting me a sandwich. I end with a bottle of water as well. She gets several more sandwiches and bottles of water for *her boys*.

"Aren't you going to eat anything?" I ask her.

She shakes her head. "I'm not hungry."

"You should have a scone. It will help soak up the acid from the coffee and your stress," I tell her and then snap my mouth shut.

She probably doesn't want my advice.

But she adds a scone to the order and changes her coffee to a hot tea.

The elevator is crowded and if I were alone, I would wait for the next empty car, but I'm not. So, I force myself to cram into the mass of people in the tiny box. I'm jostled from all sides but the front, where Mrs. Doyle stands. Sully is in front of her and creates some kind of invisible bubble around her so people aren't pressing into Cian's mom.

I wish I could create magic space bubbles like that.

CHAPTER 13

ANNA

By the time we reach the ninth floor, I want to crawl out of my own skin. I need a shower. Too many people touched me. I can still feel them.

Cian isn't there when we get into the waiting room. I'm glad his sister's visit is going well, but I want to see him.

Maybe I should have taken Lachlan up on the offer of sending me home. Cian probably doesn't need me. Why would he? He has his mom here and his men.

Lachlan comes into the room looking like thunder. Mrs. Doyle tries to get him to eat a sandwich, but he brusquely refuses and I rethink asking him for a ride home.

"I'll just join Cian in Shea's room, then," Mrs. Doyle says after Lachlan leaves. "It was a pleasure meeting you, Anna. I only wish it hadn't been on such a terrible day for all of us."

I nod and manage not to jump away when she hugs me. I even put my arms around her and squeeze back a little. When she lets go, I sag into the nearest chair. The men are back at their posts, eating their sandwiches and watching. For what? Maybe they think whoever hurt Shea will come to the hospital and try to hurt Mrs. Doyle? Or even Shea again.

Do they think what happened to Shea is because of her connection to the mob? Only things like that happen on college campuses. Fraternity parties are big on alcohol and low on security. My oldest cousin used to brag about how many drunk girls he banged when his frat hosted parties.

I thought it was disgusting and told him so.

My aunt and uncle were both angry with me, but I wouldn't apologize. Not about that. My cousins and their gross attitude toward women and sex are one of the reasons I'm still a virgin. The other is that allowing someone into my personal space is not my thing.

Except Cian. But he's not here.

My body is jittery with all the touches from the elevator. I think what happened in Cian's office opened up my receptors, because everything is so much more than usual. And the sounds, smells and touch of the world around is usually too much to begin with.

My fingernails clicking in a steady, unrelenting rhythm, I'm humming as I say my rhyme inside my head. Over and over again. It doesn't help. Why doesn't it help?

Then I feel him. Cian.

I look up, dropping my half-eaten sandwich and bottle of water on the floor. I surge up from my chair and grab his arm. But for the first time, it's not enough. Things are still too much. I want to curl up in a corner, behind a chair where no one can touch me.

Cian's expression is grim. He's upset about his sister even if his face doesn't show it. He doesn't need my issues on top of everything else.

I'm useless. I'm not a good friend. I can't stay here anymore. Cian needs better friends. Not me.

Never me.

I'm not enough. I can't be. I need space. I turn and run toward the elevator. Jabbing the button, I'm trying so hard not to lose it completely. Cian doesn't need that. He needs to be here with his family. Not to be concerned about me.

"I'll see you later," I force myself to say over my shoulder, trying to sound normal. "I need to get going."

Only Cian is right there. His arms come around me, strong and sure. He pulls me into his body wrapping me up tight. His heat and solid presence against my back lets me breathe again.

My muscles loosen and I don't care how weak this makes me. I need it. I let myself lean against him. He turns me, so all I can smell is him. All I can feel is his arms around me. All I can hear is his heartbeat. I lean hard against his chest, listening to the steady thump as my body's fight or flight response ebbs.

"Are you ready to go?" he asks, like none of this is out of the ordinary.

"Yes," I croak out. "Could someone take me home?"

I could get the L, but just the thought of all the people on the train makes nausea rise in my throat. I'll splurge for a rideshare at this point even if that means no new books for the next month.

He doesn't answer, just keeps holding me tight. I hear the ding indicating the elevator's arrival and then the swoosh of the doors opening. Without pushing or releasing me, he guides us into the elevator. One of the men that was in the waiting room joins us.

"Where is Connor?" I ask, just now realizing he didn't come inside the hospital with us.

"He went back to run the office."

"I should join him." I probably never should have left. I really shouldn't have let my boss touch me so intimately and lost track of what was going on around me so completely.

"No." Cian's arms tighten around me. "You are going home and resting."

I want to say I don't need to rest, but the truth is, I don't think I can handle any more stimulation. If I knew I would be alone with Connor in the office that might work, but right now, I'm not even sure I could be around Connor without losing it.

The doors ding and open. I know we aren't at the lobby yet. Stifling a whimper, I press harder into Cian's body.

His arms tighten around me. "Take the next car. This one is full," he barks. That happens twice more before we reach the ground floor.

Cian keeps me close to him all the way to the car, though he lets me turn and walk by his side once we exit the elevator. When we get to the car, he pulls the seatbelt across my body, buckling me in.

I force myself to meet his eyes. "I'm sorry. I wanted to help you and now you're having to take care of me."

"You saved the lives of at least two dozen frat boys today, Anna. You did help." He brushes my cheek with his fingertip and I lean toward his hand. He cups my face. "You are so damn sweet."

"Will Shea be okay?" I ask, because I want to know.

"Physically, she will heal completely."

But emotionally, she had a long road ahead of her. I don't know exactly what happened, but whatever it was put her in the hospital.

"I'll take you to see her when she gets home."

"I can go by myself," I mumble. "I'm not usually so..." I'm not sure how to term this sense that all my receptors have been opened, leaving me as defenseless as a newborn kitten to the press of humanity.

"You are exactly as you are meant to be, my Anna."

I wish I was *his* Anna, but it's a sweet thing to say, so I force a smile. "Thanks. I'll be better tomorrow."

He frowns. "I want to take you to my apartment."

"Will you be there?" I ask.

His frown darkens. "No."

He has to punish his sister's attackers. He hasn't said as much, but he told Lachlan to pick them up and take them somewhere that was not the police station.

"She didn't want to tell the officers who interviewed her who hurt her," I remark. "But she told your family."

"Mob justice doesn't have loopholes like our legal system."

I think even if Cian wasn't a boss in the mob, he would still mete out his own justice. He sees the world through a different lens. Like I do. Our lenses aren't the same, but they are both different than most people's.

CIAN

Anna decides she wants to go back to her apartment. I am not surprised, what did surprise me is that she considered going to my place. If I was going to be there, she might have been willing to return with me.

No matter how much I want to spend more time with my girl, I have two assholes to teach a lesson.

It takes us thirty minutes to reach Anna's building. She usually takes the L train and it makes me agitated every day thinking about her commute to and from the office on public transport. Anything could happen to her.

Anna is quiet. Lost in her own head, but she seems calmer than she was in the hospital. So, I spend the time on my phone, texting my men and checking my email. The dissonance between running the mob and our legit businesses is never more pronounced than today.

Images of my sister's bruised and broken body lying in that hospital bed keep flashing in my brain. Whenever my fury boils too close to the surface, I reach out and touch Anna. After a few minutes, she puts her hand on my thigh and I'm able to focus on my work.

Letting her return to her apartment after what happened in my office is harder than it should be. Even with my cameras in place. I want to assign a twenty-four hour protection detail on her, but the more people who know she is important to me, the more danger she is in.

Quinn, that bastard, suspects already. Who knows who the Murphy Boss told about my claim on Anna?

Just like Shea, Anna is now at risk because of her proximity to me. The selfish bastard that I am, I have no plans to distance myself from my girl either.

I'll know soon enough if my sister was hurt because of her connection to the mob, or if it was a random act of violence perpetrated by two college students that will have a degree in pain by the time Lachlan and I are done with them.

Looking down at Anna's small hand resting on my thigh, I can't ignore how vulnerable she is. Even more than Shea because Anna hasn't been taught to fight or how to handle a gun.

Fuck it.

I send texts to three of my most reliable men, Arlo, Eoin and Tommy. They'll work on rotation, so she always has someone alert on her. She won't need a guard at night, but they'll have to move into her building so they're nearby if there's trouble. I spell it all out for them in text. I expect them to get accommodation in her building by tonight.

How they do it is up to them. They know I'll pay to relocate tenants if necessary. They also know that failure is not an option and they need to use whatever form of persuasion necessary to get their asses in an apartment on her floor.

CHAPTER 14

CIAN

When we reach Anna's apartment building, I tell the driver to wait and I get out.

My girl looks up at her apartment building like she doesn't recognize it. That's a good sign. The less it feels like home without me the faster I'll get her moved into my place. Keeping her safe will be easier if she lives with me.

I go around to open her door.

She takes my offered hand, but frowns. "You didn't have to get out."

"How else am I going to see you safely to your door?"

Her brow wrinkles in sweet confusion. "That's not necessary."

"I disagree."

The elevator is out of order, so we take the stairs. "How does Mrs. Hart leave the building when the elevator isn't working?" I ask.

"She doesn't. Her hip won't handle the stairs, so she stays in. Ini and I get her what she needs, but I don't like her being trapped in her apartment."

"How often is the elevator out of order?"

"It usually takes the building super at least a week to fix it and it goes out every month, or so."

So, they are without a working elevator close to half of the time. This pisses me off. We're criminals, but the apartment buildings we own would never be neglected like this. "I'll take care of it."

"That's not your responsibility. You can't go around fixing everything."

"Why not?"

"I don't want to be a burden."

"Not possible." She is mine. That means I take care of her.

My girl doesn't seem to realize that yet. Even after today.

She hunches her shoulders as she grabs the handrail. "I can't rely on someone else to take care of me."

She can, but that's something else she'll have to come to terms with. Anna may have lived with her aunt and uncle, but she lost her support network when her parents died. That is obvious.

Her roommate must be working at the pet store because she's not there when Anna lets us into her apartment. She stands in the middle of her living-dining-kitchen combo space and rubs her arms, like she's not sure what to do.

"What helps?" I ask her.

She looks at me strangely, but then she shrugs. "Quiet. Being alone."

"Do you have a spot here?"

She leads me into the only bedroom in the small apartment. There are no actual beds in the space, but each woman has a single size mattress on the floor. Crates with neatly folded and stacked clothes are at the head of each *bed*. There is no closet.

I want to hit something when I see how sparsely Anna is living.

She waves toward a blanket hanging on the wall. "I pull that out, like a tent and tuck it under the outer side of my mattress. It helps."

"Okay, get in, then."

"Um...I need to change into pajamas. I won't relax if I keep my work clothes on."

"Then change."

"You're here."

I don't remind her that she showed me her bare tits earlier. And let me touch them. "I'll turn around."

She waits until I do that before I hear clothing rustling.

"Okay," she says.

I turn back and she's already on the mattress, a sheet and blanket over her legs. She's sitting up, though. Her shoulders are bare but for the two thin strips that hold her pale peach camisole nightgown up. It's satin, but from looking at what is in the crates, it's her only one. She doesn't have a lot of clothes, but everything she has looks soft. Like her.

"I'll have dinner delivered for you and your friends. You take the time you need to decompress from today."

"You're the one that needs to be pampered. It's your sister that was hurt," she says, like she feels guilty I'm looking out for her.

"You took care of me earlier today. Now it's my turn."

A pretty blush rises from the swell of her breasts, up her neck, and turns her cheeks pink. "Um...I don't..."

"Ready?" I ask, so she doesn't try to finish that sentence.

She nods, but looks confused.

I squat and kiss her gently, then I grab the blanket and pull it into a lean-to style tent, tucking it under the length of the mattress. The room is so compact that with her crates at one end, there is no space for anyone at the other end. Her little lean-to gives her an illusion of total privacy.

"Thank you." Her voice is soft.

"You're welcome. Do you have noise cancelling earbuds?" I ask.

"No, but I have earplugs. I'll put them in after you go."

Making a note to get her the noise cancelling kind, I say, "I will see you tomorrow."

She doesn't answer, but I can hear her settling onto the mattress.

"I'm using your keys to lock the door. Someone will drop them off later."

"Thank you," she says again. "Ini will be here by six."

I don't want her thanks. I want her in my place where I can watch over her. She needs a space where she can go and shut out the world. I start thinking about how to make that happen on my way back down the stairs.

~ ~ ~

Lachlan and I spend most of the night with the two frat boys.

The Kicks Bandidos are supplying the frats with party drugs. The university isn't in my territory, but that doesn't mean I'll let that shit stand. Someone else can provide the spoiled rich kids their recreational highs. The gang made an even bigger mistake targeting my sister than they did invading my territory.

I will burn down their whole fucking gang before I'm through.

After we get what we need from them, they both die choking on their own cocks. They deserved worse after what they did to Shea.

I let Lachlan do one, while I handled the other.

He needed it. After he came over from Ireland, my father brought Lachlan into our family and eventually his inner circle. My second is as protective of my sisters as I am.

Sometimes, I think he wants Shea, but she's too damn young and he knows it.

"*El Fantasma* is organized," Lachlan says, his entire body radiating fury. "She's got somebody good gathering her intel."

I have to agree. Martina Vega, aka *El Fantasma*, either knew or discovered quickly that my sister was enrolled to attend the college. She contacted her two dealers in the fraternity after we scooped up her other people on our streets and gave them instructions to get Shea invited to the party. What they did after she arrived was also on *El Fantasma*'s say-so.

I might have let Martina retreat after the incursion on our streets, but now she will die. My second looks like he's got some ideas about how to make that death as painful as possible.

"What about the little bitch that invited Shea to the party?" Lachlan asks.

"You heard them. She barely knew Shea." The sorority girl thought the blond frat boy had a thing for my sister and invited Shea as a favor to him.

"She is still the reason Shea was there."

"What do you suggest?" The young woman might not have known that she was luring Shea to an assault, but she's still culpable.

"Her friend was a drug dealer. It shouldn't take too much to find something on her and get her kicked out. Shea should never have to see her again."

"Do it, but Shea isn't giving that school another fucking chance."

"Your sister is transferring to a different university?"

"Ma thinks she should join Máire in Ireland."

"Shea already said she didn't want to do that."

I nod. "I suggested Smith." It's out of state and an all-women's university.

"You think she'll go for it?"

Before this happened? My sister was adamant she wanted to stay in Chicago. Now? She's broken in a way I didn't know she could be. "Maybe."

CHAPTER 15

ANNA

My tent usually allows me to quiet my brain. Especially if I'm the only one home.

But my thoughts whirl and whirl and whirl.

I can hardly believe I offered my naked chest to Cian to calm him down. It worked and I don't regret that. But it's the way I responded to his voice, his eyes on me...his touch. My brain floated away on a cloud of pure bliss.

While he held me, that bliss was amazing. But later, it left me even more open to everything and everyone around me. Like my whole body is one exposed raw nerve. Was it the trip to the hospital that tipped me over? I wanted to go to support Cian, but I ended up needing his help to get home.

Tears burn a path down my temples. I used to cry all the time, alone in my room at my aunt and uncle's home, after Mom and Dad were killed. Eventually, I stopped. I realized that tears never made anything better. They made my eyes burn and gave me a headache.

This is just one more example of something that started out good ended up being something I should never, ever do again.

Only, I don't know if I'll be able to help myself. I wanted to go to Cian's house so badly. To lay in his bed and inhale his scent, even if he wasn't there. He's my boss, not my boyfriend. No matter how kind he is.

Eventually, he'll get tired of being nice. Everyone does. How many teachers and school counselors reached out to me over the years? Every single one gave up when they realized that a few hugs and an offer to talk if I needed it wasn't going to make my issues magically disappear.

Ini and Mrs. Hart are the only ones who never got tired of being my friends. But I'm careful not to be too needy. And I don't crave being near them like I do Cian. If he knew how much I wish I could be with him all the time, he would run the other way.

The only other person I ever felt that way about was my mom and even she needed breaks from me. She hated summer, when I didn't have to go to school. She'd get overwhelmed spending all day with me. I heard her tell my dad often enough.

That didn't stop her from performing our rituals, the things that muffled the noise inside my brain. We ate dinner at the same time every night and then watched Jeopardy after. Back when Alex Trebek was still the host.

I still watch the show, but it's not the same without her beside me. It helps me remember her though. I watch reruns from back then and pretend she's sitting beside me sometimes.

I tried to give Mom space, like I needed from other people. But it was never enough. Even so, I know she loved me. So did my dad. When they died, there was no one left to love me. I lost my anchor.

Cian doesn't deserve for me to make him my anchor now. He has a mob and a whole bunch of businesses to oversee. He doesn't need a clingy admin who craves his nearness and touch worse than any drug.

I'm going to have to quit my job. Ini and Mrs. Hart will be relieved.

That's something, right?

I can't stop the tears falling as I bury my face in my pillow.

CIAN

Anna texts Connor and tells him she's not coming into work today. She hasn't come out of her bedroom since I left her at her apartment yesterday. My camera is in her living area. Now, I'm regretting not putting one pointed to her bed. Though all I would see is her tent.

She didn't eat dinner last night. I saw Ini take a plate of food to her, but she brought it back out a couple of hours later untouched.

Is this normal? Is this what Anna needs to cope with whatever happened at the hospital?

Ini doesn't seem shocked by Anna's behavior, but I don't have sound on the cameras, so I can't be sure. She doesn't hesitate to leave my girl alone to take dinner down to Mrs. Hart.

Tommy got the elevator fixed and my men moved into an apartment on Anna's floor last night like I told them to. I still have Anna's keys. I should have sent them back, but I don't want to.

I play with them in my pocket while I watch Ronan continue to interrogate Carmen. She's had time to stew and to realize that she was set up by her cousin. She doesn't want to believe it at first, but Ronan is a convincing guy. He's even better at psychological manipulation than physical torture.

For some weird reason, I'm glad he doesn't have to waterboard her again. I don't think Anna would like it if she knew.

Which she never will, so it should not matter.

My girl is fucking with my head.

She needs to come back to work.

My head snaps up and I start paying closer attention when I hear the name Gutierrez. "Martina's father is Eduardo Gutierrez, the head of the Gutierrez Cartel?"

Carmen looks toward the wall, but she nods.

So, Martina Vega-Gutierrez, not just plain Martina Vega.

"Our moms are sisters, but my father is only a captain. Martina is here to prove her value to her father."

"Why are you here?" Ronan asks.

"To show my loyalty to the cartel."

"Your loyalty cost you your life."

She shivers, but nods. "I know. You can't let me go."

Ronan looks at me and then at her. "We aren't going to kill you."

"You just said..." She stares up at him, like she's trying to read his mind.

"Your life as Valeria Carmen Vega-Martinez *is* over."

"Then who am I now?" she demands.

He shrugs. "Not her. Where is your husband?"

"I can't tell you that."

"You can. You will. You think you owe them loyalty, but you don't."

"Would you say the same to one of the women in your organization."

"We would never put one of our women at risk like they put you."

"You think women are weak?" she demands, a spark of fire showing in her dark eyes.

"No, but if we sent one in on a reconnaissance job, we'd make sure she had a viable exit strategy and the training she needed to get it done."

"I'm trained."

Ronan shakes his head.

"Not good enough," I say. "You believed them when they said they could track you."

"They couldn't know you'd bring me someplace with a jammer."

We didn't have a jammer down here. We didn't need one. The entire basement is built to blanket devices. There's no cell signal down here. Radio waves, infrared and laser interferometry cannot penetrate the walls of this place. No spyware, no way of discovering the existence of this place.

"They could," I say regardless.

The use of jammers isn't new technology for criminal organizations. Her cousin had to expect we would employ something to block the signal of a tracking device.

Carmen's shoulders slump in defeat. "I thought I was ready. I thought my dad wanted me to prove myself too."

"Are you saying your father was aware of your operational role?" Ronan asked.

She gives a single affirmative jerk of her head.

Ronan frowns. "Asshole."

There were easier ways to take out a rival than sending them into the lion's den without backup. *El Fantasma* had to be aware that her cousin might talk before she was killed.

Which meant what? That the father had sacrificed his daughter for what?

I have an idea, and it's not a good one.

"Take off your clothes," I order.

When she doesn't cooperate immediately, Ronan strips her of the t-shirt he'd given her and the short skirt underneath. He doesn't have to remove her thong. The scar is right there on her lower belly. Fresh and pink.

"What is that?" Ronan points to the scar.

She's shaking, scared, but she looks down. "I had my appendix out a couple of weeks before we came. Why?"

Shit. Is it on a timer? Or is it rigged to explode when she's back in signal range. It's got to be a timer. So why hasn't it gone off yet?

Ronan jabs her neck with a sedative before Carmen realizes he's pulled out a hypodermic.

"What the hel—" Her voice slurs and fades as her body collapses.

Ronan catches her unconscious form. "I'll take her to the infirmary. Call the Butcher."

"Less danger for everyone if we kill her and dispose of the body before the bomb has a chance to go off."

Ronan ignores me and heads down the hall.

I don't push it. That weird sense of not wanting to do the wrong thing here is plaguing me again. I call the Butcher and explain the situation.

The crazy fucker doesn't hesitate. "I'll be there in ten."

He must be at our club the next block over because he lives about twenty-five minutes away.

An hour later, the Butcher with Ronan's assist has removed a container from inside her uterus. It's made of material that is disintegrating. Not sure what kind of virus it houses at this point, but we suspect it was meant to infect her and anyone she came into contact with. The cartel probably thought we'd beat her, which would have made it burst faster.

If it is one of the more virulent viruses, it could have wiped out our entire organization and a hell of a lot of innocent people besides. People like Anna.

It just gives me one more reason to burn that fucking cartel to the ground.

"When she wakes up, I'll question her again," Ronan tells me. "Once she realizes that her family turned her into a biological weapon, that should destroy the last of her resistance."

"You can offer her sanctuary," I tell him.

He nods, but I get the impression he would have done it without my order.

Ronan didn't want to be the boss, but that doesn't mean he'll ever be a deferential soldier. He'll never betray the mob, but he makes his own decisions. As long as they don't go contrary to my express orders, that's what I prefer. I don't want men who won't wipe their own ass without permission in charge of our businesses.

"I want a full report of everything she knows no later than tomorrow."

Ronan nods. "You'll get it."

I doubt Carmen knows much. They wouldn't have risked it, knowing they were sending her to die. But I bet she knows more than they expect and once she learns how deep their betrayal ran, she'll be eager to share it.

If she's not, Ronan will persuade her. Whatever it takes.

But we are taking these fuckers down.

~ ~ ~

Anna doesn't come into work again today. She doesn't leave her bedroom either. Other than to use the bathroom and I'm only assuming that she does that. Because the camera angle doesn't include the hallway.

I'm expecting it when Connor lets me know that Anna has texted him again the next morning. She's not coming in.

I wait in my car for Ini to leave the apartment, and then I go into the building. The elevator is working, but I take the stairs anyway. Her security team have installed a camera outside her door. One of them will see me as I unlock her door and step inside the apartment, so I acknowledge them with a backward wave.

There is no sound from Anna's room. Didn't she hear me come in?

"Anna," I call as I walk toward her bedroom. I don't want to scare her. "Get your ass out here."

I stop in the doorway of her bedroom. Her tent is still in place.

"Anna," I bark. Yes, I have more patience for her than anyone else, but it doesn't make me Mother Teresa.

I hear rustling and then the blanket is pulled aside and Anna looks up at me, her eyes rounded in shock. "What are you doing here, Cian?" She blinks up at me like she's trying to figure out if I'm real. "Didn't Connor tell you I'm not coming in?"

Her blond hair is a messy halo around her face. She's still wearing the sleep camisole she put on the day before yesterday. She's fucking beautiful and if we didn't have so much shit to get done today, I would join her on that single mattress on the floor.

"You're not sick."

Her shoulders hunch, her gaze dropping away from me. "Are you going to fire me?"

"No."

Her head jerks up. "Why not?"

CHAPTER 16

CIAN

"I told you, you're staying." I am not letting her go.

"But I let you down."

"When?"

"At the hospital. I was supposed to be there for you and you ended up having to take care of me."

"Fuck that shit. I'll take care of you if I want to. I'm the boss." And she is mine.

"But I'm not a good friend."

"Are you hiding from me because of what happened in my office?" I'm not dancing around this. We're going to deal with it.

"No." She turns her head so she's looking away from me. "Not exactly."

"Explain it to me, exactly."

"It was..." She looks at me pleadingly, like I have the words she doesn't.

"Amazing."

She nods. "But after..."

"What happened after?"

"Everything was more. Usually being around you, it quiets all the noise, but at the hospital..." Her eyes fill with moisture.

I want to kill something, but that's not going to fix this. "I left you alone at the hospital."

"You should have been able to," she says like she's ashamed. "I wanted to support you, wanted you to know you weren't alone."

"I knew that."

"Because your mom was there. Your men."

"Because *you* were there, my Anna."

"I was useless. You had to leave because of me."

"You think I would have stayed longer?" I ask, trying to understand the root of what has my girl upset. I can't fix what I don't know is broken.

"Wouldn't you?"

"No. I'd talked to my sister. I planned to leave when I came into the waiting room to get you."

"Oh. I thought you left because I was losing it."

"If I'd known you were losing it, I would have left earlier."

"I didn't want you to," she says, agitated.

I shrug. "I didn't." Why was she still upset? "If being around me makes you feel better, why haven't you come back to the office?"

"I need to get used to not being around you."

"The hell you do." She is going nowhere.

"You'll get tired of me and then it'll be worse than it ever was. You're my boss. I can't be clingy with you. No one wants someone clinging to them all the time."

The fuck.

"Emotions are not my thing." Before Anna.

Now, I'm feeling too much sometimes, which is annoying. Not annoying enough to let Anna go though.

She nods. "Shea told me."

"I feel things with you."

"What things?"

"Everything."

"I don't understand."

"Neither do I, but I guarantee I will never get tired of having you around."

"You can't promise that. You can't."

Fuck this. I need to hold her. She needs to be held.

I drop down onto the mattress and then pull her into my lap, blankets and all. She doesn't struggle. Not my Anna. She just looks up at me, questions in her drenched violet gaze. So pretty, something hurts deep in my chest.

"I am not like other people."

"Neither am I."

"I scare most women."

"You don't scare your mom, or your sister."

"I do sometimes." When the beast inside of me gets too close to the surface it scares the shit out of my family. "Even Lachlan wouldn't come into my office the day before yesterday, but you did. You weren't afraid of me."

"You wouldn't hurt me."

She is right, but how is she so certain? "I am more than your boss." After letting me touch her tits like that, she has to know it's true. "You wouldn't offer yourself to your boss, but you did to me."

"I have a crush on you." She says it like it's a shameful secret.

I feel a rare smile curving my lips. "I think it's more than a crush. I think you need me like I need you."

"But how could you need me?"

I shrug. "I don't know. I've never needed anyone before."

When my dad moved Helen and her family away, I was pissed because I wanted to figure out what about her was different. But I didn't need her.

"Not even your family?"

"Not even them." I am responsible for them, but I don't need them.

"I needed my mom, but I was too much for her. Like the world is too much for me."

"Explain that."

"Which one?"

"Both."

She settles in against me and I'm not sure she even realizes she's doing it. Anna's sweet little hand plays with a button on my shirt. "For as long as I can remember, being around people has been hard for me. Sounds are too loud. Smells are too pungent. Colors are too bright."

Without her, I hardly feel anything, but she feels too much.

"And I help?"

"You're like a mute button."

Except after I took her into a blissed out state and then didn't give her enough time to recover. I left her wide open to everything. I'll never do that again. She's my responsibility.

She allows me to feel.

It's my job to help her not feel too much.

"Was your mom a mute button too?"

"She made me feel safe, but I was a lot. She needed breaks. From me. She'd beg my dad to watch me so she could get out of the house. I would cry the whole time she was gone. Dad hated it, but he didn't hate me. They both loved me, but I was too much."

"My ma and da loved me, but even my dad was afraid of me sometimes."

"He was the boss before you?" she asks.

"Yes." And he'd struck fear in the hearts of criminals and law enforcement alike.

Still, I'd scared my da because he knew that while he regretted some things he had to do as the boss, I regret nothing.

"He didn't understand you."

"Maybe." Maybe my da saw the beast inside me, the part of me that craved killing and felt no remorse for it.

Da knew that even he wouldn't be safe if he brought the beast to the surface.

"I hated going to school and I cried every day, fighting getting on the bus," Anna says, sounding sad. "I tried not to. I knew Mom needed time to herself, but I couldn't give it to her. She hated summer because I didn't have school."

"How do you know that?"

"I heard her tell my dad. I heard everything she said because I was always there."

"What happened when she died?"

"Nothing was the same. It didn't matter if I went to school or stayed at my aunt and uncle's house. Nowhere felt safe."

"Do you feel safe here?" I ask, not sure how I'm going to handle it if she needs to stay in this dinky ass apartment.

"More than there, less than when I'm with you." She lets out a half sob-half laugh. "You might as well know just how pathetic I am, but I'm jealous of the tracker you have on Shea's phone. I wish I could have your eyes on me all the time."

CHAPTER 17

ANNA

I admit my secret, knowing it will be the end. He'll finally understand. I'm too much.

Cian shifts and I think he's going to move me off of his lap, but all he does is pull his phone out of his inner jacket pocket. He unlocks it and taps on a button. "Look."

I do, but I don't know what I'm supposed to be seeing. It's Connor's office, but no one is there.

"That's your desk," he says.

I suck in a breath. He has my desk under surveillance?

He taps the screen again and an image of my apartment living room comes up. It's a live feed, but no one is in there. Because we are in here. He goes through three more screens. Mrs. Hart's apartment. The store where Ini and I buy our groceries. The bookstore I go to once a week, but only buy from when I can afford it. Which isn't often.

Sitting up, I look into his face. He's staring back, his blue eyes void of emotion, but I know it's there.

"You watch me," I breathe.

"I have to know you are okay."

Something unfurls inside me. Something that has been dormant, hidden away since I was a tiny child and heard my mom tell my dad the first time that she just needed a break. That she couldn't take it anymore. Couldn't take *me* anymore.

It feels like springtime in my chest, and I smile. "You watch me, even when I'm not there, you want to see me."

"I want you with me all the time and when you aren't, I have to be able to see you."

The words are an echo of my own feelings. "I want that too, but I don't think Mrs. Hart will let you keep a camera in her apartment."

And I have to tell her it's there if he doesn't take it down, or tell me how to.

"It doesn't scare you?" he asks.

He means his desire to watch me all the time.

"No," I say with certainty.

I'm probably the one person in the world that would find his obsession comforting and not scary. I feel freer than I have felt in my entire adult life.

I'll take Scary Things that Make Me Happy for a lifetime, Alex.

Suddenly every day since I started working for Cian is reframed in the knowledge that he was watching me, protecting me. "Is there a tracking app on my phone?"

He nods. "I always know where you are as long as you have it with you."

I've never been so grateful that my aunt and uncle use a phone carrier with SIM cards. I was able to reactivate my smartphone through a discounted service provider when they cancelled my line on their plan the day after my eighteenth birthday. Ini and I are on the same discount phone plan, which makes it even cheaper.

We keep our cell phones active even when money gets tight.

Sometimes, we've had to choose phones over food, but without them she could lose her job for lack of accessibility. And I'd never have been able to look for one. No one tells you that your phone bill can be as important as paying rent when you're on your own.

"Phones break. They can be lost," I say, pushing when I know I should be happy with what he's already given me.

His blue eyes are intense. "You can either have a tracking device embedded in one of your teeth, under your skin, or in a piece of jewelry."

"You've thought about it."

"Yes."

"Were you going to do it without me knowing?" I ask, curious.

Should I be bothered? Ini would flip if she knew my boss was stalking me, but I'm not her. I *need* his eyes on me.

The only thing that scares me about the mob boss I work for is the fear of what will happen when he tires of watching me.

Cian looks at me, like he's deciding if he's going to answer truthfully, or not.

I laugh. Free and happy. If only for this moment. "You were, weren't you?"

"Ma would have my hide if she knew."

That makes me smile. He might not react like other people, or express emotion like they do, but he doesn't want to disappoint his mom.

"I won't tell her," I promise.

"Are you ready to get dressed?" he asks. "We need to get into the office. I've been ignoring texts and calls since I got here."

"I need to take a shower."

He gets up with me in his arms. He's so freaking strong. Then he lets me stand. "Make it fast."

Feeling daring, but very, very safe, I drop the blankets and let him see me in my sleep cami. It stops mid-thigh, but doesn't show any of my private bits.

I grab clothes from my crates, but when I add my bra to the pile in my arms, he takes it from me. "No bra."

I don't ask why. I know. He likes looking at my boobs.

Rushing through my shower, I still wash my hair. Which means I'm going to have to blow dry it. If I put it in a French braid, I only have to get it semi-dry. So, that is what I do. I pull on a denim skirt, made soft from many washings. Chicago in August is too hot for tights, but I need no-show socks before I put on a pair of canvas tennis-shoes. I don't like scratchy things against my skin.

The lilac silk t-shirt I found at Goodwill is soft, but wearing it without a bra still makes my nipples peak. It feels good and I like knowing I left my bra off for Cian. Still, I don't want anyone else looking at the shoals it makes in the fabric, so I tug on my denim jacket.

I find Cian in the living room on his phone. I wait until he looks up to say, "I'm ready."

He frowns. "It's too hot for a jacket."

"I don't want anyone but you to see my nipples."

That makes his gaze darken. "Show me."

I pull back the sides of the denim jacket to reveal my hard peaks pressing against the silk of my t-shirt.

He crosses to me in two long strides and slides his hands under the hem of my top. "Let me?"

I nod.

His hands travel up my bare torso and cup my breasts. We both gasp at the contact.

Then he groans. "I wish we had time to play."

"I do too." It doesn't embarrass me to admit that. Not when he looks so pained to have to let go of me.

But I'm also a little nervous about the next time he touches me like he did before. It was incredible during, but afterward, when I had to try to function, it was really hard.

"Next time, we'll make sure you have time to come down after," he says, like he's reading my mind.

I trust him and I smile. He always makes me smile.

A man comes out of an apartment down the hall and joins us when we leave. He nods to Cian. "Boss."

Cian turns to me. "Anna, this is Tommy. He's one of the men I have protecting you."

"You have people protecting me?" I can barely breath from the way that makes me feel.

"Yes."

"Arlo will see you home tonight and Eoin will take you to the office tomorrow morning." Tommy falls back and walks behind us.

"Isn't this a little much for your admin?" I ask Cian as we step into the elevator.

He lets Tommy press the button for the Lobby.

"You aren't my admin. You are *mine*." Cian's tone leaves no room for dissent.

I don't want to argue. He's more than my boss, but I'm not sure he's mine like I'm his. I don't want to ask him about it in front of the bodyguard.

When we get to the office, Connor acts like I've been gone a month, not a couple of days.

"It's so good to have you back, Anna. This place is not the same without you and my cousin was like a bear with a sore paw."

"He's upset about his sister. I'm sure you are too," I say.

Connor's expression turns dark, like the sweet man I work with is someone entirely different for a second. "Pissed as hell, but that's not why Cian spent all day yesterday busting my balls."

"Language," Cian barks.

Connor stares at him in shock, but then he nods. "You bet. Sorry for that, Anna."

"Um...Ini cusses more than anyone I know."

"You haven't met Eoin yet." Connor shakes his head. "Every other word out of his mouth is fuck."

"Not anymore," Cian says ominously.

Connor grins. "Have you taken her to dinner at your ma's?"

"I will tonight."

"You will?" I ask, startled. I liked Mrs. Doyle when I met her in the hospital, but the idea of having dinner in her home makes me nervous.

"She wants to get to know you," Cian says. "Invite your friends. Ma likes to cook."

"But what about Shea?"

"Lachlan is spending the evenings at the hospital with her."

"Can I visit her?" I ask.

Cian gives me a long look. "When she gets home."

"I can handle the hospital." I think.

"She's sleeping a lot. It's the pain meds."

"She'll be happier seeing you at home," Connor adds. "Shea's not one to show weakness. She'll want to be healed a little before visitors. She doesn't even want me or my parents coming to the hospital to see her."

That makes me feel better. Not that Shea needs to heal, but that I'm not her only friend who won't be visiting her in the hospital.

It's strange that she let Lachlan visit her though. Maybe he makes her feel safe like Cian does me.

I go toward my desk, but notice my computer is not on top like it usually is.

"You'll be working in my office with me," Cian says. "When I'm away from here, you'll use your old desk so Connor can keep an eye on you."

He said he needed me to be safe. I didn't realize how much.

Cian and Connor are both looking at me. Cian's gaze is impassive, but Connor looks worried. Like he thinks I'll find his cousin's arrangements upsetting. I don't.

They're better than my lean-to for giving me a sense of peace.

"I'll still have to do the filing and some things out here," I remind Cian. He nods. Grudgingly.

I bite my lips so I don't smile again.

"Don't do that." Cian is frowning.

"What?"

"Hold back your smile. I feel good when you smile."

"Okay." I'll remember that.

I don't think a lot of things make Cian feel good. Some of his friends and family don't think he feels much of anything at all. So, this is important. He's giving me so much, the least I can do is let myself smile around him when I have an urge to.

CHAPTER 18

CIAN

I put my cell phone down after reading Ronan's text. He plans to question Carmen again, now that she's recovered enough to talk after her impromptu surgery.

I don't want to leave Anna at the office.

It's not reasonable to try to keep her with me all the time. She should not be exposed to mob business. Both for her safety, and for ours. But it feels wrong, leaving her here right now.

I get up and cross my office to her desk. It's been placed at the far end of the newly renovated room. In my fury over what happened to Shea, I destroyed several pieces of furniture and put dents in the walls. Yesterday, one of my uncle's finishing teams came in and fixed it all.

They shifted the couch and armchairs near the window that I use for meetings that I don't want to conduct from behind my desk, to make room for her desk. It sits facing the wall to my right and the angle gives me an uninterrupted view of her. She can't see what I'm working on, or hear my conversations because she's now wearing her new noise cancelling earbuds that also allow her to answer phone calls.

I don't have to tap her shoulder when I reach her. Popping one of her earbuds out, she turns her chair and looks up at me.

She doesn't ask what I want. She just waits. How is the woman so fucking perfect?

Unable to stop myself touching her, I brush her cheek with my finger. "I have a meeting offsite."

"Oh. I...uh..." Her violet gaze reflects her unhappiness. She doesn't want me to leave anymore than I want to leave her.

"You can work in Connor's office, or you can come with me."

"I want to come with you," she says instantly.

"You can't attend my meeting. You'll have to wait for me in another room."

"Will there be people there?" she asks.

"Not if you don't want there to be."

"I probably don't, but I might."

"Then we will wait until we get there for you to decide."

"Okay."

"It's not safe for you to go with me all the time." It has to be said.

"But it is safe today?"

"Yes."

"I want to go then."

I nod. "Grab your jacket."

She'd taken the denim jacket off once she settled at her new desk. The air conditioning is set a little cold in here and her nipples are peaked and pressing against her t-shirt. Her lack of a bra is obvious. No one else gets to see that. Only me.

Tugging on the jacket, she asks, "Where are we going?"

"The Lucky Charm Escort Service."

Pausing with her jacket half on, she frowns. "You have a meeting with an escort?"

"I can't give you details of my meeting, Anna."

She finishes tugging on her jacket and grabs her purse. "I'm ready."

Connor looks nonplussed when he realizes Anna is coming with us. Arlo rides shotgun while my cousin drives. Lachlan isn't coming because he's in a meeting with an arms dealer. We're increasing inventory in our armory because of these Kicks Bandidos bastards.

Anna and I sit in the backseat of my armored SUV. Normally, for a meeting like this, I would have driven myself in my favorite vehicle, a sleek black sports car that goes zero to sixty in 2.9 seconds.

However, with Anna along, I want extra security. Her safety is paramountI will always keep her safe.

We're nearly to our destination when Anna blurts out, "Do you use the escorts?"

"Use?" I ask, amused.

"You know. Do you have sex with them?" she asks baldly.

I shut the privacy window between the front and the backseats before I answer. "I have. Though it is just as easy to get a blow job from one of our dancers as it is to book a session with one of the mob's sex workers."

Anna starts tapping her fingernails together. I know this means she's agitated.

"I have not let another woman suck my cock since I met you, Anna."

Her gaze meets mine, turbulence making her violet eyes dark. "Is that what you do? Oral?"

"That has been my preference." Right now, I would give up daily blow jobs to have her offer me her tits again and watch her sink into ecstasy.

"Are you going to get a blow job at your meeting?"

"No."

She's still looking at me as if she's trying to read my mind.

I add, "It's mob business, not personal."

"Do you audition new dancers or sex workers?" she asks.

Her mind. It's fast and goes places I don't expect.

"No. I'm the boss. Those businesses are overseen by other men. The dancers audition, but our sex workers don't get auditioned, they get interviewed."

"Just like any other job?"

"Yes."

"But it's an illegal one."

"A lot of things are illegal, but people do them anyway." People outside the life break laws all the time.

That's why speeding tickets are so lucrative for local and state governments. People cheat on their taxes, beat their spouses and children, and break other laws daily, but don't consider themselves criminals. In the mob we know we're criminals, but we have a code we live by.

It's a harsher code than government laws. Abuse and rape carry a death sentence in the Doyle & Byrne mob, but stealing is a way of life. Depending on who you steal from. Steal from me or our businesses and the punishment is fast and brutal. Steal to build our organization and promotion within the ranks could be the result.

"What happens if one of your sex workers gets arrested?"

"We have excellent attorneys on our payroll."

"And you use them to protect your people?"

"Yes." It's a cost of doing business when your business isn't always on the up and up.

"That's good."

I shrug. Good and bad are relative. I don't think of my actions in those terms. I do what I need to as mob boss to protect and grow my organization.

When we get to the Lucky Charm, Connor and Arlo go directly to the Salon to wait. Ronan is in his upstairs office. His eyes widen fractionally when he sees Anna with me, but he doesn't say anything.

"Anna, this is Ronan Byrne." I nod to Ronan. "Anna will be waiting in here while we are meeting."

He shrugs. Even if she snoops, she won't find anything in this office that we don't want her to see. She won't though. She's not like that.

"Ronan, do you have a minute?" Minx, a redhead that has worked for us for the past three years comes into my captain's office.

"Make it fast," I tell him. "We'll be in the salon."

The only people in the salon right now are Connor and Arlo. They take up security positions when we enter the room.

I lead Anna to a couch against the wall and she sits down, looking around. "It's like a nice living room."

I can tell she has questions she wants to ask, but she doesn't.

"What?" I ask her.

"I'm not supposed to ask about your mob business."

"If it's something I can't answer, I won't."

She smiles at that. Despite my reason for being here, that smile warms something inside me. Like it always does.

"Do the escorts...um...do they see their clients here?"

"No."

"It's a big building."

"Wardrobe takes up one third of the space on this floor, the remaining rooms are used for offices, dressing and storage."

Her brows draw together. "You tell your escorts what to wear, like a uniform?"

"They can use their own clothes sometimes, but clients who want dates for high end events expect those dates to arrive wearing current designer fashion. Some have color preferences for the outfit they want their escorts to wear." I shrug. "The clothes take up a lot of space."

However, nothing on this floor will give the cops anything to use against us. And we never have the clients serviced on the premises. Hell, some of our clients really are only looking for a plus one for some events.

"What is this room used for?" she asks.

"Our employees hang out here before going out, sometimes between dates." It's a safe place for them to wait.

"No one is here right now."

"We don't have a lot of business before lunchtime."

"People don't want sex in the morning?"

Anna's constant curiosity charms me.

"Not from a service like this. We have other places where there are workers available in rotating shifts twenty-four seven."

"You mean like a bordello?"

"We don't call them that, but yes."

"What do you call them?"

"Houses."

"Oh." She scrunches her nose. "That's boring."

"It's safe," Connor pipes up.

She smiles at my cousin. "Because you can't get in trouble for talking about going to a house?"

I glare at Connor to shut it and answer, "Exactly."

Anna and I are talking right now. She doesn't need anyone else answering her questions.

Connor takes a hint and keeps his claptrap closed, but there's amusement in his eyes. He won't be laughing if I give him a beatdown. Anna likes him though. If he comes into work tomorrow bruised up, she'll be upset.

"It's sorted," Ronan says from the doorway.

I put my hand out to Anna. "You'll wait in the office."

"Can I wait here?" she asks, but places her hand in mine.

"Someone else may come in. I don't know how long it will be."

"If I get uncomfortable, I'll go to Mr. Byrne's office."

I squeeze her hand and then let it go with a nod. "Connor, if Anna goes to the office, you and Arlo are to stand outside it until I get back. You don't leave her alone."

"Yes, Boss," both men say in unison.

CHAPTER 19

CIAN

When we are in the basement hallway, I ask Ronan, "Has Carmen said anything useful yet?"

"I haven't had time to start questioning her. She only woke up an hour ago."

"Problems?" I ask.

"Nothing more than the usual."

I take his words at face value. Ronan is savvy enough to notice if anything was happening with the businesses he runs that might be linked back to the Kicks Bandidos.

Wearing a typical hospital gown, Carmen is lying on the cot in the infirmary. We have to keep the gowns and scrubs on hand. If our people get shot, we can't take them to the hospital. We bring them here. The man we call the Butcher is a medical board certified surgeon. He has a handpicked team that works with him.

They all do rotations at clinics or hospitals in the area, but they understand that their commitment to us comes first.

Carmen watches us approach in silence. The nurse attendant we keep on call raises the back of the gurney, so Carmen is sitting up a little.

She winces at the movement. "What did you do to me?"

"Didn't the doctor tell you?" I ask.

"He gave me a fairytale about some kind of bomb inside me." Her accent is thicker than it was, even after the waterboarding.

The anesthesia is not completely out of her system, or she's not reacting well to learning she'd been weaponized with every expectation of dying.

She grimaces. "To be honest, I feel like I dreamt the whole conversation with the doctor."

"It wasn't a bomb. It was a biological weapon. The device was created to either dissolve on its own, or rupture if you were beaten."

Her eyes round with horror, but she says, "I don't believe you."

Ronan pulls up his phone and shows her the video of him carrying her in here. The Butcher and his team arrive within minutes. They do an ultrasound of her abdomen and it shows a small cannister inside her uterus.

Showing the fucking courage I expect from our men, he quickly changes into scrubs and operating gown, etc. He doesn't hesitate to start cutting into her as soon as the anesthesiologist has Carmen hooked up to drugs that will keep her knocked out.

"How do I know it is what you say it is?" Her eyes carry the devastation of betrayal but she doesn't want to believe her people set her up like this.

"You knew your cousin wanted you dead."

"I thought she might. I didn't *know*."

"Who told you were having an appendectomy?" Ronan asks.

"I was told after I woke up, hurting like I am now and not knowing how I got there." Carmen glares up at Ronan. "I guess you aren't the only one who is handy with a hypodermic."

"They could have drugged your food or beverage. Roofied you and then put you under," Ronan says with no inflection to his tone.

The details don't matter to him, but he never likes to assume anything.

"Who told you you'd had your appendix removed?" I ask this time.

"My father."

Ronan and I share a glance. That is seriously fucked. This woman's entire family sees her as disposable.

"Your appendix is still inside you by the way," Ronan says. "The Butcher said your uterus is still intact too."

"Other than being used to carry a biological weapon."

"It didn't leak."

"I guess I'm lucky you chose to waterboard me instead of beating me for information," Carmen says to Ronan bitterly.

We're all lucky, but I don't say that. I want her focused on what her family was willing to do to her and how we saved her from it.

"Once you heal, there will be no lasting effects," I say. "Our surgeon is good at what he does."

"Oh, there will be a lasting effect all right. I will never trust anyone in my family ever again and if I get a chance, I will kill that son of a bitch."

"Which one?" Ronan asks.

"All of them."

"We can help with that," I say.

She looks at me. "You want me to rat out my family."

"Family doesn't send you on a suicide mission without warning you what you signed up for," Ronan says. "It's time you picked a different family."

"You don't get to choose your blood." Carmen looks down, her shoulders slumped in defeat.

"But you can choose family," I say.

We've inducted plenty of people into our organization with no blood ties. We aren't like the Italian mafia; we don't even require our people to be of Irish descent. They have to make the vow and that is what makes them family.

"You offering me a place in yours?" she asks sarcastically.

"It depends," I say.

Ronan gives me a look, but it's not disapproval I see in his expression. It's relief. He cares if this woman lives or dies. I wonder why?

"How will you trust me if I rat them out?"

I don't lie. "We won't at first."

"But trust can be earned," Ronan adds.

She frowns. "How do I know you won't use me just like they did?"

"You don't. Like Ronan said, trust is earned, but know this. We'll never use you as a mule to carry a biological weapon into another outfit's territory. That's not how we operate."

"I didn't know that was how we operated either." The tough exterior crumbles and tears wash into Carmen's dark eyes. "I wanted children, but he planted death in my womb instead."

"Your husband?"

"Did I mention that Bernardino is one of our doctors?"

"He performed your surgery?" Ronan asks, his voice deadly.

No question. My captain is compiling a hit list.

Since they are the fuckers who tried to infect my people with Anthrax, they're already on mine.

"Our chemist confirmed the biological weapon inside you held Anthrax."

"Anthrax?" Carmen whispers.

"Yes. Were you aware your people had access to it?"

She doesn't answer, but she doesn't have to. Her dark eyes reflect the knowledge that what I'm saying is possible.

"That thing wouldn't have just killed me," she says with horror. "It would have infected anyone I came into contact with and anyone they came into contact with until your forces were decimated."

Not to mention the thousands of other people in the city that might have died. People like Anna.

My beast paces inside me, looking for an outlet.

"It was a smart plan," Ronan says. "But it didn't account for the fact I don't beat women."

"Just waterboard them."

My captain shrugs. "You were never at any risk of drowning."

"You scared me."

"No. You were not afraid to die when you thought it was your choice, when you believed your cause was just."

"Not then, no." Carmen puts her hands over her face and turns away like she doesn't want us to witness her grief.

Too bad. That grief will get us what we want. Information.

"Do you want to see him dead?" Ronan asks.

Her hands come down and her eyes blaze with anger now, not grief. "Can you make that happen?"

"Yes," Ronan and I say at the same time.

She nods, seemingly coming to a decision. "They want to take over Chicago."

"The Kicks Bandidos? They're not that big of a gang."

"Martina is running them, but she's here on behalf of her father. My uncle has dreams of being the next emperor of the underworld."

"Who gave the order to attack my sister?"

"I wasn't aware that your family were targeted, though I wouldn't be surprised to find out they are. Martina has people watching you."

So, the order was either given after we swept up and punished all the dealers working our territory without permission, or *El Fantasma* hadn't confided her plans in her cousin.

Either way, the Kicks Bandidos were watching me and learned about my sister. Probably Ma too. Have they seen me with Anna? She works for me, but what if they realize it's more? What if they realize that even more than Shea, Anna is a weakness they can exploit?

As hard as it's going to be, I need to stay away from her outside of the office until we get this threat neutralized. I should fire her. That would be the safest course. Fuck.

Then I think of another option.

I text Connor and Uncle Jimmy.

We question Carmen until she falls asleep mid-sentence.

"I'll be here when she wakes up," Ronan assures me. "I don't want to give her adrenalin to keep her talking."

"It could make her answers erratic," I agree. "Or give her a false sense of strength so she doesn't think she has to answer at all."

"I'll keep her on low level pain meds," Ronan says. "She'll be more amenable."

"She gave us enough to get started on a plan for taking the war to them." First, we identify and neutralize every single member of the Kicks Bandidos.

Carmen has access to the files Martina keeps on her people. If the passwords haven't been changed, then we'll have access too. If *El Fantasma* was smart, they were changed the day Carmen was sent out on her assignment.

But if Martina is too confident, she wouldn't see the need. According to Carmen, her cousin's arrogance is only outdone by her father's craving for power.

CHAPTER 20

ANNA

The woman who wanted to speak to Mr. Byrne comes into the salon a few minutes after Cian leaves.

Her brow furrows when she notices Connor and Arlo standing at attention, then she looks at me. "Are you a new hire?"

"Not really. I've been working for Cian for a couple of months."

"For cripe's sake," Connor says with exasperation. "Minx wants to know if you're an escort."

Arlo coughs. Or it could have been a laugh.

"Oh, no, not an escort. I'm an assistant to his assistant." I lean my head toward Connor, indicating him.

"Is that what they're calling it now?" Minx says in a teasing tone.

"Human resources calls me a clerical assistant, but I do more than file." I frown. "Maybe I should talk to them about changing my title."

The sound coming from Arlo is definitely a laugh.

Why is he laughing at me? Did I get something wrong? Nuance isn't my thing.

"Shut the fu—hell up," Connor barks to Arlo.

Something inside me warms. Connor is defending me, even though I don't know what I got wrong. I *am* a clerical assistant. Only, I'm more. I'm sure Cian wouldn't mind changing my job title. It should match what

I do more closely. It makes me itch that it doesn't, now that I've thought about it.

"No offense meant," Arlo says, his big arms up in a gesture of surrender.

Connor says, "Tell that to the boss."

Arlo blanches.

"Are you dating the boss?" Minx asks me.

Am I? I don't know. I let him touch my breasts. He made me orgasm. But I still work for him.

I shrug. "We've never gone on a date."

Minx studies me and then looks over at Connor. "According to that one, the boss is protective of you."

"He is." And it makes me feel safe.

"Huh. I've never known him to be protective of anyone but his family."

I like knowing that and a secret thrill goes through me. He watches me, on his phone. He wants to put a tracker on me so even if my phone is lost, I won't be. He *is* protective of me.

"Do you know Cian very well?" I ask. Is she one of the women who has sucked him off? She's very pretty.

"No, but we all know about him."

"Because he's the boss?"

Minx nods. "It's only smart to know what you need to about the people in power in your world."

"He knows about all of us, too," Connor says with pride. "Cian knows the name and position of every person in the organization, down to the new recruits."

"Does he watch you all?" I ask, wondering if what I took for as special and protective, is just Cian's way.

"Even Cian can't keep tabs on all of us. That's why he has captains."

Mr. Byrne must be a captain because he runs the escort service.

"Does he watch you?" I ask Connor, tugging my jacket closer around me.

"No." Connor gives me a strange look. "He expects me to watch him and learn from him."

"You have camera feeds of him on your phone?"

Connor stares at me like I've grown horns. "What? No. He'd cut off my balls and feed them to me if I invaded his privacy like that."

If someone wants to be watched, it's not an invasion.

"Does the boss watch you like that?" Minx asks, looking worried.

"He watches over me," I prevaricate. It's not a lie, but it's clear Minx and Connor don't understand.

I don't think Ini and Mrs. Hart would either. I should move the camera in my apartment, so it can only see my bed, and not the living room where Ini hangs out too. She doesn't want to be watched.

Not like me.

Maybe Cian could move the camera in Mrs. Hart's apartment to the hall? That's more like public property, right? I wonder if I can find the camera and do it myself.

It is special how Cian watches me. Just for me, like me leaving my bra off today was just for him.

My leg stops jiggling. Every time I feel my t-shirt rubbing against my naked bosom, I think of Cian. Is that why he told me to leave it off? Or was it because he wanted to see the way my breasts bounce when they're unfettered?

Either way, it's only for him and I like knowing that.

Minx leaves before Cian returns. I'm kind of glad when she's gone. She's interesting and her presence didn't grate on me like some people because her words always matched the expression on her face, but she kept asking questions about me and Cian. And her questions only make me realize how much I don't know about what is happening between us.

He doesn't want me to quit. I don't want to leave Doyle & Byrne either. He watches me. I like being watched by him. He really likes my body. That makes me tingle when I think about it. But are we dating? Does he like me like that? I know I want to be dating him, but I don't always get it right. Assessing my interactions with other people.

Why did Minx ask if we are dating? Maybe he doesn't bring other women to meetings with him. I have lots of questions and no answers.

Connor makes a strange sound and I look up from my musings. He's putting his phone back in his pocket. "Cian says to take you back to the office, Anna."

"Now?" Without him?

Connor nods. "Let's go."

When we get back to the office, Connor stops me from going back into Cian's domain. "You'll be working in my dad's office from now on," Connor says.

I stare at him, trying to understand what he's saying. But Cian wants me in *his* office. He wants to watch me. I could feel his gaze on me throughout the morning. It calmed me, made me feel safe.

"You'll be filling in for Shea," Connor says when I don't move or answer him.

"Is that what Cian said?" I ask.

Connor looks down and away and I know it isn't. Cian just wants me out of his office. Did he get sick of me already? Was I too needy? Did he realize he doesn't like watching me? Who did he meet with that would make him have that revelation? Someone he'd rather watch now.

He said it was mob business and not personal, but I'm not personal either. I work for him. We *aren't* dating. Even if he did touch me in a way no other man ever has.

Bile rushes up my throat and I run to the bathroom. After I'm done throwing up, I wash my face with cold water and then pat it dry. I still need this job and I like working in Jimmy's office.

This pain in my chest will go away. Won't it?

I grab my phone and send him a text.

Me: **Are you still watching me?**

I have to know.

Only there is no reply by the time to go home. I don't say goodbye to Jimmy like I usually would. I don't want to talk to anyone right now. There's a lump in my throat I can't make go away.

I head for the L station at a rapid walk. If I hurry, I'll catch the train I usually miss because I chat with Shea or Connor after I get off work.

As I step into the train off the platform, it sounds like someone's calling my name, but that's just wishful thinking. No one around here cares enough about me to call out to me.

When I get home, Ini is there. She grins when I come in. "Did you go to work today?"

I nod. Words don't want to come out of my mouth. Not even for my best friend.

"I'm glad. You look worn out, though."

I shrug.

"Do you want dinner?" she asks, having experience with my nonverbal episodes.

I shake my head.

"I'll make enough for you if you get hungry later, okay?"

I nod, but I won't.

"Are you going to work tomorrow?"

I nod again. I have to pay my half of the living expenses. I can't expect Ini to keep taking care of me. What if she gets sick of me too?

I have to work. It doesn't matter that everything inside me hurts at the idea of going back there and not seeing Cian. What did I do wrong? Did I ask too many questions?

A loud pounding sounds on the door.

Ini looks at me. "Are you expecting anyone?"

I shake my head.

She goes to the door and looks through the peephole. "It's that big guy that moved into the apartment down the hall yesterday with his friends."

Uninterested, I head for the bedroom. I need my tent.

I hear Ini ask, "What do you want?" through the door.

The man's answer is muffled, but Ini replies, "Yes."

I dig in my purse until I find the case with the noise cancelling earbuds Cian gave me this morning. I put them in and the rest of Ini's conversation with our neighbor is muted.

CHAPTER 21

CIAN

Lachlan agrees that distancing myself from Anna is the best course of action. "The fewer people who have a target on their back because of their connection to us, the better. I'll triple the guard on your mom and sister. I already contacted the family in Ireland to increase Máire's protection."

He sets up a meeting for me with Walsh for the next day. I'm done playing around with this fucker. He was my da's friend, but he's nothing to me. He'll give me the information I want, one way, or another.

We've already got people following up on the location information Carmen gave us, but so far, her cousin has vacated herself and her minions from everywhere on the list. At least we are able to confirm that Carmen's intel is legit. Traffic cams and witnesses attest to the fact that Martina was staying at the hotel Carmen told us about.

We're using those same traffic cams to try to trace her movements after leaving. That will take time though.

"I've got a meeting set up for you with Quinn Murphy an hour before Walsh is supposed to arrive," Lachlan tells me after tapping some things on his phone. "Stavros will meet with you tonight."

We need to know what is happening with the Greek mafia.

As a front for the cartel, the ultimate goal for the Kicks Bandidos is control of the Chicago underworld. The Greeks are probably dealing with plenty of shit from them too.

Lachlan leaves and while I'm waiting in my office for Stavros to arrive, I check my text messages. There are a lot, but I click on Anna's first. It has been several hours since she sent it. She asks if I'm still watching her.

There's something about that question. Like she thinks I'm done with her. I'm keeping her safe, but she doesn't know that.

I text back.

Me: **Yes.**

Because I need to, I click on the feed from her apartment cam. The living area is empty. She's probably hanging out with her friends at Mrs. Hart's apartment. Sometimes, they play board games after they eat, or watch movies on the older woman's small television.

Ini is there, playing cards with Mrs. Hart, but I don't see Anna.

Where is she?

Remembering I saw a message from Arlo, I click back into my texts. I'm not worried. If something had happened to Anna, he would call me, and if I didn't answer, he would call Lachlan. It's protocol.

The last text in the stream says Anna is home. I scroll up and curse. She left the building without Arlo and rode the L home. Something stabs my chest. Fear.

Fuck this. I don't feel fear.

But she rode the damned train home. Totally unprotected. What if the Kicks Bandidos picked her up?

Dread rolls through me at what they would do to my sweet girl.

I dial Anna's number. She doesn't answer.

I text her.

Me: **Answer your phone.**

After several more unanswered rings, I text again.

Me: **Now, Anna.**

I call again, but it goes directly to voicemail. Arlo picks up on the first ring.

"Go to Anna's apartment. She's not answering the phone."

"I'll try, Boss, but her roommate wouldn't let me in last time."

"Then how you do you know she's there?"

"The roommate told me. Said Anna wasn't feeling great and was lying down."

Anna was sick? Or upset? Fuck. What happened when she was working in Jimmy's office?

A text comes through from Connor. Lachlan has returned and has Stavros with him. I'll have to call Jimmy later.

"Do not let her leave the building tomorrow morning without one of you," I say to Arlo and then disconnect the call before he answers with his usual, *yes, boss.*

He'll do what I ordered. I don't need to hear the confirmation. There's a reason he's on Anna's protection detail.

I text Connor and tell him to send Lachlan and Stavros into my office.

The meeting with Stavros goes as I expect. He's pissed at the gang because they're trying to get protection money from his restaurants. The fucking arrogance. The Greeks don't even pay us protection money. Stavros's family isn't as big as the Doyle & Byrne mob, but they're not some pissant gang upstart either.

And they operate under the auspices of Leandros Drakos, The God-father of the Night. He lives in Chicago in the Murphy territory, but he controls about a third of the Greek mafia in the US and Canada. Does the Gutierrez Cartel have any idea who they are dealing with?

We can and will take them down, but our allies increase our numbers tenfold.

Stavros wants the Kicks Bandidos obliterated.

"They're the front gang for the Gutierrez Cartel," I tell him. "We take them out first, but I'm not stopping there."

I'm burning that fucking cartel to the ground.

Stavros narrows his eyes. "We need to loop Drakos in on this. It is bigger than our territories."

"Agreed."

I wait while Stavros makes the call. He hangs up and tells me, "Drakos wants to meet with you tomorrow."

"I'll arrange it with Xander Christakos," Lachlan says, naming the God-father of the Night's second in command.

Even though Drakos is the one that wants the meeting, protocols have to be followed, so I incline my head in agreement.

"Things are going to get messy, Cian," Lachlan says after seeing Stavros out.

"They already are."

I'm not surprised to see Ronan in the doorway to my office. He would have Lachlan's position as my second except he insists on running the escort service and our *houses*.

I pull Connor in, and the four of us talk strategy while he takes notes. "Carmen's intel about her cousin here in Chicago is sketchy because Martina didn't share shit with her, but she knows a hell of a lot about the cartel in Colombia that her uncle and his lieutenants have no idea they've revealed to her."

"It will all be useful," I say grimly.

Yes, we're taking out the gang first, but I'm not stopping there, whatever my allies agree to. Their help would be nice, but I'll hire mercenaries if I have to. I'm not leaving a threat like the egomaniac leading that cartel out there to hurt the people under my protection. Once he set his sights on my mob, he signed his own death warrant.

Ronan's eyes reflect no emotion. "We promised Carmen we would kill her husband."

"And we keep our word," I tell him.

He nods, like that's what he wanted to hear. We finish up and I tell Connor I'll drive myself home. He knows better than to argue. Even Lachlan just gives me a displeased glance before leaving with the other two men.

I change from my suit into a black turtleneck and cargo pants. I grab the other stuff I'll need and leave after locking the office and setting the security system.

Taking evasive maneuvers to make sure I'm not being followed, I drive toward Anna's apartment building. I need to check on her, but I'm not putting her at further risk by letting anyone know I'm doing it.

I park a few blocks from her place and pull on my black ski mask. Sticking to alleyways and the shadows, I make my way to the unused side entrance to her building. Once my interest in her was piqued, I unblocked the door and put a lock on it that only I have the key to. I use that now, to let myself inside.

I take the stairs up to her floor and approach her apartment. With the set of keys I had made when I took Anna's the other day, I let myself into her apartment. It's dark with no lights on. I'm not surprised. Ini returned a couple of hours ago and went to the bedroom.

Moving silently, I go there now. As I gently open the door, I can hear both women breathing in the steady rhythm of sleep. I know I'm good, but it bothers me that neither are aware someone is in their place. I'll have to get an alarm system installed.

But tonight, I'm glad they don't have one.

Anna has her tent set up. Does she use it every night?

Traversing the room, I then kneel beside her bed. It takes long seconds to untuck the tent blanket and pull it back. Anna's lovely face is outlined in the dark.

I place my hand over her mouth, pull the earbud from her ear and whisper. "Anna. Wake up, sweetheart."

She jolts awake, her body flailing.

"Anna, it's me. Don't wake up Ini." I imbue my voice with authority.

It works. My girl stills, blinking up at me.

"I'm going to take you into the living room," I whisper in a near subvocal level right against her ear.

She doesn't react.

"Okay?"

She shrugs. It's not a *no*, but it's not a *yes* either. Her indifference irritates me, but I pick her up, blankets and all and carry her out of the room. I pull the door shut behind me, having to lean down to grab that handle to control the sound of the latch as I let it slide into place after the door is closed.

Her body is stiff in my arms, but I hold her close to my chest anyway. When I sit down on the couch with her on my lap; she scrambles to get off. I don't like it, but I allow it. She settles with her back against the armrest and facing me, her knees up and pressed to her chest, her arms circling them. She has the blankets over her as a barrier between us.

Everything in her demeanor screams *keep your distance*.

I hand her the earbud I'm still holding, and she takes it, before removing the other one and then clutching them with the edge of the blanket in her hand.

"You left the building without Arlo." I don't like that I can't see her.

Reaching over her, I turn on the rickety standing lamp next to her side of the couch. She pulls back from me and my confusion at her behavior morphs into irritation.

"What is the matter with you?"

"Why would I wait for Arlo?" she asks, rather than answer.

"He's your security. I told you he would be bringing you home."

"That was before."

"Before what?" I demand in a quiet tone. I don't want her roommate to come stomping in here and interrupt us before I get things settled with Anna. "It was this fucking morning."

"Don't swear at me." She's not meeting my eyes, but looking at some spot over my shoulder. She does that with other people, not with me.

"You don't like me saying fuck?" I ask.

"Not when you're mad at me."

"But it's okay if I'm pissed at someone else?"

She shrugs.

"Don't shrug at me, Anna. Yes, or, no?"

"What does it matter? We won't be seeing each other."

"Not right now, no." Fuck. I wince internally. And then I think a whole litany of curse words, but not one of them comes out of my mouth. "Things are dangerous right now. You know what happened to Shea."

"They did that to her to get back at you for something?" Anna asks, her tone disbelieving. "But she's still a teenager. She doesn't have anything to do with mob business. She told me."

My sister had been chattier than usual. She knows better than to discuss that kind of thing with friends. Damn it all to hell.

"They were sending me a message." After I sent their dealers back to them beaten and each missing a finger for their impudence in working my streets.

"But I'm not your family."

"You're my girl, Anna, but right now the fewer people that know that, the better."

"I'm your girl?" she asks, like she doesn't know.

"What the fu—dge do you think? You let other men touch your beautiful tits?"

She gasps, tugging the blanket closer. "No."

"Well, I don't stalk my employees. Just you."

CHAPTER 22

CIAN

"I wondered."

"Anna," I say impatiently.

"Don't use that tone with me. You could have called me and explained, or at least texted, but you sent Connor to tell me I wasn't working for you anymore and you didn't tell me why. I don't like feeling this way."

I hurt her. "I'm not a thoughtful man," I tell her.

"You can be, when you want to. You got new, safer doors for our apartment and Mrs. Hart's."

"I broke your friend's door when she wouldn't let me in to talk to her," I admit to Anna.

"Don't do that again. She's old. You can't scare her like that."

"I won't."

"I thought you got sick of me." Anna's voice is filled with uncertainty and pain.

"I want to hold you," I tell her.

"For how long?" she asks. And she's not talking about just tonight.

Fuck. Am I ready for this conversation?

I have an answer, so I guess that means I'm ready. "I'm never letting you go, Anna. You're mine."

"I have to agree."

"You did."

"But then you fired me."

"I didn't fire you. I created distance so you wouldn't be a target."

"What if I'm already a target?"

That is what I am afraid of. Legit afraid. I'd spent twenty-eight years never knowing what fear felt like. Now I do and I can fucking do without it.

"I'll double your protection detail."

"Won't that make whoever is watching realize that I'm important to you?"

"I'm not risking you."

"Am I really safer in Jimmy's office?"

"Yes. He has his own security and he can up the number of his guards without painting a target on you."

"Can't you do that?"

"Everyone who comes into my office sees you, Anna. There are going to be a lot of dangerous men coming and going over the next weeks."

"More dangerous than you?"

"Fu—no."

"So?"

"I don't want them all knowing about you."

"But don't they already? They've been in and out of the office already."

"Those were my men. These will be men from other syndicates."

She jumps up and the covers fall away from her, but she doesn't seem to care in her agitation. She starts pacing. "I don't like this. I feel sad. It hurts. You said you would watch me and then you sent me away."

Leaping to my feet, I pull her body into mine. She doesn't fight me, but she doesn't relax against me either.

"I will always watch you. I will never let you go. Let me keep you safe, *mo chroí*. Please."

She lifts her head and stares at me. "What does *mo chroí* mean?"

"My heart. Most people would tell you I don't have one. Hell, I thought I didn't have one, but apparently I do. Only it's not in my chest." It's sappy shit, but it's also the truth.

This woman makes me feel. She is my beating heart.

Anna's arms come around me and she hugs me tight, her tits pillowing against my torso. "You can keep me safe." She pulls back, all the way out of my arms and frowns up at me, her blond hair a messy halo around her head. "You tell me things. You text me. You call. Not Connor. Not Lachlan. *You*."

No one tells me what to do. Except for her apparently.

"If I can, I will, but if I can't *you* don't assume I'm tired of you. That cannot happen."

Her expression says she doesn't believe me, but she doesn't verbalize that disbelief. "You had time to text Connor this morning. You could have texted me."

"That's not how it works."

"With me, it is."

"With you." Only with her. Even Ma had to deal with one of the men contacting her when it was expedient.

She nods. "Will I see you at all?"

"I don't know." I should say *no*, but I don't. Because I need her like air and seeing her on my phone's camera feed won't be enough.

"Where did you put the camera in Mrs. Hart's apartment?"

I tell her. "Why?"

"I'm moving it to the hallway outside her door. And I'm moving the one in here to a spot that only sees my bed."

"No."

"Yes. You can watch me. You know I want that, but you cannot watch my friends without their permission and if I ask for it, they'll start in again on how working for your company isn't good for me."

"You're working for Uncle Jimmy now."

"Only until you get things taken care of."

She doesn't know I plan to take down a gang and then the cartel that sponsors them. It could be months before the threat is neutralized. Will

I be able to last that long with her in the other office suite? Especially if I can't watch her for most of the evenings?

The thought of her moving the cameras has my stomach tying in knots. I need a workaround. But right now, my brain and my body need the proof she belongs to me.

Sitting back on the couch, I let myself take in every inch of her beautiful body. She's wearing her satin sleep camisole again. Her pretty legs are on display. The slope of her shoulders utterly feminine. As I watch her, Anna's nipples harden, creating shoals in the satin.

"Come here," I tell her.

That fast, her eyes lose focus. Her response to me fucking turns my crank. She moves forward like we're connected by an invisible string and I'm tugging it toward me. Her knees bump mine and she stops.

"Come up here." I tug her thighs.

She climbs onto my lap, spreading her legs like that day in my office. I grab her soft, curvy ass and squeeze as I pull her closer and closer, hungry for the feel of her pressing against my hard dick.

She pushes against my chest, stopping me. "I want you to take it out. I'm not ready for penetrative sex, but I want to touch you."

Her honesty is going to kill me. Undoing my cargo pants takes longer than usual, but finally I get my cock free and it stands at attention between us. Her focus zeroed in on my hardon, she licks her lips.

ANNA

I've never seen a hard penis in person before. Cian's is thick and long. I curl my hand around it and he groans. It feels like silk suede, one of my favorite fabrics because it's so soft. I squeeze my hand, sliding up and down the hot skin. It's soft, but he's so hard, there's no give under my fingers.

He cups my breasts through my sleep cami, sliding his thumbs over the slick fabric. It feels different than when he touched me before. Not better, but just as good in a different way. He kneads and caresses me and that sensation of being alone with him in the universe starts to come over me.

I can feel my hand on his sex, but I don't register the couch under us. My senses are flooded with the feel of his hands on my body and my hand on his. His scent, that mixture of aftershave and him. Cian Doyle. I hear our hearts beating, our breathing...the sound of his hand sliding over the satin of my camisole nightgown.

Cian leans forward and takes my aching nipple into this mouth right through the satin. Pleasure shoots directly to my vagina and I spasm, feeling empty.

I've never been full, so how can I experience this sense of emptiness?

Placing my other hand on his hardness, I use both to explore the shape and texture of him.

He slides a hand between us, delving under my panties to touch my most intimate flesh. I'm so wet, his thumb glides over my folds. It's an abundance of sensation, but not too much. Because he is there.

My eyelids lower, shutting out everything but physical sensation and smell. There's a new scent between us and when my hand brushes over the wetness at the tip of his erection, I know it's him. He hasn't come, but something viscous and earthy smelling rubs against my fingers.

I bring one hand to my mouth and taste. Salty. A little sweet. Cian.

He groans. "That's right, baby, taste me."

I lick all of him off my fingers before putting my now saliva soaked hand back on his arousal. It slides more easily. He grows impossibly hot and hard in my hands, the fluid leaking from his tip mixes with my saliva and my hands move slickly on him.

His hands leave my body and I make a sound of protest, but I don't open my eyes. I feel jerky movement and then he's yanking at my camisole, forcing me to let go of him so he can pull it off over my head. His hands grab my boobs and everything inside me stills at the feel of his skin against my nakedness.

Moaning, I rock a little, needing for him to touch me there. Between my legs, but he shifts us so I'm riding his hard thigh. Without thought, I begin to hump against his corded muscle. My panties are so wet, it's almost like they're not there. The roughness of his cargo pants increases the stimulation against my clitoris and I move faster, pressing down harder.

All the while, he's touching my breasts, mapping them with his fingers, bringing my nipples to stinging rigidity.

It all feels so good.

My brain shuts down, going to that place he took me before. The only thing tethering me to reality is the feel of his hard penis in my hands. Even that feels distant in relation to the bliss making my mind go quiet and my body buzz with a different kind of tension.

Then it happens. The bliss inside me shatters into shards of ecstasy and my awareness of anything else disappears.

CIAN

Anna climaxes with a soft cry, her body bowing against me. Her hands keep sliding on my cock, her pussy moving against my leg, but the slack look on her beautiful face tells me she's not aware of any of it. She's gone. On a different plain, and I took her there.

Or we took her there together.

That's what sends me over and cum explodes from my cock like a geyser, landing in plops on her hands. I pull her forward so her naked tits press against my chest. Skin to skin. Anna goes completely still at the first contact and then she slumps into me, boneless.

I savor the sensation, feeling peace steal over me. Calmness that is not born of lack of emotion, but a sensation only she can give me. In this moment, nothing else exists but our two bodies pressed together. I *feel* calm, not empty. Devoid of stress.

Maneuvering our bodies, I get us laying side by side on the couch our naked chests pressed together, her face burrowed in my neck. I yank the blankets over us and make sure she is secure between me and the back of the old couch, one of my thighs wedged between her legs, holding her in place.

Her sigh of contentment tells me this is what she needs.

This time, I'm not leaving her until she comes down from her sexual high. I'm holding her safe until she settles and the barriers between her and the world are back in place.

CHAPTER 23

CIAN

I wake up when I hear movement from the bedroom. Anna's warm little body is still pressed against mine and it feels right in a way that I don't want to think about.

The roommate is awake. If she takes a shower before coming out, I have time to wake Anna up gently.

First, I hear the toilet flush and then the old pipes clang as the shower goes on. Good.

Brushing my hand along Anna's arm, I say, "Wake up, *mo chroí*."

She nuzzles into my chest making a disgruntled sound. It's adorable.

"Come on, my girl. Do you want Ini to come out here and find you naked in my arms?"

"Don't care. I like this." Anna's leg curves over mine as if she's going to stop me moving.

I grin. I want to stay, but I can't. I should have been up hours ago. There's a war to plan, things to put in place before meeting with my allies later this morning.

"If you get ready quickly, I'll drive you to work." As incentives go, it wouldn't be much for someone else.

But my girl is like me. She wants every second with me that she can get. Just like I want to be with her, even when it means we'll have to sneak to my car like a couple of teenagers cutting school. I'm rethinking the idea of keeping my distance from her, because after less than twenty-four hours that is already working so well. Not.

Anna sits up and the blankets fall away. Her nipples peak in the air, but her eyes are clear. Alert. I need to keep her this way. So, no touching.

"I need a shower," she informs me as she climbs over me to get off the couch. She grabs her sleep camisole and puts it on.

I stand and pick my turtleneck up from where I tossed it on the floor last night. "Make it quick."

"You dressed for stealth last night," she says, eyeing me up in my black clothes.

"I didn't want anyone to see me coming here."

"You really are worried about me."

"Did you think I was lying?"

She shrugs. "No. Not really, just...it's easy to get lost to the voices in my head. They aren't always nice."

"I will never get sick of you," I tell her. Should I kill her aunt and uncle? Would that hurt or help? Maybe it wouldn't change anything at all, but the way they raised my Anna to think of herself as a burden pisses me off.

"What the heck is he doing here?" Ini demands as she comes into the living area.

"He's taking me to work," Anna says.

Ini gives me the stink eye. "After spending the night on our sofa?" She looks between me and Anna in her nightgown. "With you? When did he even get here. You were alone when I went to sleep."

"I came over to check on Anna after I finished work last night."

"How late do you work, mobster King?"

"Most people just call me Boss." But I kind of like mobster King. It has a nice ring to it.

"I'm not calling you Boss. I don't work for you."

The roommate's attitude is eating up Anna's time to get ready. I don't want to leave without her, but soon I won't have any choice. I look at my girl and tap on my watch.

She takes the hint and scurries off to the bedroom.

I go into the kitchen and ask, "What does Anna eat for breakfast?"

"She does better if she has eggs and toast, but..." She shrugs. "We don't always have it."

I open the fridge and pull out the eggs. "Scrambled, fried, boiled, or poached?"

"She only eats scrambled, but not too dry or too runny. Are you going to cook for her?"

"Yes. Do you want eggs?" If I'm cooking for one, I can cook for three just as easily. Ma taught me that.

I might have been her only son, but she taught me to do for myself. Said a man wasn't an adult if he couldn't wash his own clothes or make basic meals. And she wasn't raising any man-child.

Don't know what that says about my da because if he ever stepped a foot in the kitchen in his entire life, I never saw it.

"Sure, if you're offering. I'll start the toast."

It's an olive branch and I take it. Anna will be happier if I get along with her friends. "Thanks."

"She really spent the night with you?" Ini puts two pieces of bread into a small toaster and presses down the lever.

I assume by *spent the night with* she means had sex. I'm not about to answer that question. "Shouldn't you ask her that?"

"I will, don't you worry."

"I worry about very little." An impending war with a street gang and the cartel that supports them? That concerns me.

Whether Ini approves of the intimacy that Anna and I shared doesn't.

Anna comes out wearing a dress with flowers on it. It has short, cap sleeves and a full skirt that doesn't reach her knees. She looks beautiful, but her gorgeous tits are clearly confined by a bra.

We eat quickly and Ini offers to do the dishes so we can leave.

"Thanks!" Anna touches her friend's shoulder, but doesn't hug her.

My girl doesn't like to touch other people. Except me.

Just another way she's perfect for me.

We leave the building the same way I came in last night. My clothes aren't meant for day stealth and she looks too pretty in her dress to be ignored. However, even if Martina has watchers on me, or even Anna, it's unlikely they're watching twenty-four-seven, much less all the angles of her building.

Still, I scan the area for any threats before I let Anna follow me outside.

Her bodyguards are in their SUV waiting near my car like I told them to be.

"I thought I was riding with you," she says when she sees them.

"You are. They'll follow at a distance to make sure we aren't tailed and to be available if I need backup protecting you."

"Is this because you're a mob boss?"

"Yes. And you're mine."

"But you don't want anyone to know that."

"Not sure how well that's going to work with me showing up at your apartment and staying the night." I don't have issues with self-control. If something has to be done, I do it.

"You were worried when I didn't answer the phone last night."

"I didn't like it."

"I had my earbuds in. I didn't hear it ring, or the text chime."

"When you wear your earbuds, will you pair them with your phone, so you hear it ring?"

"Is it important to you?"

"I broke into your apartment and pulled you out of your bed last night because I couldn't talk to you."

"You didn't break in. You have a key."

"Because I made a copy without asking you."

She looks out the window, her posture tense.

"What's the matter."

"You know that's not normal behavior. I know it's not either, but I was glad when I realized you were there. That you hadn't forgotten about me."

"You would have known that if you had answered your phone."

"I liked having you show up more."

Fuck. I did too. But that wasn't what was safest right now.

"Are you still planning to move my cameras?" I ask.

"Yes."

Anger surges in me, but I refuse to let her see it. She has every right to move the cameras. If she wanted to get rid of them completely, she could. My brain takes a dark and twisted turn when I think of her doing that. Damn it.

I take a right when I should go left to reach our office building.

"Where are we going?"

"To a specialty jeweler." I'd intended to have Connor pick the anklet up for me later today, but now I want it on her immediately.

I use my voice feature to text the jeweler and tell him I'll be at his place in thirty minutes or less. It will make it tight for me to get to the office in time for my meeting with Quinn. If I'm a few minutes late? Too fucking bad.

ANNA

Cian pulls the car to a stop in front of a house.

"I thought we were going to a jeweler," she says.

"We are. Yiorgos works out of his home."

"That's a Greek name, isn't it?"

"He is cousin to Stavros."

"The man who owns the Deli? He's friendly when I call to make a lunch order."

Cian shoots me a look. "He's dangerous."

"Like you?"

"No. Because I am not and never will be dangerous to you."

"But he is?"

"Yes."

The door opens as we approach and I don't pursue the conversation, but I wonder how someone taking an order for food over the phone can be a danger to me.

The man standing in the doorway is big and imposing, but he doesn't scare me because I'm not alone. I'm with Cian.

He nods to the man, but doesn't greet him with any words and we go into the house without talking to him. Cian seems to know where he's going. He leads me down a hall and into a room on the left that at one time was probably the parlor. Now, it's set up like a waiting room with armchairs along two walls and a table in the center.

There are no magazines on the table, like at a doctor's office. Just a square box covered in blue velvet so dark it's almost black. We don't sit down, but stand near the table and a couple of seconds later a thin man with stooped shoulders and a thick head of white hair comes in.

He's carrying a small box and he sets it down on the table. "Hello, Mr. Doyle. The item is exactly as you specified."

Item? The box is long and rectangular. I hope it's not a necklace. I don't like having anything around my throat, but for Cian I would try to wear it. For a little while at least.

"Show me," Cian says.

The older man opens the box and pulls out what looks like a thick flat gold bracelet. He lays it on the velvet and then takes out a tool he uses to point. "The clasp is a puzzle lock. Only someone with the sequence key can open it. The tracking device draws power from the metal's conduit connection to the body. It is fully waterproof and can withstand temperatures well beyond the human body's capacity. The titanium is bonded with gold overlay as you wanted."

As soon as he said tracking device, I knew this was for me. I'm glad it's not a necklace, but I'm not sure I can wear a bracelet all day, every day either. I should have told Cian I would prefer having a tracker embedded in one of my teeth. I mean, that would be just like getting a filling, right?

Cian picks up the gold chain and then kneels in front of me, one knee bent. He taps his thigh. "Put your foot up here."

I lift my foot and set it on his leg. He puts the gold chain around my ankle and then closes the clasp. He looks up at me. "How does that feel?"

Pulling my foot off of him, I shake my leg a little. "I can barely feel it." I bend down and run my finger all the way around my skin between my ankle and the jewelry. "It's very smooth."

"Never take it off and I'll always know where you are."

"According to the jeweler, unless I know the key sequence, I couldn't if I wanted to."

I can see Cian having an internal argument with himself, but he takes the anklet off, shows me how to open and close the clasp before putting it back on me. Knowing I can take it off settles the anxious butterflies that had started fluttering inside me. It's not that I don't want him to know where I am, but not being able to remove it would make me obsess over having it on.

It wouldn't be pretty.

Knowing I can means I don't have to.

CHAPTER 24

ANNA

Working in Jimmy's office is better today because I'm not doing it under the emotional storm cloud I was yesterday. I still miss Cian and I want to be where he can see me. Where I can feel his eyes on me.

I don't care if that's normal, or *emotionally stable*. For the first time since my mom died, I feel like I have a person again. I've always been grateful for Ini and then Mrs. Hart's friendship, but it's not the same.

With Cian, I feel *seen*. All the time. And I crave that feeling.

Regardless, I know I can't drag my friends into the dynamics of my relationship with Cian. Maybe if I asked them if they minded the cameras, but I know they will. And if I tell them that it makes me feel safe to have him watch me, they might join my aunt and uncle's bandwagon of getting me *professional help*.

They sent me to therapist after therapist while I lived with them and when the doctors couldn't fix the way my brain works, they said I wasn't trying hard enough. I know my brain is wired differently than most people's but so is Cian's. And he doesn't mind that I'm different.

He wasn't angry that I got overwhelmed at the hospital. He doesn't treat me like I'm broken because the world gets to be too much for me.

Before him, the only people who treated me like I was a fully functioning human were Ini and Mrs. Hart. Which is why I won't risk losing that with them either.

So, when I get home, I move the camera in our apartment to a spot at the head of my bed. Even when I have my blanket tent over me, he can watch and the angle won't allow him to see any part of the room that Ini might be in.

Getting the camera out of Mrs. Hart's apartment will be trickier. She takes a walk every day that the elevator is working, but that's during the day. When I'm at work. I'm mulling that problem over when I get a text from Cian.

Cian: **You moved the camera.**

Me: **I told you I would.**

Cian: **I'll watch you sleep tonight.**

Me: **Blushing smiley face emoji.**

Me: **I don't know how to move Mrs. Hart's camera without taking time off from work.**

Cian: **I'll take care of it.**

Me: **Without scaring her.**

Cian: **Devil emoji.**

Me: **I mean it, Cian.**

Cian: **I already turned it off. Tommy is installing cameras in the halls of your floor and hers as well as the stairwell and elevator.**

I'll take Mobsters Who Listen for five hundred, Alex.

His willingness to accommodate me makes me smile, but part of me is worried. Cian's solution sounds like a lot, but will still leave long swaths of time he can't see me, that I'll know his eyes won't be on me. The anklet calms me. He always knows where I am, but it's not the same.

I gnaw the problem over in my mind and do some research on the Internet. When I find the app that turns an extra phone into a nanny cam, I search for it immediately in my app store. It's there.

I download it and set it up. Now all I have to do is pair it with Cian's phone.

~ ~ ~

I'm sleeping with my noise cancelling earbuds in when the ding of a received text wakes me up. I grab my phone and pull up my text messages. Cian sent me a picture. Of me sleeping.

While I'm looking at it, another text comes in.

Cian: *Mo chroí.*

I smile, feeling that peaceful bliss settle inside me. I text back a heart emoji then I snuggle into my pillow and go back to sleep.

CIAN

The meetings with our allies went well. Even Walsh gave over every piece of information he had on the Kicks Bandidos. The threat of losing his territory and his life loosened his lips. He tried to make a speech about working with my father and the value of wisdom. I told him to shut the fuck up and that it was wise not to test me.

He listened.

Pooling our information and resources, we have a location for *El Fantasma* and a watch on her. Because of Carmen, we also have a list of the major players in the street gang that we need to take out. We should have locations for all of them in the next forty-eight hours.

Leandros Drakos is putting his Greek mafia behind eradicating these fuckers. Between the Greeks, my men and Quinn's mob, we have the manpower to make a devastating coordinated attack.

And that is what we're going to do. Obliterate those bastards in one bloody night.

Ma says the doctors are releasing Shea from the hospital tomorrow. I convinced her to take my sister to a rehabilitation clinic in Spain so they'll both be out of the country when we strike back at the Kicks Bandidos. Her doctors okayed the flight in our private jet, but they'll be taking a medical team with them anyway. Allies in the Irish mob in Spain will watch out for Ma and Shea, but they'll take a ten man squad of bodyguards with them too.

Our plans for taking out the street gang are only days away from fruition. Once we do, I'm moving Anna into my place. This shit where I can only see her for glimpses at a time is not enough. I check the tracking app for her anklet several times an hour, but knowing where she is without being able to actually check on her is messing with my head.

So, as soon as the Kicks Bandidos are handled, she's coming back to work in my office and moving in with me.

It will take the cartel time to regroup and before they do, we'll send the war to them. For that, Carmen's intel has proven invaluable. Think they can fucking try to kill my people with a biological weapon? I'll blow their fucking compound, or send in a platoon of mercenaries to take out every last one of those suckers.

We promised Carmen proof of death for her father, her uncle, that bastard she married and her flaming bitch of a cousin who not only thought she could take over Chicago but forgot the most important rule in any syndicate. Loyalty.

Martina Vega-Gutierrez is the reason Anna isn't working at her desk in my line of sight right now. She is the reason my sister has months of physical rehabilitation and psychotherapy ahead of her. I will see to *El Fantasma*'s punishment and death personally.

"What?" I growl when Lachlan comes into my office.

"You sound like a pissed off lion. I thought you'd be happier. We're close to taking out that *El Fantasma* bitch."

"Not close enough." Anna is still in danger.

And not where she needs to be: with me.

My phone lights up with a text message. It's Anna. She's in early. It's only 7:30. She'd better have ridden with her bodyguards.

I check the message.

Anna: **Could you come to Jimmy's office for a couple of minutes?**

Getting up, I head out, not bothering to tell Lachlan where I'm going. When I reach my uncle's office suite, I'm not surprised to find Anna alone. He won't arrive for another thirty minutes at least.

Anna jumps up when she sees me. She's holding her phone, her face creased in that beautiful smile that I hardly get to see because I don't get to see her. "Give me your phone."

I pull it out and hand it to her after unlocking it. She taps on the screen for a few seconds and then says, "I need your finger."

Lifting my hand, I let her use my fingerprint to access whatever it is she's trying to do. If someone else had asked to put something on my phone I would have insisted on seeing what it was and asked what the hell it was for beforehand.

Not Anna. She's mine. Unlike everyone and everything else that belongs to me, I am also hers.

She hands me back my phone, her smile shy as she looks up at me through her lashes. "Now you can watch me whenever."

My cock goes hard as stone with those words, but I don't understand them. "What do you mean?"

"Tap on that app." She points to a new icon on my homescreen.

I tap to open the app. It's called a nanny phone cam and my brain starts racing. She found this. For me.

I tap on the link titled **Mo Chroí**. It's even spelled right with the accent on the *i*. A video feed pops up. It shows Anna and me. It's live. On her phone.

"You can choose the front camera view or the back camera view." Her voice is filled with delight.

Then she sits down at her desk, pops out the ring on the back of her phone and props it up like she's going to join a video call.

I look down at my phone and I can see part of her face, but not enough of her body. "Move it back a couple of inches."

She does and the curve of her tits comes into the frame.

"Perfect." I pull her up from the chair and against me, lowering my head so my mouth is only a hair's breadth from hers. "Thank you, *mo chroí*."

Her lips soften immediately against mine as I kiss her. My hands roam over her body and I ache to take things further, but although Jimmy's workday doesn't start until later, mine has already begun.

I break the kiss and step away. "Soon, you will be back in my office."

It's more than I should say, but less than she needs. I can see that by the look in her pretty eyes.

"I'll be watching you," I promise her.

That makes her smile even though there are still shadows in her violet gaze.

On my way back to my office, I contact one of my best tech guys. "I want a military grade spycam put on a phone that I can access from mine."

Anna's idea is sweet, but standard apps are too hackable and I don't want anyone else watching my girl. Or using her phone to spy on me when she's with me.

My guy agrees and I give him Anna's details. "This is not a stealth mission. Tell her you're putting the software on there and make sure you delete the *nanny cam* app she has installed. Update her phone with the latest security protocols too. If it can't support them, get her a new phone."

That taken care of, I force my brain to focus on the battle ahead. It won't be a war because there won't be any of the street gang left to fight after we attack.

CHAPTER 25

ANNA

A man I don't recognize comes into Jimmy's office in the late afternoon. He tells me that Cian sent him. I'm about to text Cian to confirm when Jimmy comes out of his office and greets the man like a long lost son.

Okay. Part of the mob then.

He gives me a new phone. "It has security that will keep you and the boss safe and an app he controls from his devices that allow him access to the cameras on yours. If you give me your phone, I'll transfer your data and contacts. I would have already, but you don't have it backed up to the cloud."

Of course, I don't. Cloud storage costs money.

I don't say that. I don't think mobsters have much experience with being broke.

It only takes him a few minutes to transfer everything on my phone, including my number. "I'm deleting any apps that could be used to spy on you or the people you are with if hacked."

I never considered that. Cian did though and rather than chide me for putting the *nanny cam* app on my phone and his, he took care of the security aspect. He's such an action oriented, decisive guy and that's only one of the things I find irresistible about him.

"Do you want me to recycle this phone for you?" the man asks.

I put my hand out and shake my head vehemently. "No, thank you. I'll use the line I have with my service to activate it again with a new number and give it to a friend of mine."

Both Ini and I will feel better if Mrs. Hart has access to a cell phone.

I don't see or talk to Cian over the next couple of days, but there's an air of tension around the building. Even Jimmy isn't his usual affable self. So, I know something is going on.

Cian sends me texts though. Screenshots of me throughout the day to show me he's watching me. Every time I get one it gives me a warm tingly feeling, but I still miss seeing him. I want to breathe the same air as him. I want to inhale his scent and block out all the other scents that make me feel anxious.

I want to touch his penis again and feel his hands on my body. I want his strong arms around me blocking out the world. I want him to tell me to leave my bra off, but not until I'm back in his office working. There's no point when I'd have to wear a jacket or sweater all day in Jimmy's office for modesty's sake.

I get a text ping in the middle of the night and see it's from him. I grab my new phone and check the text. It's not a picture this time.

Cian: **Take off your sleep camisole.**

I don't think about denying him.

It's hot in our apartment. We don't have air conditioning and summer temperatures in Chicago can make it stifling. Even so, I've been using my blanket lean-to every night so when my phone's screen lights up with a text it won't bother Ini.

Besides, I like the feeling that Cian and I are in here, in our own little world. Even if he's somewhere else in the city, his texts let me know that he's watching. That he's with me.

I don't like sleeping without a blanket. It feels wrong, but tonight I'm trying to make do with just my sheet. I push it off and pull my nightie up my body and toss it to the end of my mattress, leaving me in only my panties.

Making no effort to cover my breasts, I lie on my bed and let myself feel the weight of Cian's eyes on my body. Despite the warm air, my nipples bead from pure arousal. My panties are wet.

My phone pings with another text and I check it.

Cian: **Beautiful. Sleep well, *mo chroí*.**

And I do, without the sheet or my camisole. I dream about Cian's hands on my body.

~ ~ ~

The next day, Jimmy sends me home early, saying he doesn't have anything for me to do. I get the sense that he's lying, but I don't press him. As I exit the elevator into the parking garage, I see two big SUVs pulling into spots. Arlo and Tommy both step forward and flank me, sort of frog marching me to the car.

As we pull out of our parking spot, I watch as several men with grim faces and the aura of danger I'm coming to recognize get out of the SUVs.

Did Jimmy want me out of the building before they got there?

"Today is bookstore day," I tell Tommy, who is driving. "I'll go early since I have the time."

He nods. Unlike Arlo, Tommy doesn't talk much, which I appreciate. Arlo is not exactly chatty, but he usually responds verbally. Tommy doesn't unless he has no choice but to speak. I rarely see my other guard, Eoin.

I spend an hour browsing in the bookstore. I find a used book on Irish history and another about the mob in America, but one of my favorite authors has a new release out too. It takes me most of that hour to decide which book to put back.

Asking the clerk if she can hold the book on Irish history for me for a week, I put the other two on the counter.

"No problem, Anna. But you know the policy. One week max and then it goes back on the shelf."

"Thank you." I don't get paid again for ten more days, but maybe if I skimp on something else. I sigh, knowing it's unlikely, but I don't tell her to put it back on the shelves.

Maybe Ini will lend me the money, if she has it. She knows I'll pay her back with my next check.

Stepping outside, someone grabs my arm. "Anna Lake?"

Trying to pull my arm away, I don't answer. Why aren't Tommy and Arlo stepping in to help? Isn't that what bodyguards do?

"You are Anna Lake?" It's a different voice. A woman. She steps in front of me and I see the shiny badge on her belt, right next to the not so shiny gun.

I swallow and nod.

The man holding my arm says, "We need to ask you some questions about your association with Cian Doyle."

"No." Panic is clawing at my insides, but I don't let it out. I have a lot of experience hiding my anxiety from my family and that makes it possible for me to keep my expression placid now.

Even though my heart feels like it's going to beat out of my chest.

"Are you sure that's the attitude you want to take, Anna?" the man still in possession of my arm asks.

"Who are you?" Aren't police supposed to announce themselves?

Okay, my only experience with law enforcement is what I've seen on television, but still. This feels wrong.

"Please, let go of me," I say.

"I'm Detective Grieves." Rather than releasing me, his hold tightens on my arm. "And that's my partner, Detective Samuels."

"We need to ask you a few questions," Detective Samuels says.

Detective Grieves starts dragging me toward a car parked in front of the bookstore. "Down at the station."

"Are you arresting me?" I ask as the panic swirls.

"Do we need to?" Detective Samuels asks.

"Because we can arrest you for obstruction of justice if that's what you want, but most folks want to keep their records clean."

I look around wildly, trying to find Tommy and Arlo. They'll know if these detectives can do what they are threatening. I see no sign of Arlo and Tommy is watching from a distance.

He has a phone to his ear, but he mouths, "It will be okay."

Now he uses his words? When they are very much the wrong ones, because they imply I should go with the detectives.

Somehow, I find myself shoved into the back of the detectives' car. There's no grill between the back and the front, like you see on television, but Detective Grieves gets in the back with me.

He leans across me and grabs the seatbelt, buckling me in. It's nothing like when Cian does it. Then I feel cared for and protected. Right now, it feels like I'm being confined.

His hand brushes over the apex of my thighs as he pulls away from me and I gasp. He laughs. "I bet Doyle enjoys how responsive you are."

"Detective Samuels?" I call out.

She ignores me, pulling into traffic.

"Don't expect my partner to worry about your sensibilities. If you didn't hang out with criminals, you wouldn't be in this situation. Are you one of his whores? Or is yours a private arrangement?"

Trying to scoot as close to the door as I can get and away from the odious man, I ignore his questions. Even if I wanted to answer him, I couldn't. The situation is taking every bit of my coping skills to manage.

The car smells funky, like dirty sweatsocks and puke that's been cleaned up but not well. The air conditioning is on, but I'm so hot I'm sweating. My hands feel cold though.

His hand is hot when it lands on my chest.

I squeak, and he laughs.

"Stop touching me," I force out of my mouth, even though making words is the last thing I feel capable of doing right now.

He doesn't listen. He shoves his hand down my top and grabs my boob. Hard. Pain shoots from all five points where his fingers dig in and radiates outward.

I scream and grab his wrist, trying to pull his hand away from me. "Please, Detective Samuels, make him stop."

But she doesn't. She ignores me.

"You're going to tell us what we want to know or my hand on your tit is going to be the least of your worries," Detective Grieves threatens.

He molests me, pinching my nipple so hard that tears spring into my eyes. I just want it to stop, but I don't promise to cooperate. I'm not telling them anything about Cian. Not that I know a lot, but if I say anything these two crooked cops could twist it.

When I realize that the female detective isn't going to do anything to stop her partner, I seal my lips tight and retreat inside my mind with my rhyme. I say it over and over again, even though I can't act out the ritual to calm myself.

I'm still trying to yank his hands away from me, so I can't click my fingernails together. I'm breathing too erratically to do the deep inhales and exhales I need to. I can't even look down at my feet because that awful man's face is blocking everything as he leans over me.

"We're almost there," Detective Samuels says from the front.

With a final squeeze I'm sure is going to leave bruises, Grieves pulls his hand away and sits back on his side of the seat. "We'll pick this up when we get you into an interview room."

Aren't interviews recorded? Don't they have windows, or two-way mirrors, or something? He can't molest me in the police station.

"We've got our own special set up," he says like he knows what I'm thinking. "It helps people like you remember that you want to help the cops, not piss us off."

Tommy said it would be okay. But it's not. What are these two going to do with me? Now that he's not touching me, I'm clicking my nails on both hands. I still can't deep breathe. It's just not possible.

I'm trying hard not to puke. No wonder that sour smell is in the air in here. They probably have people throwing up in their car all the time from having his hands on them.

CHAPTER 26

ANNA

They hustle me into the station when we get there, both of them holding one of my arms. Ants are crawling under my skin and I have to grit my teeth to stop from screaming.

Maybe I should scream? Would anyone in here help me? Are they all corrupt?

I frantically count the steps from the door in my mind. One. Two. Three. Four. Five. Six. Se—

"Hey, Grieves. Samuels. Who do you have there?" The tall Black man who steps in front of us, halting our progress, has a warm, melodious voice, but his dark eyes are narrowed on the tableau we make.

Samuels says dismissively, "A person of interest in a case."

"I don't want to be here," I tell the other man. "They forced me."

"That happens in a police station," he says, but he frowns at Grieves.

"He hurt me," I add, jerking my head toward Grieves, trying to pull my arms away from the two detectives.

"She's full of shit." Grieves' grip on my arm tightens. "I didn't do anything, did I, Samuels?"

"Nah. She doesn't want to get in trouble with her boyfriend for talking to the cops, but she came of her own free will." Samuel glares down at me.

Do they think I'm going to agree with them? They're scary, but I'm terrified of what might happen if they get me into a room alone.

"That's a lie," I say, hoping the other detective will listen. "Let me go." I keep trying to yank my arms away from them, but it's no use.

The other man steps forward, making it impossible for Grieves and Samuels to get me past without releasing me. "I've got some time; I think I'll sit in on this interview. Make sure she's here as voluntarily as you say she is."

Will he stop Grieves from touching me again? Samuels didn't.

"No way. This is our case," Grieves says hotly.

"Detective Grieves. Samuels," a deep voice booms from behind us. All three of the officers tense up. "Let that woman go."

Grieves turns his head. "Captain, she's a person of interest in an important case we're working."

"Did I fucking stutter?" the captain asks.

The detectives drop my arms like I'm diseased. I feel dirty...infected by Grieves' horrible touch, but I don't hesitate to move away from them as fast as I can. I go toward the captain. One step. Two steps.

"I want to go home," I tell him. "Please. I didn't do anything."

"Are you arresting her?" he demands.

Grieves and Samuels remain silent.

The captain's expression turns thunderous. "You brought a witness in to interview against her will?" he asks furiously.

"She agreed to come. She just started having second thoughts when we got here," Samuels lies.

I would argue, but my throat is closed. I've got to say something. I'm trying to force words out. They won't come.

"Second thoughts, third thoughts, it does not fucking matter. You cannot hold a witness against her will."

Samuels grits her teeth. Grieves glares menacingly at me. The other detective shifts his body so he's between me and them.

"You are free to leave, Miss Lake," the captain says.

Grieves and Samuels react to his use of my name like they've been tazed. I should get a taser. If these two come for me again, I'm not going quietly.

Maybe I should move out of Chicago, but I don't have the money and I can't leave Ini stuck with the full rent. My mind spirals and I can't make it stop. My rhyme stutters after one, two every time I try to say it now.

The other detective looks at me worriedly. "The captain said you can go, miss."

"Grieves, Samuels, in my office. Now," the captain barks.

They start protesting, talking over each other, but I don't wait around to hear how that's going to play out. My feet finally unstick themselves from the floor and I turn to rush from the police station. I don't even count my steps to the door, I just bolt through the doors to the outside.

Someone puts their hand on my shoulder. I scream.

"Fuck. Miz Lake, it's all right. It's just me."

I jerk my head up and see Eoin standing there. I shake my head and start walking away. The station is only a few blocks from my apartment building. I can walk from here. I'm not getting in another car with a man.

Remembering the ride here, I have to swallow against the need to throw up.

"Anna," I hear my name called, but I recognize the voice this time. It's Arlo.

I stop, but I don't turn.

"Let us take you home."

I spin to face him. "Take me to Cian." I want to see Cian.

Arlo grimaces. "I can't do that, Anna. He's in a meeting right now."

I nod and turn back around and start walking again. I hear footsteps behind me and realize one of them is following me. I look back over my shoulder. It's Arlo.

"It's hot out here. Let us drive you home. Walking ten blocks in this heat is going to give you blisters."

A vehicle is keeping pace beside me. I can hear the quiet purr of the engine and the whisper of the tires against the street. I look to my left and see that it's Tommy driving the SUV I was in earlier. Eoin is in the front seat now.

He shouldn't be going that slowly on the street. The SUV is barely moving. Other drivers will get mad.

"I'll walk with you, but I'd rather you got in the SUV," Arlo says.

I hear voices behind us and realize there are people coming out of the police station. Are two of them the detectives that took me?

I leap toward the SUV and yank the backdoor open, throwing myself inside while it's still moving. The truck lurches to a stop and Arlo comes rushing up, panting. "Okay, that works. Let's get you home."

Scooting as far over on the seat as I can, I ignore my seatbelt.

Arlo climbs inside and seems to realize I want my space because he settles near his door as well.

"Buckle up," Tommy says from the front.

The idea of being trapped by the seatbelt has me shaking my head side to side and chanting, "No. No. No."

One of the bodyguards curses, but the car starts picking up speed. They aren't going to force me to put on the seatbelt. I let out a breath and then suck in another.

"I want to see Cian."

No one says anything. They aren't going to take me to the Doyle Building.

I grab my phone out of my purse and send Cian a text.

Me: **I want to see you. Tell them to bring me to you.**

He doesn't reply immediately, so I send another.

Me: **Please.**

We arrive at the street where we usually park near my building. The bodyguards get out of the car, but I stay where I am. I'm safe here. I'm not safe out there. They know my name. They know where I live. They can come for me again, and this time I can't expect their captain to save me.

I don't know why he told them to let me go the first time, but what are the chances I'll get that lucky again.

My door opens and I scramble to the middle of the seat.

Arlo's face twists. I don't try to read his emotions. I'm too stressed right now to deal with anyone else's feelings. I want a shower, but I know it won't make me clean. I'm dirty now. He touched my boob. Like Cian.

No, not like Cian. Grieves hurt me with his touch, but no one else except Cian has ever touched my breasts. I shudder when I remember the feel of the awful man's hands on me. And that drag of his hand across the apex of my thighs. He didn't touch my skin there, but I feel dirty there too.

Tears spill over my eyelids, running hotly down my cheeks.

I hate being touched by almost everyone. Being touched like that has me feeling like I want to crawl out of my skin.

My phone dings. I lift it to see. A text from Cian flashes on the screen.

Cian: **I told them to take you to my place. I'll meet you there as soon as I can**.

I nod, but don't text back. Instead, I message Ini and tell her to spend the night at Mrs. Hart's tonight.

She calls and I swipe to answer, wondering if I'll get any words out.

"What's going on, Anna?" Ini asks, worry lacing her tone. "It's that criminal you work for, isn't it? He's got you mixed up in his business."

"No." I'm not mixed up in Cian's business.

The cops said they wanted to talk to me about him, but that's not his fault. They're bad cops. Good ones wouldn't have done what they did to me. That other detective, and the captain...I think they're good cops. They wanted to protect me.

Why didn't Cian protect me?

Cian told me he didn't want me associated with him to protect me from his enemies, I remind myself. Are the detectives working for his enemies?

"Where are you going to be?" Ini asks after several seconds of silence.

"Cian's place," I get out.

"Why can't I spend the night at home?"

When no more words will come, I hang up and text her.

Me: **Because it might not be safe**.

Ini: **Why???**

Me: **IDK**

Ini: **That doesn't make sense**.

Me: **Wouldn't be the first time**.

Ini: **Not funny**.

I wasn't joking. Was I? I don't think I was. Ini loves me but there are lots of times my thought process doesn't make sense to her. I want to tell her about the police picking me up, but I don't have the words right now.

Besides, if I tell her, she'll get angry with Cian and blame him. She'll insist I come back to the apartment.

I can't do that.

Me: **Please.**

Ini: **Okay. But I'm giving that boyfriend-slash-boss of yours a piece of my mind the next time I see him.**

Relieved and out of words, I don't reply. I know Ini won't be mad. She understands when I get like this.

I'm surprised when we pull into the underground parking garage for the Doyle building, but I don't ask why we're here. I'm done talking. Arlo is carrying my bag from the bookstore. Tommy has my purse. I left both behind when I got out of the SUV.

We stop at the floor which has both Jimmy and Cian's office suites, but no one steps out of the elevator. Giving me a small smile, Connor steps in and then he swipes a card against the space above the buttons before pressing his thumb against it as well.

The elevator starts to move again. When it opens, there is a lobby with a set of double doors opposite the elevator, a hallway to the right and another to the left. Cian lives here? In the building? How did I not know that?

"My apartment is down there." Connor waves toward the hall on the left. "Lachlan's is too." He indicates the hall on the right. "That's where the workout room and pool are.

I nod because it feels like Connor expects some sort of acknowledgement.

He heads to the double doors opposite the elevator. Connor puts his entire palm on the reader to the right of the door and then a mechanism pops out that scans his eye. He types in a code on a box above the door handle and then a small whir and click sound.

He opens the door and ushers us all inside.

He's careful not to touch me as I move by him. "Cian might be a while. He wants me to get you dinner. If you want a shower, use his bathroom." Connor rolls his eyes. "My cousin is a control freak. Anyway, he says wear whatever clothes you want from his closet."

I nod and tilt my head in inquiry.

We are standing in an open concept living area with a gleaming modern kitchen, a sunken living room with a huge leather sectional facing a television that takes up half of the wall. Behind it is a dining table that seats six and beyond the floor to ceiling windows is a large terrace.

There is a short hall to my right and another to my left, past the kitchen. "His bedroom is down that hall." Connor points to my left.

I nod and head in that direction. What I find is not a bedroom, but a master suite even larger than my aunt and uncle's. The bathroom is to my left and it's what I imagine a spa would be like. Stone tile floors and walls in shades of brown encompass a shower with a sparkling clear glass wall. It doesn't have a door, just an opening. To the right is a large, jetted tub.

I haven't taken a bath since moving out of my aunt and uncle's home two years ago. I used to love the quiet of a long soak, letting my head submerge until only my face was above the hot water. Our apartment only has a cubicle style shower in the small bathroom, the entirety of which would fit inside Cian's shower area.

I turn on the taps, letting the tub start to fill before peeling out of my clothes. I leave them in a neat pile on the floor. They are dirty. I cannot put them back on. Not after *he* touched them. They smell like the detective's car too and every time a whiff of the scent assaults my nostrils, I want to vomit.

I kick the whole pile to the furthest spot from me and the bathtub in the bathroom.

Looking in the mirror, I see bruises forming on my left breast, the nipple is still red from being pinched so hard. There is no visible trace otherwise that the detective put his hands on me, but I can feel his touch still, like he left a layer of dirt behind.

I've been stimming constantly since the police station and my fingertips are sore, but I can't make myself stop. Searching in the cabinets, I find some eucalyptus bath salts. They are probably good for after Cian has been in a physical altercation. I'm hoping the eucalyptus will make my skin feel clean again.

I pour a couple of handfuls of the bath salts into the water and then swirl them around with my hand. Once the bath is half-filled, I step into the hot water and sit down. The heat begins to seep into me and only then do I realize how cold I am. Shivers wrack me as the water rises. When it reaches a couple of inches below the tub rim, I sit up and turn off the taps.

Then, keeping my arms away from my body, I lay back in the water and float. I don't want any part of myself to touch another part and spread the grime from the detective's touch further. My breasts are not submerged. I will have to turn over for that, but not yet.

I let my head sink into the water until only my face is out of it like I used to do. My fingernails cannot click together in the water, so I can finally let my hands rest, splayed out and floating.

I savor the muffled silence the water creates around my head, the sense of being alone and safe. I am in Cian's home. No one can get me here.

My bookstore isn't safe anymore. Is anywhere outside of this building? What if those detectives come here? They can't get up to this floor without someone letting them. Without a warrant, they can't force it. Can they?

Cian won't let them. But he let them take me. Why?

That is the question my mind won't let go of. It is the reason I have to speak to him tonight.

CHAPTER 27

ANNA

I don't know how long I float in the tub, but eventually the sound of my name being called penetrates my bubble of isolation created by the water.

I sit up and Connor is there. In the bathroom. He's not looking at me though.

He's facing the wall opposite the tub I'm in. "Crap, Anna. You about gave me a heart attack. I guess you didn't hear me yelling your name with your head under the water like that. Is that safe? What if you fell asleep? You could drown." He makes a weird noise in his throat, like a laugh, but not. "I sound like my ma."

"Is she a good person?" I ask, surprised the words come almost easily.

"What?" He runs his hands through his hair. "Yeah. Ma is great."

"Then it's not bad to sound like her, is it?"

"No, I guess not."

"I don't want to get out of the water yet."

Connor steps backward and sits down with his back against the side of the tub enclosure. "Okay, but I don't think you should do that floating thing without someone in here to notice if you go under."

I almost smile. He's watching out for me and that feels good. I wonder if he would have let the detectives take me if he'd been there instead of Tommy and Arlo. So, I ask.

His hand messes with his hair again and he sighs. "It's protocol, right? To cooperate with the cops, and stay silent until the lawyer arrives."

"No lawyer came for me."

"He was on his way, but it was faster to get the captain involved. We don't like to do that when it's not necessary."

But it was necessary with me? Did they know that detective was grabby? If they did, why let him take me?

I'm not asking Connor these questions. I'll wait until I talk to Cian. Only he can tell me definitively why *he* let that happen. He's the boss. It's down to him.

Leaning forward, I allow the front of my body to submerge into the water. I still don't let any of my limbs rub against each other and I hold onto the rim with both hands shoulder width apart. "Do you think soap and water can wash away the touch of another human being?"

Connor's shoulders tense and he expels a long breath. "Who are you trying to wash away? Cian? Because I gotta tell you, lass, I don't think you'll ever get rid of my cousin." He rubs his face and mutters, "And I don't like the city of Chicago's chances if you do."

I'm not sure what he means, but I'm not trying to wash away Cian and say so.

"Good. Anyone in particular then?"

I don't want to answer, so I ask again, "Can it?"

"Sometimes. Sometimes the touch feels so wrong that even when you've washed every inch of skin, it still feels like it's there."

"You sound like you know."

He shrugs.

"Do you want to talk about it?" I know I don't want to talk about what happened to me today.

"There are no gay mobsters. At least that's what everyone likes to believe. It's what my ma and da think."

"That's a statistical improbability."

He laughs, but the sound is harsh. Hurt.

"Are you okay?" I ask him. Connor is my friend. I don't want him to hurt.

"Not really, no."

"Can I help?"

"How are you asking me that when you're still stressed out by what happened with the cops?"

"Because you're my friend. You came in here to make sure I am okay."

"And now you're making sure I'm okay?" he asks, sounding both amused and something else.

Sad?

"I don't like talking sometimes."

"Is this one of them?"

I have more words than usual, but yes. "Uh huh."

"So, I should talk?" He sounds almost grateful. Like he wants to talk.

"Yes."

"I'm gay." He says it like he's admitting something huge.

"I'm not."

He laughs. "Is that your way of saying it doesn't matter?"

"Uh huh." I turn my head and let my cheek rest on the tub rim between my hands, none of my skin touching.

"It matters to my family. I mean I think it does. Ma and Da, they've never said anything antigay to me, but the mob...it's not LGBTQ friendly, you know?"

"Why?"

"Tradition? Ignorance? Religion? Take your pick."

If I got to pick it would be none of the above. I always liked that option on tests. It made it less stressful to pick my answers when I knew I didn't have to choose one on the list.

"Since I was a teen, every once in a while, when I'm out with the lads, I pick up a woman. We have sex and they think I'm normal like them."

"I emulate people too, so they'll think I'm *normal* like them." That's how I'd kept my jobs before, but it never lasts long. Eventually, they see the differences and things don't work out.

Everywhere but at Doyle & Byrne.

"Yeah? How does that work out for you?"

"Not great."

"Well, it didn't work out great for me either. I got someone pregnant."

"You don't want children?"

"I always wanted to be a da, but now...it's perfect for me but not for everyone else."

I float in silence, letting him decide if he wants to tell me more.

"About a month ago, I ran into this guy. Something about him seemed familiar, but I didn't place it. Not at first."

"Who is he?"

"My baby's daddy."

I think for a minute and realize what Connor is saying. His baby's father is trans and was presenting as a woman when they slept together.

"You just ran into him?" I ask.

"He bumped into me by accident on purpose."

"And?"

"I like him."

That's good, right? "When is the baby due?"

"Dot is ten months old."

"Oh."

"Elliott had a lot of fears about telling me he'd had my kid. Not least of which is that I'm part of the Doyle & Byrne mob."

"He knows?"

"If I wasn't a Doyle, if I didn't work for Cian, he probably wouldn't. But yeah, he knew and it scared him. I can't blame him. Look at what happened to Shea."

"But he told you anyway?"

"Yes. He said he had to give me a chance to be part of Dot's life if that is what I want."

I can hear the longing in his voice. "It is."

"She's my kid. She's so beautiful, Anna. And her dad..." Connor's voice trails off. "He rocks my world."

"What are you going to do?"

"I *want* to make a family with Elliott and Dot."

I turn and sit up, pouring water over my shoulders and arms. "Elliott doesn't want that?"

"He wants me too. He kind of fell for me that first night, but he thought there was no hope for us when he transitioned."

Tears prick my eyes, but I'm not sure why. It's a beautiful story though. A family that was meant to be. "Congratulations."

"If my cousin kills me for being gay, there won't be a lot to celebrate."

"Cian won't kill you. He cares about you."

Connor sighs. "I know you think my cousin walks on water, Anna."

Not so much. Not after today.

"But he's the boss. He has to do what's best for the mob."

Is that why he let the detectives take me? Because it was the best thing for the organization? "Well, killing you isn't best for anyone." That's one thing I'm sure of.

"Definitely not for me." There's a smile in his voice.

"I want to meet Elliott and Dot." A few months ago, that would never have come out of my mouth.

Especially after a day like today when I hit my mental limit. But my life has changed. There are more people in it than just my two friends. And I'm okay with adding to that number. Which is the opposite of how I've operated since my parents died. I've kept my inner circle to two because I couldn't trust anyone else.

Until I started working at Doyle & Byrne.

I don't feel as safe as I did when I started working for Cian, but I'm still glad I know these people. Because I fit here. Even if fitting in with a mob is riskier than I realized.

"I want you to meet them too. After Shea was attacked, I sent them out of town. Elliott wasn't happy. We'd only had a couple of weeks being back together, but I need him and our daughter to be safe."

"Have you told your parents yet?"

"About their grandchild?" Connor sighs. "No."

"Cian will help smooth things over. Shea told me that he lets women into the mob."

"That's different."

"I bet it isn't to Cian." He's too logical to cling to emotionally fed prejudices.

Jimmy might be less understanding. I don't know. We've never talked about stuff like this, but I have heard him lament not having any grand-children. I think Dot will be the bridge between Connor's new family and his old one.

"Oh, crap."

"What?"

Connor grabs something from his pocket and then holds up my phone. "Cian wanted me to give this to you. He's probably texted you and is waiting for a response."

I don't take the phone. "Put it in the other room. I'll check it later."

"Okay, but are you about ready to eat some dinner? I'm starving. If you come out to the living room, I'll show you some pictures of Dot I have on my phone."

"Let me finish up." The water isn't as hot as it was and I'm starting to get cold again.

Connor nods and stands. "No more floating." He doesn't wait for me to agree before leaving the bathroom.

Standing up, I use a washcloth and some glycerin soap from a dish beside the tub to wash my body. I don't feel clean when I'm done, but I start the tub draining and get out. I don't think soap and water can wash away the touch of someone when your whole being is revolted by that touch.

Maybe eventually, it will stop feeling like bugs are crawling over my skin.

I should have asked Connor how long he feels uncomfortable after having sex with someone he doesn't want to in order to make his friends think he's like them.

CHAPTER 28

CIAN

I look down at my phone again. No text from Anna. Although the cameras on her phone are now showing my bedroom and not the dark interior of her purse, she is not there.

What the hell is going on?

I text Connor and demand a situation update.

I've been in this meeting for the past six hours. I can't end it no matter how much I want to. If things go according to plan, we move against the Kicks Bandidos the day after tomorrow. Everything has to be prepared and every element to the plan must have a backup. The logistics are interesting, but I'm not deriving my usual satisfaction from solving a problem, or even planning to take out my enemies.

Anna is in the forefront of my mind. I knew she wouldn't react well to being taken to the police station. That's why I called in a marker from the captain for her. It was a calculated risk. Now, he's another person who knows of Anna's importance to me.

According to him, she was barely in the building for five minutes before he ordered his detectives to release her. Arlo said she was stressed though. That she refused to get into the SUV with him and the other guards at first. Then she texted me that she wanted to see me.

I gave instructions for her to be brought to my place. I know they're up there, her, Connor, Tommy, Arlo and Eoin. But she hasn't responded to any of my other texts and she's not letting me see her.

I don't like it. When one of the Greek mafia men under Drakos suggests we scale back the assault on the street gang, I let my frustration loose. Lachlan calls in two of our men to carry the man out of the room. He'll wake up. Eventually.

No one else makes any more fucking ridiculous suggestions and we finally wrap up the meeting.

"I'll see everyone out," Lachlan says to me. "You go check on her."

~ ~ ~

Opening the door to my apartment, I find Anna and Connor sitting at opposite ends of my sectional, watching some kind of nature show. Anna is wearing one of my t-shirts. If she has anything else on, I don't see evidence of it.

Connor looks up. "Hey, Boss."

Anna does not acknowledge my presence. I watch her profile. She seems engaged in the show. Her phone is still in my bedroom. The camera feed has not changed in the last hour. She didn't bring it with her in here. Why?

"Where are Arlo and his men?" I ask.

Connor stands, gives Anna a concerned look and then says, "Over at my place. I figured Anna would appreciate the quiet."

"I do." She turns her head slightly and smiles at Connor.

It's not a big smile, but it's more than she's giving me.

Connor nods. "I'll head out then." He looks at me. "Arlo and his crew can stay at my place."

It's a good idea. I want Anna's bodyguards nearby but I don't want them in my guestroom.

"Send Tommy to keep an eye on Ini and Mrs. Hart." Anna's friends shouldn't be targets, but I'm leaving nothing to chance.

The two detectives who picked up my girl today aren't clean, but they aren't on my payroll either. That police station is in Walsh's territory, as is Anna's apartment. He said they aren't on his payroll either.

If I find out differently, Walsh is done. And I'll make an example of him for anyone who thinks they can fuck with me and mine.

I'm not sure what to do with Anna. This is the first time we've been in a room together that her attention isn't on me. I don't like it.

Grabbing the remote, I turn off the TV.

She doesn't react.

"What's going on, Anna?" I ask.

Her head comes up, those violet eyes looking at me with accusation. "Why did you let them take me?"

"The detectives?"

She nods.

"It's protocol. When possible, we don't escalate with the cops."

She doesn't reply, just stares at me.

I rub the back of my neck and sit down. She scoots into the arm of the couch. What the fuck is going on?

"I knew you wouldn't like being in the police station." But I didn't think it would affect her like this. "I didn't want you upset like you were in the hospital so I called in a marker with the captain."

"He knew my name. It shocked the detectives."

"We don't know if they picked you up because they're trying to make a case against me, or if someone ordered them to do it."

"How did they know about me?" she asks, her body still tense, don't-touch-me vibes rolling off her.

"That's the question. It could be as simple as you're the most recent hire in my office and they found out about you."

She doesn't react to my words.

I admit, "It could also be that the Kicks Bandidos tipped them off that you're connected to me. We know they had people watching me and my family."

It's more than I would usually tell an outsider, but Anna is different. And she deserves to know that I might be the reason she was taken in for questioning.

"They said they wanted to ask questions about you."

So, she already knows I'm to blame. Is that why she asked why I let them take her?

"I can instruct your guards not to let them take you in for questioning again."

"I'm going to get a taser."

What the fuck? "You don't need a taser, Anna. You have three body-guards."

"They didn't protect me today."

"Did the detectives say something to you that scared you?" I'm trying to understand why she's reacting so strongly. "They don't have anything on me. They can't arrest you. You're not an accessory to anything."

Maybe she needs to be given the talk by our lawyer. He has a whole spiel prepared for when our mobsters date outside the organization. It's a watered-down version of what he tells new recruits.

"He touched me. I'm tainted." Anna starts to cry. "I'm not yours any-more."

"The fu--. You are mine, Anna. Today doesn't change that."

She just shakes her head. "It's all ruined."

What is ruined? I know my girl doesn't like other people touching her, but she reacts differently to me and I need to hold her right now because something is seriously wrong. Anna's brain isn't wired like other people's but she's strong. No way is this reaction just because she took a ride in a car with strangers to the police department.

What the fuck did they say to her? What does she mean, that *he* touched her? To put her in the car?

"I'm going to hold you."

"You can't. I'm dirty."

"You're not dirty. Your mine," I reiterate. Then because I can't stop myself, I pull her into my lap.

She's stiff as a board, but then she collapses into me and starts to sob. The sound makes me want to kill someone. But it also makes me want to comfort her. I don't know how to comfort a woman.

I do the only thing I can think of and that is to wrap my arms around her and rub her back. It's something my da used to do for my ma when she was upset.

Anna doesn't seem to mind, but I don't know if it's helping. Eventually, her crying subsides and I hand her my handkerchief. She mops up.

We sit in silence for several long minutes.

Eventually, I say, "I know words can be hard for you when you are upset, but I need you to tell me what happened. Will you do that for me?"

She starts to talk, her voice monotone. She recites the events like she's reading a book with narration and dialogue. She details every action and repeats every word of dialogue. When she reaches the point where the detective laid hands on her, red rage fills my vision.

I *will* kill him but first I have to fix this.

I don't interrupt to ask questions. I let her tell me the entire episode, including how she texted me and ended up in my apartment.

I was going to fucking send her home? I only told Arlo to bring her to my place after he told me Anna refused to get out of the car when they got to her apartment building.

Something strange twinges in my chest. Is that guilt?

It's not a sensation I'm familiar with, but I'm feeling something right now and it's not pleasant.

"He will never touch you again."

"No, he won't. I'm buying a taser."

"I'll get you a taser and Connor will teach you self-defense." She likes my cousin. Trusts him.

So do I.

"Thank you."

"Don't thank me. It's my fault you went through that today."

"I don't like your protocol."

"It's not the protocol for you. Not anymore." I'll tell Arlo that he and his crew have permission to use deadly force if necessary to prevent the cops, or anyone else, from taking Anna again.

"I don't want Grieves to touch me again, but nothing can change that he already did." She starts crying again.

Fuck.

Her words from earlier come back to me. I pull her body back and tilt her chin so our eyes meet. "You think him laying hands on you taints you?"

She doesn't answer, but that drenched violet gaze says it all. She does.

"It doesn't."

She doesn't acknowledge that claim anymore than she did when I told her she is still mine.

"Is that why you didn't keep your phone near you? You don't think you belong to me anymore?"

"He touched me!" She's furious and so damn sad. "No one has ever put their hands on my boobs. Only you."

And while my touch sends her to a blissed-out headspace, Grieves' makes her feel tainted.

"No one else has ever touched you that way? Not even your boyfriends?" Her tits are a work of art. I would be miserable trying to date her and never being able to see or touch something that beautiful.

"I've only been on a few dates. I never had a boyfriend."

And now she has me. What we have is a hell of a lot deeper than that. We belong to each other. If I have a soul, it's connected to hers.

"I don't like being touched," she adds.

"Except by me."

"I can hug my friends," she says, almost defensively. "If it's not too long."

"I know. I'm a possessive man when it comes to you, Anna. It's good that you aren't touchy-feely. That would drive me to murder."

Her lips tilt. Not quite a smile, but it's something. She thinks I'm joking. I'm not. I would kill anyone who got too familiar with her. Like I will kill Grieves. I've got something else in mind for Samuels.

"You can't want me anymore. Not now. After he touched me."

"You're wrong. I will always want you."

"But I'm dirty."

Fucking Grieves. He's going to take a long time to die and hate every fucking minute of it.

"You are not dirty."

She just looks at me.

"I'll wash his touch away," I promise her.

CHAPTER 29

CIAN

"Y ou can't. Soap and water won't clean it," she tells me, distressed. "I tried. It's like ants crawling all over my skin."

Fuck this.

I tug at the hem of my t-shirt she's wearing and ask permission with my eyes. She looks away, but she shrugs and doesn't stop me removing it.

She's not wearing anything underneath. Not even her panties.

Her left breast has dark red finger size splotches on it. So do her upper arms. They'll be purple by tomorrow.

Fury surges through me. I know where every mark comes from because of her meticulous recitation of events.

"You are so beautiful."

Her head snaps around her eyes searching mine. "Still?"

"I hate seeing these bruises mar your soft skin, but they don't make you any less gorgeous." I maneuver her body so she's straddling my thighs. "Do you want me to take my clothes off too?"

She shrugs again.

I'm taking that to mean yes. It's easy to get my jacket and shirt off, but I have to shove first one side of my trousers and boxers down and then the other, while I hold her to me with one arm so she doesn't slide off my lap. I don't know why, but it feels imperative to keep her exactly where she is.

Despite my rage, her nudity affects me as it always does and my cock stands up hard between us.

Now that we are both naked, I pull her forward so her pussy touches my hardon.

She doesn't react, just looks at me, like she's waiting for me to reject her.

That's not going to happen.

I gently cup her tits. The difference in her usual reaction to my touch is obvious right away. She remains tense, her eyes locked on mine totally focused.

"These belong to me."

She cocks her head to one side. "Do they?" She's not teasing. Her expression is questioning, her tone completely serious.

"Yes," I growl.

A little gust of air expels from her mouth, her shoulders relaxing infinitesimally.

"I'm going to show you that you are mine and mine alone," I promise her.

Then I lean forward and using my tongue, I bathe every inch of her fleshy mounds, paying particular attention to the skin discolored by bruises. I lift her arms and wash the marks on each one with my tongue as well. She makes a soft sound, like relief, but her body is still rigid, like she's holding herself back from me.

That is not going to happen.

I return to her breasts, kissing and licking them again. Her nipples get hard, flushing with blood. I kiss them and then take the nipple on her tit, that asshole touched, into my mouth. I suckle until she starts making the sounds I love so much, her hips shifting so her pussy rubs up and down my shaft. But every movement is metered, like she can't let go.

This is not enough. She needs to feel me on her skin. Not the bastard that signed his own death warrant when he touched her.

I slide her off my lap and arrange her so she's sitting with her back against the sectional. She doesn't protest like she normally would, but looks up at me in silence.

I stand above her. "Give me your hands."

She lifts them for me and I put them around my cock, my own hands over hers. I slowly start to jack my cock with both our hands. It feels good and I know I'll come soon, but getting off isn't why I'm doing this.

"Those tits are mine," I grind out. "Always. You are mine, every fucking inch of you."

Her pupils dilate and that hazy expression that tells me she's into this as much as I am comes over her lovely face. I increase the pressure of my hands over hers, speeding up our movements until I'm leaking copiously from the head of my cock.

"Taste it," I tell her.

She leans forward without a word and licks my tip over and over again, bringing me right to the verge.

I release her hands, pulling them from my rock hard dick. "Sit back."

For a second, she hesitates, licking her lips, her eyes on my cock.

"We'll do that another time, *mo chroí*," I promise.

She nods and then sits back against the couch.

I cup her cheek while jacking my cock with my other hand. "I'm going to cover you in my cum and all you will feel is me."

Her lips part but no sound comes out of her mouth.

Ecstasy punches me in the base of my spine and then it explodes out of my cock as my jizz spurts. After the first couple of shots hits her left tit, I aim my cock at her right and paint it with my cum too.

When I have squeezed the last drop of semen out of my dick onto her tits, I rub it in, all over each globe until every bit is absorbed into her beautiful skin.

Anna's body slumps against the sectional, her eyes now completely unfocused, her breathing shallow.

I join her on the couch, pulling her across my legs. Sliding one hand between her thighs, I feel her wet pussy. Silky and soft, it keeps me sporting a semi. "I'm going to lick all over your body now," I tell her. "Bathe you with my tongue."

"Yes."

I lick and kiss every inch of her delectable curves, turning her on her stomach so I can give the same attention to the round globes of her ass as I did her tits. She's so fucking perfect.

Moving a hand around her body, I play with her clit while I kiss and nip along her back. Moaning, she humps against the couch and my hand. When she comes, she cries out. My name. Because she fucking belongs to me.

I come again, this time coating the small of her back and top of her ass cheeks with my seed. I rub it in again because that feels right. She smells like me. Like sex with me. Like us.

We lay together like that for long minutes. Finally I think my legs will hold me up if I stand and I pick her up. I carry her into the bathroom, but when I step toward the shower, she puts her hand on my chest and shakes her head.

"No. I don't want to wash you off."

"Okay."

"Do you need the toilet before we go to bed?"

She thinks and then nods.

So, I let her use it while I brush my teeth. I put a new toothbrush out for her. She uses it while I piss. Then I take her hand and lead her to my bed. She's still blissed out, just like she should be.

Once we are plastered together under the covers I tell my smart speaker to turn off the lights.

"Thank you." Her voice is slurred, but I can feel her smile against my chest in the dark. "I'm clean."

I don't say anything about her feeling clean with my cum all over her body. I just say, "You're mine."

"I'm yours."

ANNA

I wake in Cian's arms. I don't know what time it is, but I think it's still dark out. I'm not sure because the blackout blinds on the sliding door leading to the terrace might be that good.

Cian is still sleeping and I don't want to wake him up. This feels too good.

I never thought I would feel clean again, but he knew what to do to erase that awful man's touch.

I can smell Cian on me and I like it. He changed his protocol for me. He won't let me be taken again, but he's still going to get me a taser and have Connor teach me self-defense. Cian wants me to feel safe.

I've never felt safer than when I am in his arms.

The thought of leaving his apartment to return to my own hurts, but he's not going to want to keep me here. He's busy with mob stuff right now and he needs to keep me away from him. He said so.

So, I don't wake him, wanting to revel in the peace I feel being where I am for as long as I can.

His phone rings, disturbing my reverie. Frowning, I stifle a sound of protest. It's only a matter of time now, before I have to go.

One arm tight around my waist, he drags me across the bed with him so he can grab his ringing cell. He barks into it, "What?"

I don't hear the other side of the conversation and Cian does little more than grunt before disconnecting the call. He instructs the smart speaker to turn the lights on at fifty percent.

A soft glow fills the large bedroom and I can see Cian's handsome features. His golden red hair is sticking up in places, but it looks sexy, not messy. His beard stubble is a shade darker than the hair on his head.

Curious what it feels like because he's always smoothly shaven when I see him, I reach up and brush along his square jawline with my fingertips. "It's softer than I expected. I thought it would be bristly."

"It would feel bristly enough against the tender skin of your face. If I kissed you right now, you'd end up with beard burn."

"Does that hurt?"

"I don't know."

"But you've given it to other women?"

"Once or twice. I'm not big on kissing."

"You kiss me."

"And I'll keep kissing you."

I love when he talks like we have a future. It makes me feel secure.

His arm still around my waist, he sits up. "I have to go."

"I wish you didn't." I feel safe telling him the things I would usually keep silent inside me.

The arm around me tightens. "I do too, but I'm the boss."

And he takes his responsibilities seriously.

CHAPTER 30

ANNA

"Y ou have two choices." Cian releases me and stands up beside the bed, his morning erection mouthwatering. I want to taste him again.

He groans. "Do not look at me like that *mo chroí*. We do not have time."

I shift my gaze from his sex to his face, my own burning. "Two choices?"

"You can join my mother and sister in Spain, or you can stay here in my apartment until the current threat is neutralized."

Whatever that means. It sounds serious though. "Are you going to war with another criminal group?"

"I can't answer that question, *mo chroí*. The less you know about mob business, the safer you are."

"You thought I was safe going with the cops," I remind him. I'm not convinced his protocols are as spiffy as he thinks they are.

"Do you trust me?" His expression is unreadable.

He's not trying to sway me toward one answer over another. He wants my honesty. Do I trust him?

There's no doubt in my mind. "Yes."

"Even after what happened yesterday?" he pushes.

Shifting, so I'm sitting up too, I let the blankets fall around my lap. "Yes."

"That means trusting my rules." His eyes roam over my body and then settle on my breasts.

It makes me hot.

"If we don't have time for me to taste you, we don't have time for you to taste me," I remind him logically.

"True. More's the pity." He meets my eyes again and I can see there's still a question in his.

I mull over what he said before getting sidetracked by my body. Trusting him means trusting his rules. "I'm not sure it does. Trusting you doesn't mean I think you are always right. It means I believe you will always try to do right by me."

There are very few people I believe that of. Ini. Him. Mrs. Hart. Connor, now. Cian's cousin confiding his truths to me last night allows me to trust him too.

"We aren't always going to agree what's right for you, what is safest." Cian says the words like they are a warning.

"When it comes to my safety, I will do what you think is best." I pause and consider the promise and then add, "Initially."

He doesn't get mad at my qualification. Instead, he gives me one of his rare smiles. "I will always give you a choice." His smile turns into something more, something challenging. "Initially."

"Right now, my choice is Spain or staying here? And why Spain by the way?" Cian isn't a random guy. Everything he does is deliberate. So, if he sent his family to Spain, there's a reason why.

"The Irish mob is strong in Spain. My allies are watching over Ma and Shea along with the security detail I sent. It is also not a country where my current enemies have known ties."

That makes sense, but the idea of being across the ocean from Cian makes everything inside me twist painfully tight. "If I stay in your apartment, can I still work for Jimmy?"

I don't like the idea of spending the entire day alone, even in someplace as nice as this. Yes, there are times that being by myself is all I want, but now is not one of them. Not after yesterday. I'm still feeling vulnerable if not tainted anymore. I want people around me, which is weird for me, but

I'm not even a little tempted to go back to my apartment and hide in my blanket lean-to.

I can't help frowning. "I wish I could work in your office again."

"I've never seen you pout before. It's cute." He taps my bottom lip. "But there's no need. You can come back to work in my office if you want to."

"I can? But I thought it wasn't safe."

"Everyone is going to know you belong to me and the risk they are taking when they try to get to you."

"Because you are a scary guy?"

"Yes."

Too bad the detectives yesterday didn't realize that, but I have a feeling they will come to regret their decisions. Cian is not the forgiving type. I don't know what exactly happened to the men who hurt Shea, but I'm pretty sure it's worse than what they did to her.

"If I can be with you, I want to stay here."

"In my apartment," he reiterates.

"Yes, but I need my clothes." I don't ever want to leave it, but he's not going to want me to just move in on him.

That's not how things work. I'm not even sure how to define what we have. Am I his girlfriend? His lover? We haven't had intercourse, but he's touched me more intimately than anyone ever has.

Still, wanting to move in with him is both impetuous and irrational. It also wouldn't be fair to Ini. She needs my half of the rent. I know all this, but I can't help feeling the way that I do. I don't have to act on those feelings though. That's something one of the many therapists my aunt hired to fix me said.

I can feel whatever way I need to, but I do not have to act. It sounds a lot easier in theory than reality. I tried to explain that to the therapist. To my aunt and uncle. None of them agreed. They all said I had to try harder.

I've done my own research on ASD and they're all wrong. You can't rewire a brain just by trying. Sometimes, we are what we are.

Ini gets that. She always has. Which is why, I won't leave her high and dry for the rent. No matter how much I want to move in with my boss.

"I'll send Tommy over to collect your things. Make a list for him."

I nod. "What am I supposed to wear to work today?" I can't go in his t-shirt.

"You'll have to wait to come into the office until after Tommy gets back with your clothes."

Considering he hasn't left yet and I don't even know if he's awake, that could be a while. I sigh, but nod. "Okay."

"You can go back to sleep."

I shake my head. "I'm too awake."

"Want to make me some coffee while I'm in the shower?"

"Yes." I climb out of the bed and walk into the other room.

Cian groans behind me. "It had better be a cold shower," he mutters.

I smile. I like tempting him. A lot.

I find the t-shirt he threw aside last night and put it back on. It's big on me and hangs to a couple of inches above my knees. Most importantly, it doesn't feel wrong against my skin. It's soft. It breathes. I like it.

There's an espresso machine in the kitchen. I have no idea how to use it, so I look it up on YouTube. There's a video that takes me through it step by step and by the time Cian comes out wearing a suit and looking grim, I've got a cup of espresso ready for him.

He takes it and kisses me. "Thank you."

"You're welcome. Do you want some breakfast?"

"I don't have time."

I noticed he had nutrition bars in one of the drawers I searched looking for the coffee scoop. I spin around and grab one and then hold it out to him. "You need to eat something. I'll bring you real food when I come down later."

The look he gives me. I'm not used to seeing it on anyone's face. Not even Ini's. It's like I'm something special. Like I just offered to do the best thing ever.

My face heats with a blush of pleasure. Cian doesn't think I'm weird or incompetent. I make him happy. That's what that look is.

And seeing it makes my own heart soar.

I have a person. *My person.* And I'm his.

Whether we live together, or not.

CIAN

Lachlan and Ronan step off the second elevator, coming up from the lobby, at the same time the doors open on mine. Ronan doesn't have access to this building, so Lachlan had to let him in. All secondary access codes have been temporarily disabled. When the issue with the Kicks Bandidos is handled, they will be reinstated.

Right now, we are on red alert status in the building. Which is one of the reasons I want Anna staying in my apartment.

I should have moved her in when we realized the extent of the cartel's involvement. Instead, I opted to distance myself from her to keep a target off of her back. That didn't work.

Mistakes aren't something I'm used to and I won't make another one when it comes to Anna's safety. Or Shea's. I've had tracking devices implanted in her and Ma and their security detail is doubling going forward.

Connor is working at his desk when we arrive. He looks up, his expression grim. He's settling into his enforcer role. There's a seriousness in his demeanor that wasn't there a few months ago. And he's handled his duties as enforcer well without showing signs of cracking under the pressure.

Jimmy said Connor was meant for the mob side of the business, but I wasn't sure. Now, I am. My cousin is younger than me, but he has a ruthless streak that I understand well.

He still has more conscience than me, but then almost everyone does.

Maybe not Drakos. The Godfather of the Night shares my brutal, unemotional outlook about syndicate business. He was married once, but I don't think he saw his wife the same way I see Anna.

As necessary, but he understands loyalty.

"I want the two detectives that took Anna in for questioning under investigation by Internal Affairs," I say to Lachlan before we head into my office. "Grieves assaulted her." Remembering what the man did, groping my girl, rage boils inside me. "Samuels didn't even try to get him to back off. No way was it a one-off. There will be a string of victims behind them for IA to leverage."

"You want IA to handle it?" Lachlan asks with shock.

"He fucking touched her?" Connor's fury makes his voice deeper than normal. "No wonder she was so upset."

"When Grieves disappears, I want it to look like he went on the run from IA," I correct Lachlan. My plans for him don't include his body ever being found. "I want Samuels in prison, paying the price for her culpability day in and day out for every fucking year of her sentence."

If she survives prison, the detective won't survive her release. Anna asked her to stop Grieves and Samuels ignored her. I've got no doubts that she's stood by while he's done worse.

"I'm on it," Lachlan says.

Then we all get down to what we're here for. Going over the intel that came in last night.

"If we don't move tonight, Martina and that asshole Carmen's married to are going to be on their way to Colombia," Ronan says. "According to the wiretap we have on Martina's phone, others will be sent to accomplish what she hasn't been able to."

Like hell. That is not fucking happening. We are taking down the street gang and then going after those fuckers in Colombia.

Chicago is off limits.

"Connor, send out the coded messages to our allies," I tell him.

"Everyone but Walsh, right?"

"Right. I don't trust that bastard." He gave me the information I asked for, but I'm not convinced he isn't playing both sides.

He was too reluctant in the beginning.

"You think he's trying to make a deal with the Kicks Bandidos for more territory?" Lachlan asks.

"Or just to keep the territory he's got. Once we've got *El Fantasma* and her lieutenants in our hands for questioning, we'll find out. If I'm wrong, then no harm. No foul." But if I'm right, then Walsh loses his life and his territory. It's as simple as that.

Quinn wants to split the territory between us and at first that's what I was thinking, but our grandfather's kept the Walsh mob in place for a reason. They're a buffer between two powerful mob families. We're going to keep them that way, just with a boss that Quinn and I handpick.

CHAPTER 31

ANNA

As I move around Cian's apartment after he leaves, I keep my phone with me, set up so that the camera lens can always see me.

He texts me.

Cian: **Thank you**.

And I know he means the phone access so he can watch me. But it's not just for him. Having his eyes on me brings me more internal calm than my rhyme.

I'm watching a show about building houses in Nova Scotia on my phone when my bodyguard arrives.

His knock is loud, startling me. I pull up the app Connor installed on my phone that accesses the cameras in the lobby, allowing me to see who is standing outside Cian's door. It's Tommy and he has a set of luggage with him that I've never seen before.

I'm showered and wearing a fresh t-shirt from Cian's closet, so I open the door to let him in.

I didn't like washing Cian's scent off of me, but I don't want to share our intimate times with anyone else either. And the scent of his semen on my skin was unmistakable.

"Here's your stuff. Just text me when you're ready to go downstairs. The boss said you aren't to leave his place without an escort."

"Okay, I'll text you." When I got my new phone, it had all my previous contacts in it and a few I hadn't had before.

Tommy, Arlo, Eoin, and Lachlan. I already had Cian's number. Connor and Shea's too. But his mother's number is in my contact list too as well as Jimmy's.

I don't know if Cian wants me to unpack my things, so I leave what I'm not using right now in the suitcases and store them in his walk-in closet after I pull out one of my softest tops and a pair of yoga pants that never chafe. It's a comfort outfit and I don't think Cian will mind me wearing it.

Leaving off my bra, I dig out my one hoodie and pull it on. With the air conditioning in Cian's office, it won't be too warm, regardless of the summer weather outside. And I'll only be wearing it when other people are around.

Which might be most of the day, I remind myself.

After I get dressed, it's barely past eight o'clock, so I pull out food to make breakfast for Cian. He has very little in his fridge and cupboards. But he does have what I need to make breakfast burritos. I make him two and myself one, which I eat while standing in the kitchen. Cleaning up the dirty dishes and pans goes quickly and I'm ready to leave a few minutes later.

I text Tommy and he knocks on the door less than a minute later. He's wearing a hoodie too, but when he shifts I see that it's to conceal the gun he's wearing in a hip holster. He nods to me, but doesn't try to talk and I appreciate it. I prefer silence with people I don't know.

Small talk is stressful.

When the elevator doors open, Connor is waiting. He looks me over, like checking for injuries. I know he's not worried that Cian hurt me last night. Our boss must have told him about what the detective did to me.

"They'll pay, don't you worry," he says to me as we head into his office outside of Cian's.

And I know I'm right. I nod in reply to Connor's words, but don't say anything. What is there to say? I'm not sure how Cian will deal with the detectives, but I know he will. Maybe it should bother me to think that a ruthless criminal is going to exact vengeance on my behalf, but it doesn't.

I'll take Scary Things that Make Me Happy again, Alex.

Too many people get away with cruelty. People with power rarely have consequences for their actions while people like me and my friends, pay the price for the actions of others all the time. Ini has no parents because hers were killed in a completely preventable fire. The shell company that owned their apartment didn't even get fined for the lack of proper fire safety.

Their pricey lawyer found a loophole in the interpretation of tenancy law and took advantage of it.

I feel nothing but relief that Cian will stop Grieves and Samuels from treating others like they did me. And I know he will.

Connor looks down at the container in my hand. I found it in Cian's cupboards and it's keeping his breakfast warm. The clear lid shows his egg and sausage burritos though.

"Did you make me one?" Connor asks, pointing to it.

I shrug. "I made Cian two. Maybe he'll share."

We walk into the office suite and Cian is standing in the open doorway to his office, like he's waiting for me. My face breaks into a smile when I see him even though he looks intense, almost angry.

His hard blue gaze softens for just a moment before he glares at his cousin. "Get your own damn breakfast. She cooked for me."

"I'll remember that the next time Ma sends home her corned beef and cabbage with me," Connor says.

Cian ignores his cousin and goes back into his office. I follow and place his food on his desk for him. "Eat before it gets cold."

"You need to wear your noise cancelling earbuds today. If anyone comes in, do not speak to them unless I bring you into the conversation. Even if they try to talk to you first."

"Okay." I'm not offended. I know this is for my security as much as his.

He never spelled it out when we had extra people coming into the office, before he moved me to work with Jimmy, but that was the way it played out. Cian has always been picky about who talks to me, and I always assumed it was about my safety, considering his role in the mob.

Besides, I'd rather follow this stricture than have to leave Cian's office again.

I put in my headphones and pair them to my phone for work before I get started on the things piled on my desk. There is paperwork that needs to be filed, documents that need to be filled out and copied and I've got a ton of email in my inbox. Connor and Cian have trusted me with more and more administrative work the longer I've been here.

When it's time for lunch, I call for delivery from the Greek deli.

Stavros tells me to inform Cian he's seeing to the food personally. I'm not sure why. So, I ask after I hang up.

"Stavros said he's seeing to the food personally and to tell you. Why?"

"Safety," is all Cian says in reply.

Is Stavros part of the mob? But he's Greek. I don't ask because I'm positive Cian wouldn't answer that particular question.

We all eat together in the conference room. Lachlan, Connor, Jimmy, Cian and me. No one talks about mob stuff, but Jimmy looks stressed. Did Connor tell him about Elliott and Dot?

Connor doesn't seem any tenser than he has been all morning. Everyone is on edge. So, I think maybe that's not it.

When we get back to the office, it's just me and Cian.

CIAN

Anna doesn't put her headphones back in after lunch but stands in front of my desk biting her lip.

"What is it *mo chroí*?"

"I..." She looks away, hiding from me, but then her head comes back around, her violet gaze locked on mine. "I want you to put your hands on my breast. I keep thinking about Detective Grieves touching me. I only want to think about your touch."

"Shut and lock the door," I grind out, pushing my chair back from my desk.

Anna's curvy hips sway as she crosses the room. The doorlatch snicks into place a moment later and I hear the whisper of the lock turning.

She turns around and walks toward me, her eyes beautiful and dark with arousal.

I stand up and move toward the leather couch. "Yesterday, you told me you had never been touched before."

Anna nods.

"Does that mean you've never had sex?"

"Only with you."

That tells me all that I need to know. My girl has never had a cock in her pussy and she will never have another besides mine.

It also limits what can happen right now. Anna is too fucking precious for her first time to be on the couch in my office. That can wait for tonight. Right now, I'm going to replace her memories of Grieves's hands on her with mine.

I'll do it as many times as I need to until she never thinks of that bastard's touch again.

Pulling her to stand where I want her, I sit on the couch so I have a perfect view of her body. "Take off your clothes."

Her eyes widen, but the tension in her body lessens. She likes when I tell her what to do and it turns me on in ways I've never experienced to have her respond to my orders the way she does.

After toeing off her sneakers, Anna shrugs out of her hoodie, revealing the points of her nipples behind the thin fabric of her top. Without hesitating, she grabs the hem and tugs it over her head. Her generous breasts sway as she moves to push her leggings and underwear down her hips together. She kicks them off, leaving her in nothing but her tiny no-show socks.

She lifts her leg to remove one, but I jerk my head in the negative. "Leave them on."

Her head cocks to one side, like she's trying to figure out why I would tell her to do that, but she shrugs and obediently drops her foot back to the floor.

She's so fucking sexy wearing nothing but her little white socks.

Taking in my fill of her sensual but innocent beauty, I get my jacket and shirt off without breaking eye contact with her. I leave my slacks on because I'm not sure I would be able to stop burying myself in her sweet pussy otherwise.

Then, I pat my thigh. "Come here."

Anna immediately moves forward and I guide her to sit sideways on my lap. If she straddles me, it would be too easy to unzip my trousers and pull my cock out before driving up into her virgin depths.

"Put this around my neck," I tell her, brushing her left arm.

She does it, leaving her breasts and the rest of her body open to my seeking hands.

I reach around with my right hand and cup her fleshy mound. Anna moans softly from that simple connection. Rhythmically squeezing and releasing, I gently pinch her nipple at the end of every contraction of my hand.

Her ass shifts restlessly on my thighs.

"You are mine to touch," I tell her.

She lets out a soft sigh, her body relaxing against me. "Yes."

I take my time bringing her to a climax, bringing her to the brink and then backing off over and over until she's breathing like she's run a marathon and her pussy is leaving a wet patch on my pantleg.

"Can you feel my hands?" I ask her, one buried between her legs, two fingers slowly fucking her slick channel and the other plucking at her nipple.

"Uh huh."

"Do they make you feel good?"

She nods, her lips parted, but no sound coming out.

"Your body was made for me," I tell her. Then I slam my lips on hers and violently claim her mouth.

She returns my kiss with fervid passion, her tongue tangling with mine, her teeth grinding against my lips. There is nothing sweet about this kiss. I am not feeling sweet. Neither is she. She belongs to me, and I will imprint my touch onto her skin so she can remember no other hands on her than mine.

CHAPTER 32

CIAN

I grab Anna's tit tight and squeeze. She'll have matching marks on this one to the ones *he* left on her other soft globe. These marks will belong though.

They are my right to give, and she *wants* them.

The way she presses her soft flesh into my hand says as much. But then she moans. "Yes, like that. I want to feel you."

Continuing to roughly knead her tit, I press against her clit with my thumb and shove my fingers deep inside her. I feel the barrier no one else has breached. I push deeper and she screams against my lips as her vaginal walls contract around my fingers in a climax.

My girl likes a little pain with her pleasure. I'll remember that.

But tonight, when I put my dick in her, the pain will be minimal because of what I am doing now.

Coaxing her through the aftershocks of her orgasm, I eventually pull my hand out of her soft, soaked pussy. Pink tinges my fingers, blood mixed with her cum.

Lifting my hand, I say, "Look. You are mine and mine alone."

Her hazy eyes widen and then she smiles. "Yours."

Putting my fingers in my mouth I suck the sweetness of her cum and the coppery tang of her blood off. She watches me, her violet gaze focused on my mouth as her already blown pupils widen.

Tugging her body close, I kiss her forehead. I've never done that with another woman. Not even my sister. It feels as intimate as the taste of her virginity on my fingers. I am not a gentle man, but with her, I am whatever she needs me to be.

She goes boneless against me, her chest rising and falling in shallow breaths I've come to associate with that zoned out place she goes from my touch.

Satisfaction makes me smug as I hold her. No other man has ever touched her the way I'm going to. Only one other man has touched her at all and he's a dead man walking.

My phone chimes and I grab it out of my suit jacket beside us.

Connor: **Your two o'clock appointment is here**.

Fuck. The arms dealer. I'd cancel the meeting, but we need the weapons and ammo for our upcoming move against the Kicks Bandidos.

Me: **10 minutes**.

Connor: **Thumbs up emoji**.

Grabbing our discarded clothes, I carry Anna into my office's en suite and sit her on the counter. Running the water until it's nice and hot, I grab a washcloth and get it wet before washing between her legs. Afterward, I rinse the cloth and get it wet with even hotter water before folding it and pressing it against her pussy.

She sighs. "That feels good."

"Touching you always feels good."

Her smile is still loopy and I know there's no way I'm leaving her to sit at her desk alone right now. This is when she's like an open circuit and I won't let her get overwhelmed again, like that day at the hospital.

I dress her in her leggings and go to slide her arms into one of my black dress shirts I keep on hand to change into when mob business gets messy. I don't want to put her hoodie back on her, but I also don't want her beautiful tits on display under her top.

Besides, I like when she wears my clothes. A hell of a lot.

But she shakes her head. "That's scratchy."

I grab the other shirt hanging in the tiny storage cupboard. It's a silk cotton blend by a designer I like. Still black. Still large enough to be roomy on my girl.

"What about this one?" I ask.

She rubs the sleeve between her thumb and forefinger and nods. "Better."

After I get her dressed, I put my own shirt back on and my jacket. Once we are presentable, I carry her out of the bathroom and cross the office to unlock the door. I don't open it though.

I sit down behind my desk, with Anna positioned sideways in my lap. She immediately rests her cheek against my chest. "I like this suit. It's soft."

I make a note to have her go through my clothes so I can get rid of anything she doesn't like against her skin.

I text Connor.

Me: **Bring him in**.

The arms dealer isn't affiliated with a syndicate. He works freelance and supplies to more than one criminal organization. I have never liked that aspect of working with him, but he gets what we need when we need it.

Connor brings the dealer into my office, showing him to one of the chairs in front of my desk. My cousin sits to the side, out of the peripheral vision of the dealer, but in a position to take action if I give the signal.

He's learning the tricks of the trade for enforcers and things like this are becoming second nature to him.

Lachlan has already met with the dealer, but Smithy insisted on meeting with the boss before finalizing the deal. It annoys me, but I want the weapons, so I had Connor set up the meeting.

"You know what we want," I tell him.

He looks at Anna in my arms and smirks, giving her a once over with his eyes that makes me want to gouge them out. Second mistake.

The first was demanding to meet with me personally. I couldn't kill him if he wasn't here.

"Mr. Farrar gave me a list of requested supplies, but it is a much bigger order than your organization usually makes. Is there a reason you want incendiary grenades?"

My eyes narrow and then I look to Connor. "Was he wanded?"

Connor jerks his head in affirmative. "His cell is in the safe drawer."

No one but a select few are allowed to bring anything that could be used as a listening or recording device into my office. Anyone who wants to meet with me also submits to being scanned for bugs.

"The fuck are you doing trying to get information?" I demand.

Anna stirs a little, patting my chest, like she's calming me down and then she snuggles into me again.

The dealer shrugs, like he hasn't realized how close to death he has gotten. Huh. I guess that kinder, gentler me that reacted to Carmen Vega isn't here right now even though my girl is in my arms.

Fury about what happened to Anna yesterday roils just under the surface and this guy looking at her like she's his next perverted meal is making it rumble like magma in an active volcano.

"My inventory is low right now, but I can get your items in a couple of weeks."

My eyes narrow. "My second told you the order needs to be expedited."

"You aren't my only customer."

"Who the fuck takes precedence over me?" I demand. I'd be on my feet if I wasn't holding Anna.

"That's confidential. I am known for my discretion."

"You are known for getting shit to me on time. Two weeks is not timely."

"That's the best I can do."

Is he working for the Gutierrez Cartel? It's one thing to be an independent operator; it's another to provide weapons to my enemies.

I pin him with my glare. "Are you supplying the Kicks Bandidos?"

"Look, maybe I can get half of your order a week earlier, provided the right incentive." He looks right at Anna and there's no question what he means.

"Stupid fuck," Connor mutters. "And I'm going to have to clean up the mess."

I pull the gun from under my desk. My office is soundproofed, but it is fitted with a silencer anyway. You never know when you'll need to shoot someone with the door ajar. Better safe than sorry.

Anna makes a sound of distress. Did she see the gun? No. She couldn't have. I still have it in the hand behind her back. Something has her upset though. I look down and she's watching the dealer, revulsion on her pretty face.

"What is it *mo chroí*?"

"The way he's looking at me makes me want to vomit. It's like Grieves." Her voice is losing the sweet, just-a-little-out-of-it tone she gets when she's lost in her post pleasure haze.

Like hell is this fuckwit taking that from her.

Opening my desk drawer, I pull out an extra pair of noise cancelling earbuds I bought to have on hand.

I paired them to my phone to test them, which works out well for me now. Pressing them into each of her ears, I turn on the music, then push her face into my chest as I bring my Glock up and fire. I hit right where I'm aiming. The asshole's kneecap.

He screams and Connor curses, saying something about getting blood out of the carpet.

"Last chance. Are you supplying weapons to the Kicks Bandidos?"

"You shot my knee, you psychopath. How are you going to get your weapons if you kill me?" he asks angrily.

"I find another weapons dealer. You're convenient, but you aren't special," I inform him.

Finally, his face registers concern. "You need me," he insists.

"Tell me what inventory you got for them." Why the hell hadn't the cartel sent weapons through their usual channels? Were they really hoping that their connection to the Kicks Bandidos wouldn't be sussed out?

Stupid.

The dealer doesn't answer fast enough, so I shoot out his other knee. He's crying now. You never know what kind of pain will be the one to push a criminal over. For this dickwad, it's his knees, I guess.

I aim my gun at his junk. "Tell. Me."

He starts spouting off a list of guns and ammunition. Connor takes notes. Good man.

"When did you deliver?"

"Yesterday."

"After you met with Lachlan and got our order." It's not a question. I know when the bastard met with my second. It was right after we discovered the biological weapon inside Carmen Vega.

"They offered me twice my going rate, what was I supposed to do?"

Unmoved, I shrug. "You can't spend money when you are dead." I look at my cousin. "You ready to interrogate this piece of shit?"

Connor stands and approaches the man. It takes him forty-five minutes, but he gets what we need from the dealer. Contact information. Where the weapons were delivered. When the next shipment is due. Where.

The fact he was paid to insure we didn't get our arms shipments on time, if ever.

There's a price for selling to my enemy, but colluding with them? No way is this asshole getting out of here alive.

"Step to your left," I tell Connor.

He does and I shoot the dealer right between his legs. "That's for thinking what you were about my woman."

The man is sobbing and shouting all sorts of shit about my parentage. I offer my gun to Connor. "Do you want to finish him off?"

Connor takes the gun and shoots the dealer through the temple. The yelling stops.

I look down and smile. Unaware of what happened only a few feet away, Anna has fallen into a doze against my chest.

I stand and shift the angle of my body so she won't see the dead man on the floor as we leave the office. "Get a cleanup crew in here and tell Lachlan we need a new arms dealer. Shaughnessy's mob in New York specializes in weapons."

The Murphy mob gets their stuff through the New York Boss. Maybe it's time we do too. I'd use Stavros and his syndicate, but he doesn't sell to locals. Safer that way.

My now-dead arms dealer should have been so cautious.

CHAPTER 33

ANNA

Cian carries me all the way to his apartment. The whole time music plays in my noise cancelling earbuds. I don't know what happened in the office, but he didn't want me to see it.

I heard some agonized shouting though. Not what was said, but the tones. I think maybe I'm not a good person, because I never looked to see what was happening. Not once.

But that man? He looked at me just like Grieves. It made me sick. Cian kept me close, and the feelings of nausea dissipated.

I think maybe Ini would be disappointed in me. I've never seen the world the way everyone else does. Not even her. I don't want to hurt her though, so I'll never tell her I think I was in the room when Cian killed someone.

I'm not sure he did kill the man. Connor was there too. The truth is, I actually fell asleep for a while. I don't really know what happened. What I do know is that Cian and Connor are two of the best men I've ever known. They protect their people. When they make promises, they keep them.

That's why I know things with Elliott and Dot are going to work out okay. Connor isn't a weak man. He'll bring his boyfriend and baby into the rest of his family.

All thoughts of Connor disappear when we reach Cian's apartment. He gently removes my earbuds and puts them on the kitchen counter.

His gaze searches my face. "Are you okay?"

"Don't tell me if you killed him," I blurt.

Cian kisses me. Gently. So different from earlier, but just as incredible. "I didn't kill him."

That's good to know. I think. "Will he come after me? He wants me."

I know what that looks like and when it's mixed with that other look, it means the man will take what I don't offer. Like Grieves. If I hadn't gotten out of the police station when I did, there would have been no blood on Cian's fingers today.

There would have been no hymen to penetrate.

I pulse between my legs. The way he sucked my blood and wetness off his fingers turned me on so much.

It felt so earthy and intimate. I liked it.

Ini would probably think that is weird. Maybe. Maybe she would understand. I'm not telling her and finding out. I love my best friend, even if we see things differently sometimes.

"You will never see him again," Cian promises me.

I believe him and let out a sigh of breath I didn't realize I was holding. Then I yawn. Oh, that's so sexy. Not.

"I'm sorry. I just..."

"Yesterday was a lot and I blew your mind down in my office." He winks at me.

I smile up at him. "You did."

"Time for a nap." He guides me to his bedroom.

I shuck off my tennies and leggings, but leave my socks and his shirt on. The heat in his blue gaze tells me he appreciates my choices.

"Let's get you tucked in before I can't make myself leave."

I love that I have this effect on him and I inwardly preen as I climb onto the bed.

He sets my phone up so he can watch me and tucks the sheet and summer weight comforter around me. "I have another meeting, but I'll be back for a late dinner. Anything you want especially?"

I think about it. "Soup?"

"Soup it is."

I smile and let my eyes drift shut, but my lips respond when he kisses me before leaving.

~ ~ ~

The smell of something delicious pulls me from sleep. I open my eyes and find Cian there, a food laden tray between us.

"It smells good."

"It should. I had Connor raid Ma's freezer for some of her seafood chowder. She hasn't been home to make bread, but Connor swung by his parents' place and got some soda bread from his ma. "

Scooting into a sitting position, I look over the food on the tray. There are two bowls filled with a thick, rich looking soup, bits of fish and whole prawns floating in the creamy broth. A plate piled high with thick, buttered slices of a dense looking bread sits between them.

My stomach growls.

"Sounds like I got here just in time." Cian winks at me.

Picking up a bowl of soup, I ask, "Did your meeting go well?"

I don't hear his answer because that first bite? Is so good, I moan. The flavors burst on my tongue and even though it has been defrosted and reheated, the seafood isn't chewy. I wonder if his mom will show me how to make this.

"I think I'm jealous of your reaction to my mother's cooking." Cian's tone is filled with humor.

So, I don't think he means it.

"She's a very good cook."

"She'll be glad to know you think so. When she and my sister get back from Spain, Ma will want you over for dinner."

"Because I'm your girlfriend?" I ask.

"Because you are mine. Period."

"What does that mean?" He says that a lot, but I don't want to make assumptions. Mine aren't usually the right ones when it comes to inter-personal relationships.

"I want you to move in with me."

Happiness surges through me. Maybe my desire to live with him isn't as irrational as I keep telling myself. "You do?"

"Yes."

"Ini needs me to pay my half of the rent." Some of my joy deflates. I can't let Ini down.

"So, pay it. You aren't paying rent here. I own the building."

Hope flutters inside my chest. "Really? You don't need me to pay rent? But what about utilities, food?" With as often as he orders in, my whole paycheck could get eaten up. Literally.

"Let me be clear. You are mine to take care of, Anna. When you are with me, you don't pay for any of that. When you are not with me, you use the credit card I give you to pay for it."

"But I earn a salary. I don't want to quit working with you." Not only do I like being around Cian, I enjoy my job.

Which isn't something I ever thought I would feel.

"I don't want you to quit either. Use your money however you want."

"As long as it's not paying for my rent, food, or utilities?"

"Or clothing. Or getting your nails done. Or any of the other shit women like to do. I take care of you," he emphasizes.

"That's not how it works. I'm an adult. I should take care of myself."

"I'm the boss of the biggest mob in Chicago. Taking care of people is what I do. You are mine as much as the men who swear allegiance to me."

"I haven't sworn allegiance."

"You have with your body."

"That's not how sex works." My aunt drilled into me from a young age that a boy having sex with me didn't mean he was committed to me.

She didn't want me to get pregnant and have no way to support a child, the refrain was a common one between her and I. Almost as common as the "Why can't you at least pretend to be normal?" one.

"It does between us. The day you offered your body to me to calm my rage, you sealed your fate."

"That should worry me."

"Does it?"

"No."

"Good. Finish your dinner. I have plans for after."

We're going to have intercourse. My body buzzes with anticipation. I want that. So much. I want to feel more than his fingers inside me, I want to experience the sensation of his semen inside me, not just on my breasts.

Though that is something I never want to give up.

"I'm not on birth control," I tell him.

"Okay."

Then I admit, "I don't want to use condoms."

"Neither do I," he growls and puts down his half-eaten soup before grabbing my nearly empty bowl and placing it back on the tray.

"What if I get pregnant?"

"Then we'll have a baby."

Shock courses through me. "I can't be a mom."

"Who says?"

"My aunt."

"She's wrong."

"But what if she's not? I don't know how to interact with children."

"There are plenty of kids in the mob. You can practice being around them. And Ma will help. She raised me and the girls, she's got it down."

"You make it sound so easy."

"If you're afraid to get pregnant, we'll use condoms until you can get on birth control. Or you can take the morning after pill." His eyes burn with desire, but his tone is calm and pragmatic.

I'm not just afraid of being a mom, I'm terrified, but the idea of having a family again fills me with yearning so strong, tears burn the back of my eyes.

How did we go from planning sex to considering starting a family?

"I don't know what I want," I admit.

He nods. "Until you do, we'll use condoms."

He doesn't want to. He said so. But he will. Because even if he's not afraid to become a dad, I'm not sure I'll ever be ready to be a mom. No matter how much I want it. And I'm his to take care of. So, condoms.

"Will you come on my breasts after? Like you did last night?" Heat climbs into my face.

Yes, it's hard to ask for this, but I want it. I might actually need it.

Lust flares in his blue gaze. "Yes."

He takes the food tray out of the room. When he comes back, he stands beside the bed, his gaze laser-focused on me. Nothing else. He's not thinking about whatever is making everyone in the office edgy right now. Or what happened earlier. He's not thinking about work at all. Only me.

His expression intent, he strips out of his suit and the rest of his clothes until he joins me on the bed naked.

He pulls the covers back so I'm exposed to his view. "You're so beautiful, Anna."

"Are we going to have penetrative sex now?" I ask, wanting to be sure. I like knowing what to expect.

"Yes. Are you ready for that?"

I remember telling him in my apartment I wasn't. He remembers too.

"I am." I reach out and lay my hands against the hot skin of his chest. "I want it."

"Good." He undoes the top button of the dress shirt I've been wearing to sleep.

It was surprisingly comfortable. I wonder if he'll notice if I keep it?

His knuckles brush the upper swells of my breasts as he undoes the next button. I shiver. He leans down and kisses the skin he just touched.

Warm pleasure spreads from the gentle kiss outward, making my body sing with anticipation.

It takes excruciating seconds for him to finish unbuttoning my shirt. Every brush of his fingers against my skin heightens my awareness. But he's not the only one touching. My hands reach for any part of his body I can connect to, caressing and claiming.

I shrug out of the dress shirt and he pulls it away and tosses it on the floor.

My socks follow. "You're cutely sexy in your little socks." He grabs my foot and raises it to his lips, kissing my instep. "I've never had a foot fetish but everything about you turns me on."

"The f-feeling is m-mutual," I stutter out, my breath coming in gasps as he mouths the surprisingly sensitive skin of my inner ankle.

Grasping both ankles, he pulls and I end up flat on my back on the bed. Then he pushes until my knees are bent and my legs are spread wide, opening my most intimate flesh to his gaze.

And his mouth.

He licks up my wet folds making an *mmming* sound. He likes the taste of me. A lot. Because he goes back for more and more and more.

"Cian... please..." I moan, humping his face.

The feel of his tongue along my folds and even delving inside me is not enough. He nips at my inner thigh, making me jump and groan. Why does that feel so good even though it stings a little?

His mouth moves up and his tongue circles my clitoris while two fingers slowly slide inside me. That stings too, but not much and the pleasure I feel is nearly overwhelming. But still not enough.

Ecstasy for one more finger, Alex.

Then Cian gives it to me, stretching sensitive tissues, filling me and ratcheting my pleasure higher.

He sucks my clitoris. Hard and my body goes off like a supernova. Explosions of pleasure turning the world white around me.

I scream and buck and he rides me with his mouth through it all, pulling more and more pleasure from my body until I fall limply back to the bed.

He sits up between my thighs and wipes his mouth with the back of his hand. "Are you ready for me?"

CHAPTER 34

ANNA

I have no words, but I nod.

Cian leans across the bed and grabs something from the nightstand. Then I hear a wrapper tear and watch as he slides a condom down his huge erection. The look on his face as he does it makes my core clench.

Then he surges up my body, only stopping when the blunt head of his penis presses against my sensitized opening. I'm so wet, it slides in a little.

But I'm still tight. I've never had anything this big inside me. The closest was just now when he put three fingers in.

"You already belong to me, but after this, I'll never let you go." He bites down slowly on the inner curve of my breast.

He doesn't break skin, but I can feel his teeth and the pain mixes with pleasure in a way I'm learning I like. Watching for his reaction, to see if he's the same, I grab his bulging biceps and dig my fingernails in. Not hard. But he feels me.

His eyes shut for a second, his jaw going granite hard. "Be careful *mo chroí*. You don't want this over before it even starts."

"You like it too," I say with awe.

His gorgeous blue eyes open and look straight into mine. "A little pain with my pleasure? I fucking love it, especially when it's you marking me with your nails."

"When we're like this and you say that word, it excites me."

"Good to know. I can try to be better around you outside the bedroom, but in here? I'm too fucking turned on having my cock ready to take your pussy for me to watch my mouth."

I grin as warmth gushes from my center to where his erection sits barely inside me. "Say something else," I demand.

"I'm going to fuck you so long and so hard, you're going to forget what it feels like not to ache from my cock inside you."

I tilt my pelvis up, forcing him in further. "Now, Cian, I want you to do that, now."

But he doesn't move. His face is stretched in a rictus of strain as he holds his body rigid.

"Sex can be casual, but this isn't, *mo chroí*. This is us making promises with our bodies. Vows as binding as the ones I made to the mob."

That penetrates the fog of lust covering my brain. "You make it sound like we're getting married."

"Marriage allows for divorce," he growls, his gaze trapping mine. "This between you and me, it's forever."

My heart thumps heavily in my chest. Forever. He will *always* be my person. I will always be his.

"We'll be a family." Even without children.

Like Ini is my family. Like Mrs. Hart.

"Yes."

"Yes," I repeat back to him.

Like that was what he needed to hear, Cian pushes inside me with one powerful thrust. It stings and tears wet my eyes but the pleasure is right on the heels of that small pain. I don't know if it would have been worse if he hadn't broken my hymen earlier, but the more he moves now, the more I want him to move.

Cian pleasures himself with my body while giving me one ecstatic sensation after another.

I can feel another orgasm building even though only moments ago, I thought my body was utterly spent. This time when I climax, everything disappears except Cian. The entire world centers down to him and our bodies joined.

He shoves into me once, twice, three times and then he seizes, his shout making my ears ring and he comes.

I want to feel the heat of his cum inside me, but my heart swells with the knowledge he took care of me just like he promised he would. I need to think long and hard about whether I want to get pregnant. Until I'm ready for that, I need to get on birth control.

After he disposes of the condom, we fall asleep, our bodies entwined. I wake sometime later to find him jacking off above me and then I feel the splatter of his semen on my breasts and my whole world settles into that quiet place only he can take me to as he rubs it into my skin.

He wakes me three more times to make love. The last time, I'm so swollen and tender, he has to use lube to get inside me. The next morning, Cian insists I take a hot bath with muscle relaxing bath salts making the water smell like eucalyptus and menthol.

It feels so good, I float in peace, not even resenting the loss of his smell on my skin. We are together now. Permanently. I can get his smell all over me again.

After I've been soaking for about half an hour, he brings me breakfast and joins me in the bathtub. We feed each other the fresh pastries and fruit he had delivered. I love the intimacy of that almost as much as when he touches me in ways no one else can.

~ ~ ~

When I tell Ini I'm moving in with him, she's not surprised, but she's not happy either. "This is fast, Anna. I'm worried about you. What happens if he gets tired of you?"

He won't. We made promises with our bodies.

"I'm going to keep paying my half of the rent for the next year at least." Hopefully, that will put her mind at ease.

"Can you afford that?" She sounds doubtful.

"Cian won't let me pay him rent, or anything else, so I'll be able to put money in savings."

"I'm glad you're not going into this blind, sweetie. I'm scared for you, but I also like hearing you sound so happy."

The savings and the rent are for Ini's sake and her peace of mind, but that's what you do for family. You help them not to worry about you.

"I am happy."

"I hear a but..." she says leadingly.

"I want children, but I'm scared I won't be a good mom."

"Isn't it a little early to be talking about having kids together? Maybe see how things are a year from now before making decisions that big."

"But I'll be the same person in a year that I am now."

"First, that isn't exactly true. You're not the same person you were four months ago. Neither am I. We all change. Every encounter we have, ever experience changes us, even if it's such a small change no one else can see it. Like a built memory."

"Okay."

"Second, if, after you've made sure you and Cian are in this for the long haul, you decide to have a baby, you'll be an amazing mom."

"How can you be sure?" Ini, of all people, knows my limitations.

"Because you're kind and loving. Anna, that's what matters. You'll love your children and you'll do whatever you have to in order to take care of them. Just like you kept looking for job after job that made you miserable so you could pay your half of our living expenses. You're strong enough to do what you need to for your family."

"What if I don't want to hug my child?" I voice one of my biggest fears. I don't even like hugging Ini.

"You don't have any trouble touching Cian." There's a disapproving tone in her voice when she says his name, like every time she uses it. "You'll be the same way with any children you two have together."

"I wish I could be sure."

"Did you mind your parents hugging you?" she asks.

"No."

"Not even your dad?"

I know why she's asking. Because I loved my dad, but he wasn't my person. That was my mom.

"No." I liked my dad's hugs, but he knew not to hold me too long.

"So, why would you think your children wouldn't be the same?"

"What if I need to retreat into my quiet place?"

"That only happens when you are triggered. Your life now isn't set up to have a lot of those."

"When the kids are in school, there will be back to school nights. Stuff like that."

"And if you aren't in a good place to go, have their dad take them."

Even though she doesn't like Cian, Ini knows he would do that. Just like I do. He's not emotionally available to most people, but he is to me. He will be to our children.

I only have to look at how he is with his family to know that even if he doesn't feel the same way as he does with me, he'll be a good dad. He's a good son and brother. And cousin.

He may not be a good man, but he is good to the people that matter to him. A lot of so-called good men can't claim that.

Ini is there when my bodyguards and I go to the apartment to pack up my stuff. She helps and even has one of my favorite cupcakes to celebrate me falling in love and moving in with my boyfriend.

It's only when she says that I realize neither I, nor Cian, have used the word love.

Does he mind? Does he expect me to say it first? Because I do love him. So much it hurts. Does he love me? He's never said. I'm not sure he knows how to love. Not like I love him. He said once that he didn't, but he also said that being with me makes him feel.

Wanting to keep me doesn't mean that's changed, but how he treats me? It's all I need.

CIAN

I stop by Mrs. Hart's apartment and then Ini's. I need them to know about their account at the grocers I set up. Mrs. Hart offers me tea and thanks me.

Ini's reaction isn't nearly as positive.

She glares at me and snaps, "You can't buy my approval with groceries."

"I don't need your approval. Anna is moving in with me." There is no question about that. She's already packed up her things and taken them to my place.

I gave her the code to the panic room. She can use it as her safe space, like her lean-to tent.

"Then why?" Ini asks suspiciously.

"I want Anna to be happy. Knowing you have food and a place to live will make her happy. If you want to quit your job and go to school full time. Done. If you want to transfer to a university, done. Just stay the hell away from the frat parties."

Ini looks shaken. "You don't mean that."

"I don't say things I don't mean, Ini. You are important to Anna." She's my girl's sister-by-choice and that makes her family.

I take care of my family.

ANNA

Things around the office remain tense but when we are alone in our apartment together, Cian lets the stress go. Sometimes our lovemaking is volatile, but I like that and I give as good as I get.

We make love every night and most mornings.

Before we go to sleep, he always spends on my breasts and rubs it into my skin. The scent has become so comforting to me that even when I wake from a bad dream, I go right back to sleep because it's there.

~ ~ ~

A few days later, things are even more tense than they have been, with a dozen men coming to talk to Cian throughout the day.

At four o'clock, he has me shift to my old desk in Connor's office area while he meets with Lachlan, Mr. Byrne, and some men I don't know.

I'm finishing up an email when Connor stops by my desk. He asks for my phone and I give it to him.

He taps on the screen for a few minutes and then hands it back. "I put Elliott's contact information in there. If something happens to me, you need to make sure my dad and mom take care of Elliott."

I have a feeling this is about what Cian is planning. I'm not supposed to know what it is, but I've eavesdropped a little. Enough to know that what's going down is dangerous and it's big. They are going to war with a street gang and are planning a coordinated single strike to take the gang out in one night.

Apparently, that night is here.

"Stay safe. Elliott wants you back, not your parents providing for him and Dot," I tell Connor.

He shrugs. "Maybe it would be easier if I don't make it home tonight."

"Don't say that!" I mean it. "You will do whatever you need to in order to come back from whatever you all are doing. You are going to live to be Dot's dad and Elliott's partner. You all deserve that, Connor."

There is no substitute for a parent's love. I still miss my mom and dad. Living with my aunt and uncle was never even close to like having them.

The way Connor talked about Dot the night he told me about her? He will be a good and loving dad.

"This life is dangerous, Anna. None of us can promise that. Not even the boss."

A cold chill goes down my spine, but I don't let my fear show. "I know. All the more reason to go into this situation with the determination to come out of it alive. Do you hear me, Connor? You watch out for yourself and let your friends watch out for you too."

"We're more than friends. We're brothers."

"Good. Brothers take care of each other." Even my odious cousins have each other's backs.

They never had mine, but then they never saw me as real family.

CHAPTER 35

ANNA

Cian takes me up to our apartment an hour after my conversation with his cousin. "Tommy and Eoin are staying with you. Arlo is over at your old place keeping an eye on your friends."

"Thank you, but shouldn't Tommy and Eoin go with you?" I ask. "I'll be safe in the apartment. No one can get in."

"No."

I sigh. That tone of voice? I'm not changing his mind. But what is happening tonight is dangerous, for all of them and he needs all the soldiers he can get at his disposal.

"Please." I have to try. "Keep them with you. I won't leave the apartment. I promise."

Cian kisses me until the elevator doors ding and open. Even then, he conquers my mouth with his tongue until I'm pressed against him, my arms wrapped around his neck.

When he ends the kiss, he looks down at me. "You are mine to protect."

That's all he says, but I realize it's futile to ask again.

Tommy and Eoin are waiting outside our apartment. Cian wants me to open the door, to show that I remember the sequence and the code I have to type in.

When he put me in the security system, it made me nervous, but since he doesn't just use a key like I did with Ini, I know it's necessary.

Cian has me stand by the front door with Eoin while he and Tommy check every single room, closet and the terrace to make sure no one is there. How he thinks they would have gotten in, I don't know, but his protective actions make me feel safe and cared for.

When they are done with the room check, he cups my face and kisses me. Hard. But his lips don't linger. "Do not order food in tonight. You're going to have to make do with what we have on hand."

"Okay." That's hardly a problem. We bought groceries right after I moved in, and the cupboards are stocked. I grab his sleeve, stopping him from going. "Stay safe."

Blue eyes lock onto mine. "I'll keep the city safe. I promise you, *mo chroí.*"

It's not the same as promising to keep himself safe, but he's the boss and this is his city to protect. What a strange world I've found myself in where the criminals are more committed to the protection of my city than some of the people whose job that is.

CIAN

We execute our coordinated attack on the Kicks Bandidos with our allies once all the teams are in place.

Each syndicate is responsible for their territory. The ones that are shared by more than one crime family have worked out the logistics of their shared responsibilities.

Drakos has all the Greek mafias involved. We also pulled in two smaller Irish mob families besides us and the Murphy Clan.

We aren't starting a war; we are obliterating our enemy.

I coordinated this assault, but I'm no one's fucking mother. As long as they execute the objective, I don't care how they share the responsibility.

Stavros and I have split our territory by streets. Others are using joint teams. Our agreement is to get the Kicks Bandidos off our streets. How we do that is up to each Boss. Lachlan says we need to recruit, so we're assessing every gang member for potential loyalty and specialty within our mob.

That assessment will come with the pain of torture, but a price must be paid for giving loyalty to the wrong syndicate to begin with.

Anyone who already has their finger cut off and is found on the street, working for the gang in my territory again, dies tonight. That kind of stupidity can't be trained away. This is war and there will be casualties.

Lachlan is coordinating our attack because I am going after *El Fantasma*. Martina Fucking Vega-Gutierrez.

Connor is on my team, along with two other enforcers, including a sniper. Drakos sent four of his top soldiers with us, including Christakos. He wants access to the intel, because he wants the cartel dismantled as much as I do. He's furious they dared to come after Chicago, the city where he lives.

I run a mob, not a territory that covers the Midwest and part of Canada, like him. Between the two of us, I'm the one the cartel has to worry about the most though. Because Chicago is *my* city. I will do whatever it takes to destroy the cartel threatening it, including bringing together a coalition of Irish mobsters from all over the city *and* the Greek mafia.

Eduardo Gutierrez is a fool to think he can take over Chicago.

His daughter, *El Fantasma*, is staying in a house an hour outside of the city. It's too well fortified to be some random house they decided to use. This place has been built, or upgraded, to protect its inhabitants.

Which just confirms that Carmen was kept in the dark about a lot of her cousin's plans.

Security is tight, but my tech specialist is ready to shut down the alarm system when I give the word. It will appear as if it is running normally until we infiltrate the second perimeter. Then he will cut all power and backup power sources to the house.

Martina Vega-Gutierrez has a dozen men guarding her and Carmen's husband. The soldiers can die, but I want to bring *El Fantasma* in alive. Bernardino too, her cheat of a lover. They will have the intel we need to take out the Gutierrez Cartel in Colombia.

They'll both die as we promised Carmen, though.

Eventually.

I don't think she'll mind knowing they're enduring worse at our hands than she did.

ANNA

Not knowing what is happening with Cian is much harder than I thought it would be. I wish I had a spycam on his phone like he has on mine right now.

Unable to sit and read, or watch a show, I pace through the apartment saying my rhyme over and over. I keep my phone with me, just in case, but I know his eyes aren't on me right now.

They can't be.

Cian doesn't think I know what is happening. But although I wear my noise cancelling headphones, I don't always turn on the music or the white noise. Sometimes, I don't fit them snuggly to my ear either, which makes it possible to listen to conversations if the voices are loud enough.

The men he's been meeting with have been tense and often loud.

I'm very good at pretending not to hear things, something I learned to do when living with my aunt and uncle. So, neither he, nor any of his men, suspect I've overheard enough to put it all together.

While I don't know the specifics, I do know that the city's underworld is going to war and the rest of Chicago has no clue.

Tonight dozens, maybe even hundreds will die. How will they hide the bodies? How will they hide their involvement? Will Cian come home to me tonight? Tomorrow?

Will Connor survive? Lachlan?

I've never had so many people I cared about before and now the majority of them are in the mob and their lives are at risk.

My phone rings and I glance down. It's Elliott. He must be worried too.

Pushing aside my initial reticence at talking to strangers, I answer. "Hello. This is Anna."

"Anna. This is..." He hesitates. "This is Elliott, Connor's friend."

I scurry into Cian's room where I can speak without being overheard. Since I'm so good at listening in, I'm very aware of how easy it is to do.

I shut the door to the bedroom. "You're Connor's baby-daddy."

Elliott makes a choking sound. "He told you?"

"Yes."

"He must trust you."

"He wouldn't have given me your number otherwise." Connor cares about this man and their baby.

Warmth unfurls inside me at the knowledge that Connor really does trust me. Not just as a confidante, but as a friend. I need to call Ini and check in with her after I get off the phone with Elliott.

Friends do that for each other.

"No, I suppose not. He gave me yours too. He said I should call if I needed something and I couldn't get ahold of him."

"Do you need something?" Can I help Elliott without leaving Cian's apartment? Am I obligated to stay here if a friend needs me?

Anything Elliott asks for is a byproduct of my friendship with Connor.

"It shouldn't be a big deal." He sounds nervous.

"What is it?"

"I've been staying at a hotel in Rockford with Dot." He stops talking. "I don't know if Connor told you anything about my family?"

"No, he didn't."

"They're not thrilled about my transition and that's putting it mildly, but I thought..." He breaks off. "I thought they still loved me, that we were still family."

"I'm sorry." I know what it feels like when your family doesn't accept who you are. My aunt and uncle spent eight years trying to make me into someone different. Someone *normal*.

"My dad was going on and on about how I can't raise Dot on my own. I got so sick of it, I finally told him about Connor. When he realized Connor accepts me as I am and wants to be with me and raise Dot together, my dad went ballistic."

Ballistic could mean a lot of things, but none of them are good. "Does he know where you are?"

"Yes, and he's on his way here to try to take Dot."

"Did he threaten you?"

"Yes, and I know it's not just hot air. I told my sister where I am because she was worried when we couldn't get together for dinner like we usually do tonight. I missed last week too."

"And she told your father?"

"Yes. She says she's Switzerland. Calling to tell me that Dad is on his way here is her way of being neutral. He doesn't know what hotel I'm staying in, but I didn't use an assumed name when I checked in."

"Why would you? You and Connor thought the danger was in Chicago. As long as no one knows about you, you shouldn't have to hide."

"Which is why I wanted to stay in the city, but he insisted."

Knowing what's going to happen tonight, I understand why Connor did. The mob will try to avoid collateral damage, but the gang they are fighting might not be that conscientious.

"When did your father leave the city?"

"Just a few minutes ago. I could refuse to let him into my hotel room, but he has friends in the police. If he tells them I'm a risk to my baby, they'll believe it."

I remember how helpless I felt when the detectives came for me. No wonder Elliott is nervous. "Do you have a car? Can you come here?"

"Yes, but I'm not sure where to go. My apartment is out. I've never been to Connor's place. I can't just spring myself on his parents. And what if they're as off the road about me and Connor raising a child as my parents are?"

"Jimmy isn't like that." I don't think. "But I don't know Connor's mom. You need to come to Cian's apartment. You can stay with me and the bodyguards he has assigned to me, but you need to hurry and don't stop anywhere along the way. Not for anything."

"I'm not like Connor. Violence isn't my thing. I'm a geek kind of guy," he rambles. Like he has to explain himself.

He doesn't. Not to me. Not everyone is a fighter and that's a good thing, or there would be a lot more fights. Right?

"That's probably for the best. Dot doesn't need more than one mobster for a dad."

Elliott laughs. "You got that right. You talk about it so casually though. Are you in the mob?"

"No. I wouldn't make a good mobster at all. I hate being touched and my anxiety goes through the roof when I'm around too many people. Especially in a small space." I don't know why I'm telling Elliott this, except maybe I want him to know that we all have our issues.

"I don't think anything scares Connor."

"You and Dot being hurt does, or he wouldn't have sent you out of town."

Elliott is silent for a beat. "Thanks for saying that."

I'm not sure how to respond. I can't say you're welcome for just telling the truth. So, I focus on the situation at hand. "Get yourself packed up and on your way."

Connor will be furious with me if Elliott is on the streets of Chicago when things get started.

If Elliott hurries getting their stuff together, he should get here a minimum of fifteen minutes before the time I overheard Cian say they are going to attack the street gang.

"I've been packing while we talked. I'm ready to go."

Oh, good. That gives seven minutes more leeway. The time I estimated it would take Elliott to pack. "Okay. Call me back when you're on your way."

"Will do."

CHAPTER 36

ANNA

H anging up the phone, I rush into the living room. Tommy and Eoin
are playing cards at the table, but they're alert and both turn to face
me the moment I enter the room.

"One of you needs to head toward Rockford. You're going to meet up
with a friend of Connor's on the I-90 and follow him back here to make
sure nothing happens to him."

"Can't do that," Tommy says to me.

"Yes, you can. I've seen you drive. You're competent behind the wheel."

"The boss gave strict instructions. You aren't to leave this apartment and
we stay here with you. No deliveries. No visitors."

"Did he really say no visitors? Because I'm inviting Ini and Mrs. Hart
over. Are you going to try to stop me from letting them in?"

The two bodyguards look at each other.

"He didn't say no visitors," Eoin admits.

"Okay then." I give Tommy my best impersonation of Ini in a snit. "You
get your butt out that door and on your way toward Rockford. I'll text you
with the exit to pull off and meet Elliott."

He looks conflicted, but he's not moving.

"Elliott has Connor's daughter with him." I don't tell them the baby is
Elliott's too, but they'll probably figure that out on their own. Or not.

It's hard to say how Elliott will react to spending time around Connor's mob brothers.

"Connor has a kid?" Tommy asks in shock.

I nod. "And that baby is in danger in Rockford. We have to get her and Elliott here before tonight's events get started."

Tommy's eyes widen. Is it because I know something heavy is going down tonight, or because he realizes his boss's family is in danger? Connor is Cian's cousin and that makes Dot his family too.

No one suggests calling or texting Cian to ask. None of us are willing to distract him tonight.

"I'm heading out," Tommy says.

"I'll tell Cian I made you," I offer.

"No." He shakes his head decisively. "We take responsibility for our own choices and this one is mine."

"Thank you."

"If you want Ini and the old lady to come over, you'd better call them now," Eoin says.

I agree and do just that.

Ini doesn't even argue when she hears the tone of my voice. That's one of the benefits of having a friend as close as family. They trust you and when you say they need to do something to stay safe, they believe you.

"I was making dinner," she says. "I have to put the food away in the fridge."

"Okay. Remember that big guy who came knocking at the apartment?"

"Yes."

"That's Arlo. He'll bring you and Mrs. Hart in his car." Which reminds me I need to text Arlo.

"At least I know what he looks like," Ini says. "Mrs. Hart isn't going to want to miss the end of her gameshow."

I do a quick calculation in my head. "Leave the second it is over."

"I'll do my best."

~ ~ ~

An hour and seventeen minutes after talking to Elliott, he reaches the building with Tommy following.

The usual driving time from Rockford to Chicago in good traffic is an hour and thirty-two minutes. Speeding increases the fatality rate in accidents associated with it, but there was no accident, and he is here safely with his baby, so I push the anxiety I feel knowing he had to have driven well above the speed limit away.

Ini and Mrs. Hart are not here yet, but Ini texted me when they left and again when they hit a traffic snarl. They should be here any minute.

"I know Connor will be glad you're here when he gets back." I usher Elliott inside.

He looks at Tommy and Eoin and grimaces. "Not so sure about that."

Connor's baby-daddy has brown eyes and hair, his delicate facial features enhanced by a close-cropped beard. A few inches taller than my five-feet-four-inches, he's slender and dressed like a hipster. He's very good looking, though not nearly as sexy as Cian. I can see why Connor is so into him though.

He indicates the baby in his arms. "This is Dot."

She clings to her dad, but looks at me and the others around us with curiosity. The baby has Connor's bright red hair and square jaw, but the shape of her brown eyes is all Elliott.

"This is Connor's kid?" Eoin asks.

Elliott shoots a panicked glance to me, and I shrug. "I had to tell them to get them to agree to you coming here. The building is on lockdown."

A firm knock sounds on the door. It opens a second later, revealing Arlo, Ini and Mrs. Hart.

He nods to me. "Since they'll be here with you, I'll just make myself useful to the boss."

I know what he means. He's going to go into battle with the rest of his mob. After a few words with Tommy and Eoin, Arlo leaves.

"What is going on?" Ini demands as she and Mrs. Hart come inside.

"Let's get dinner going and we can talk after." Though I'm not sure what I can or should say.

Thankfully, my best friend doesn't push for answers while we work to get everyone fed.

But as soon as we're all sitting at the table, Dot in Elliott's lap, Ini looks at me with a frown. "Why are we here?"

I open my mouth, and nothing comes out. I can't tell Ini that Cian and his mob are waging war on the streets of Chicago tonight. I'm not supposed to know that.

"I'm here because my parents are all kinds of extra," Elliott says, like he's trying to buy me time to come up with an answer. "They threatened to take Dot and I'm not letting that happen."

"If Connor trusts you with his kid, we aren't letting anyone take her away from you," Tommy says, his eyes flat, his tone adamant.

Elliott grimaces. He doesn't like that Connor's friends don't know he's Dot's dad too, but he doesn't correct them.

"Okay," Ini says, drawing out the word. "But that doesn't explain why I'm here. Or Mrs. Hart."

"Don't mind me," Mrs. Hart says. "Spending the evening with three hunky men isn't my idea of an imposition."

Ini rolls her eyes. "Enjoy your eye candy." Then she looks at me with the expression that tells me she's done waiting for answers.

So, I tell her about what happened with Detectives Grieves and Samuels. How I was picked up by dirty cops and that one of them groped me. That Cian thinks I might be a target for his enemies.

"You are in danger because you're involved with a mobster." Ini glares at Tommy and Eoin. "Working for Doyle Construction would have been bad enough, but I told you working at Doyle & Byrne wasn't a good idea."

Ini knows I don't just work for Cian, but that I've moved in here. Maybe that's the problem.

"He's my person, Ini." I need her to understand.

She's my dearest friend. I don't want her to be angry with me, but I am not giving Cian up.

"He's your stalker, girl. How do you not see that?"

I never told her about the cameras or the spy cam app on my phone.

She glares at me. "I found a camera on the crates at the head of your bed after you moved out. He watched you sleep. That's creepy."

I forgot about that camera. Ooops. "It made me feel safe." Seen.

Ini, who never cries, looks like she's about to. Her eyes are wet, and her expression is grief stricken. "You're not safe with him though. Are you?"

Is Cian's world dangerous? Yes. But I'm staying, because my heart feels like it's in a vice when I even consider living in a world without him in it.

"My dad is a plumber. My mom works as a secretary at their church. We lived in a regular, middle-class neighborhood in New Jersey." Elliott shakes his head, his eyes haunted. "I was attacked and nearly killed on my way home from school when I was sixteen. Some kids didn't like the way I dressed, that I wanted to use *they* for my pronoun instead of *she*."

The table goes still.

"My parents said it was my fault. That if I had hung around with the *normal* kids and acted like the girl they thought I was, it wouldn't have happened." Elliott stops, gathering himself. "Those so-called normal teenagers were the ones that hurt me."

"That's fucked up," Tommy says.

Eoin's eyes are filled with death. "Give me names, Elliott."

"That's what Connor said when I told him about it." He gives Ini a wry smile. "Connor is in the mob too, but I'm safer with him than I ever will be with my parents."

"Connor is a good guy," Tommy says. "You sure as hell are safer with him."

Do Tommy and Eoin realize that Elliott isn't talking about being friends with Connor, but more?

"It's not the same thing," Ini says, her tone nearly desperate. "Anna would never have been traumatized by that dirty cop if she didn't work for Cian Doyle. She was targeted because of him."

"And I was targeted because I didn't conform. Anna's life won't be the same with Cian than it would be without him, but if she loves him, maybe that's okay with her."

I get the feeling Elliott is talking about more than me. He had to decide whether to let Connor into his life and Dot's too and he chose to tell Connor about their baby.

"I know you care about him, but Cian is a psychopath, Anna." Ini is not letting this go.

But she's wrong. "No, he's not."

Everyone at the table, except Elliott, looks at me with disbelief. I give them all a good frown, especially his men.

"He's not a psychopath," I say firmly. "I did some research and his behavior is more in line with someone who has antisocial personality disorder."

Not that he needs a label. Does it matter why Cian is the way he is? Not to me.

"So, you're saying he's a sociopath. That's *so* much better."

"It is. He can feel emotions and while he has no regrets for the things he does as a mob boss, he's capable of caring about the wellbeing of his family, the men under him, and me."

"That's a lot of words, Anna." Ini regards me intently. "Especially for when you are stressed."

I *am* stressed. I hate being at odds with Ini. And the man I love is out on the streets of Chicago waging a very real war against our enemies.

"They are words that needed saying."

She looks at me for several long seconds. No one else says anything.

Finally, Ini sighs. "He's your person."

"Yes."

"I get that, but I'm always going to look out for you, too."

"Thank you." I'm doing my best to look out for her and Mrs. Hart.

Maybe she understands that because she gives me that look she does when she wants to hug me but knows I prefer she not.

"I still don't understand why Mrs. Hart and I had to come over tonight."

Eoin says. "Anyone Cian cares about could be used as leverage against him."

"One. He does not care about Mrs. Hart or me." Ini ticks off on her fingers. "Two. We aren't moving in here, so why tonight specifically?"

"I can't answer that," I tell her baldly.

"Anna is Cian's woman," Tommy says. "Anyone important to her is important to him."

Ini narrows her eyes. "Something is going on tonight, but you can't tell me what. And because we are your friends, we need to be here to be safe. Have I got that right?"

I nod.

"Okay. Fine. Where are we sleeping?"

I let out a sigh of relief. Once again, Ini trusts me and I'm so grateful.

She looks at the full dining table. "As swanky as this place is, I'm guessing it doesn't have a bunch of guest rooms."

"Elliott and Dot will sleep at Connor's place." I give Elliott a little shrug. "It's right down the hall. Either Tommy or Eoin can let you in."

Relief crosses Elliot's features. "That's a good idea. Dot's going to have enough trouble going to sleep in an unfamiliar place. Having so many people around will only make it harder for her to settle."

I've never been around babies, but I have no doubt Elliott knows what he's talking about. He's been Dot's dad for almost a year.

Eoin says, "Tommy and I will take turns sleeping on the couch. We can't sleep at the same time anyway."

"Maybe one of you should take a nap now?" I suggest. "You can use Cian's bed."

Tommy shakes his head. "We're both staying lively until ten. Boss's orders. We'll trade off every three hours after that. Elliott, you tell me when you want to go to Connor's."

"Now would be great," Elliott says, looking tired.

"Okay, let's go. I left all the baby paraphernalia you said to bring up in the hall."

"This sounds like we're in some kind of military installation," Ini grumbles, but then she adds. "Need any help, Elliott? I don't know much about babies, but I bet I can figure out how to set up the bed while you entertain Dot."

"That would be awesome," Elliott says gratefully. "I want to let Dot crawl around to wear herself out, so she sleeps deeply tonight, but I doubt Connor's place is baby proofed."

"That's something that will have to change," Tommy says. "Him being a dad and all."

Elliott doesn't reply, but the look of hope in his eyes? It's there for anyone to see if they are watching. I'm hoping too, for both of them.

Connor deserves to be happy. So do Elliott and Dot. They deserve to be the family they were meant to be.

"I assume Ini and I will be getting the guest room here?" Mrs. Hart asks. "I'm not staying up until ten. Eight-thirty is about my limit, as you girls know."

I nod. "Do you want one of Cian's t-shirts to sleep in?"

Tommy chokes and Eoin looks like he swallowed something that got stuck in his throat. Ini bursts out laughing.

"What?" I ask her, knowing she'll explain what has everyone acting so weird.

"I doubt a mob boss is used to having his clothes offered to random women for sleepwear."

I shrug. "He didn't mind me wearing his t-shirts. He has some made of silk fiber. They're soft and breathable."

"I brought a nightie in my purse, Anna. While I've never dated a mobster, I've been around the block a few times. When Ini told me you wanted us to come over immediately, I didn't assume we'd be returning home tonight."

"I wish you'd said something to me," Ini gripes. "I didn't bring anything to sleep in and I don't particularly want to borrow a mobster's clothes."

"So, sleep in the altogether, dear. It won't be the first time I've been in bed with a naked woman." Mrs. Hart winks.

Everyone but me bursts out laughing. I'm worried about Ini not having her sleep shorts and tank top she likes to sleep in. It's stressful not to have appropriate sleepwear. Though I liked sleeping naked with Cian.

I know that's not what Mrs. Hart means though.

"It's okay, Anna," Ini says to me, her expression understanding. "I can sleep in my shirt and underwear. Sweetie, I don't need a certain nightgown to get my rest."

Heat burns my cheeks. Because she knows that usually I do.

She just shakes her head though. "Remember, friend, we're all different. Not better. Not worse. Just different and that's good."

"Because otherwise life would be boring," I finish.

Elliott says, "Amen to that."

As hard as it is for me to have so many people around, I'm glad they're all here as the evening darkens to night. We haven't heard anything from Cian, or the others and I'm worried. Having the extra people gives my anxiety a more manageable outlet than my fear he'll be hurt.

CHAPTER 37

CIAN

*E*l *Fantasma's* house has a six-foot high brick wall surrounding it. No broken glass at the top. No electrified barbwire. Just a useless, easily scalable brick wall and motion sensors that are already disabled.

The dogs would be a bigger problem if they hadn't already been neutralized with tranquilizers. We aren't here to kill animals conscripted and trained to protect the cartel scum.

Martina and Bernardino don't expect to be attacked here. They think no one will find their base. Maybe if they were in another fucking city, not Chicago, where we own the streets and those we don't control, our allies do.

Connor and one of my other enforcers breaches the north wall while the other one and I go over the south. Christakos's team splits in two and breaches from the east and west.

Using a fingertip lift, I pull myself to the top of the wall and drop silently to the ground on the other side of the wall. A muffled thud tells me the enforcer with me is over too.

"In," I say over the comms. The other three teams confirm their breaches. "Scáth?"

"I have a bead on the front guard," my sniper replies over the ear comms.

His name is Oscar, but his military unit called him Scáth and it stuck. Irish for shadow, it fits the man whose kills will never see his face.

I say, "Go."

A few seconds later, Christakos confirms, "Front guard down."

After that things go fast. I take out the south guard while the others eliminate their targets. Suppressors don't completely mask the sound of a shot, so I don't waste any time telling my tech guy to take out the power and its backup.

We converge on the house from all sides.

My enforcer and I shoot out the bullet resistant glass on a window in unison. The armor piercing rounds shatter it a microsecond before we dive into the darkened dining room, tucking and rolling in opposite directions.

I come up on one knee and take in the room. My night vision goggles allow me to see what I need to.

A shot comes at me from my left and I spin on my knee to face the threat, aiming and shooting in one smooth movement. I hit my target twice. I don't shoot to kill. None of us are, now that we're inside the house.

We have to confirm Martina and Bernardino's identities before we dispose of the rest of their people.

I hit the shooter in the leg and shoulder of his gun arm. He goes down and I stalk toward him on silent feet, trusting my enforcer to have my back and be covering the other side of the room.

Kicking his gun away, I drop beside him, putting mine to his head. "Name?"

He curses at me in Spanish. Wearing tactical gear, it's unlikely this is Bernardino, the doctor, but I take the time necessary to compare his face to the picture we have of Carmen's husband.

It's not him.

I shoot the soldier in the head and look toward the door to the hall. My enforcer nods. "Dining room clear," I say.

I head upstairs, my enforcer and Christakos behind me. The rest of the teams are clearing the first floor room by room. We split off at the top of the stairs, each of us taking a door.

The house plans we studied show that there are two master bedrooms, one at each end of the hall. If Martina and her lover are smart, they don't sleep in the same room every night.

Trying to move in on a city already occupied by syndicates and gangs, they should be on high alert.

I take the master bedroom to the left and Christakos the one on the right. My enforcer takes the room closest to the stairs.

I shoot out the door handle and shove the door open, staying low. A bullet hits the door, making more noise when it cracks the thick wood than the gun did when the woman took her shot.

Jackpot. Martina is shooting at me from one side of the bed. Her lover is fumbling with a gun on the other side. Neither are wearing night vision goggles so I have the advantage.

It gives me the extra time I need to take aim and shoot the gun from Martina's hand. She screams with pain filled rage and runs toward the window. I shoot the floor in front of her to stop her fleeing while grabbing the tranq gun with my other hand.

I shoot and she grunts. I hit her. She'll be out cold in seconds. Turning my attention back to the doctor, I see it's just in time. He's got his gun up and it's pointing at me.

He gets a shot off and I feel the impact in my chest, but I don't go down. We train to keep going when our vests get hit. I shoot him with a tranq.

He gets another shot off before he goes down, but I'm already tucking and rolling.

A few seconds later, first one heavy thump and then another tells me they're both out. "Target one and two down," I say over the comms.

"Fuck. Man down," comes through. It's one of my men.

"Get him out," I bark.

"We've got this. Get your guy to medical," Christakos says over the comms, confirming the man down was not one of his.

I don't hesitate. "DBM pull out." Even over our secure comms we are circumspect. DBM is Doyle & Byrne mob.

The plan was always for Christakos and his team to do cleanup while me and my guys get the targets to the interrogation chamber.

Once the house is cleared and the bodies are brought inside, Christakos will set the place to blow with incendiary devices. What doesn't explode will burn to cinders before the fire department can arrive.

The fact that the dispatcher at the closest fire house has been paid to ignore the distress call will help.

It's only when we reach the SUV with the prisoners that I see the man who was shot is Connor. He's holding one arm with the other, but he's standing.

"Get in the SUV," I order him, before dropping the deadweight of the doctor into cargo hold of the truck.

My enforcer drops Martina on top of him. Their wrists and ankles are bound with zip ties I put on them as soon as they were out.

I pull the cover over the cargo hold and shut the storage area. Getting into the backseat with my cousin, I tell the enforcer behind the wheel to drive. Scáth is already on his way to give backup to one of our teams on the street.

CHAPTER 38

CIAN

We head to Lucky Charm. I want the prisoners in the basement holding cells and I want Connor seen to immediately. The doctor and his team are already set up there to receive casualties.

"Where are you hit?" I ask Connor.

He drops his arm and I see the blood covered entry point. Below his shoulder. Fuck. Did the bullet hit his lung? But there's no rattle as he breathes; his chest is rising and falling steadily if rapidly.

Sweat coats his brow and I know he's in pain, but he doesn't say a word. Good man. He's proven he's tough enough to be a mob enforcer.

I leave Connor with the Butcher and make sure Martina and Bernardino are secure in their holding cells before checking in with the other teams.

~ ~ ~

We lose seven mob brothers taking out the Kicks Bandidos, two from my mob and three from the Murphy clan and two from the smaller clans that joined us. The Greeks lose five men too.

Twelve men is twelve fucking too many, but between us, we take out seventy-three gang bangers. Some are kept alive with the chance at recruitment, but twenty-six are dead and in the process of being incinerated.

Including everyone above foot soldier status.

Martina is deluded if she thought she could take control of even part of Chicago with an army that size. Did her father really think she could do it?

Or were they relying on something else?

If the Anthrax gambit had worked, that would have taken hundreds if not thousands of lives before we knew what hit us. The real question is: are there other patsies like Carmen that have been weaponized for biological warfare?

It's not a question that can wait to be answered, so after checking in on Connor with the Butcher and learning he doesn't need surgery, just sewing up, I take a couple vials of adrenalin down to the holding cells.

Ronan is already in the room with the doctor and the fury on his face tells me he wants to question this bastard.

I toss him a vial of the adrenalin and a syringe. "Have fun with him. I'll go next door and wake up *El Fantasma*."

"My pleasure." Yeah, he means it.

Ronan Byrne will get every piece of information Berdardino has to give, and he will enjoy doing it.

I don't enjoy torture, but it is necessary in my line of work. The fact that *El Fantasma* is a woman doesn't make any difference to me. She's not innocent.

She sent her underlings after my sister. For that alone, she will die. That she planned to kill my mobsters and anyone they came into contact with through that fucking implant in Carmen? That just means I won't regret the method I have to use to get the information I want out of her.

~ ~ ~

I drag Martina Vega-Gutierrez into the interrogation chamber and attach her to the same bench her cousin was on before waking her up with the adrenalin.

Ronan has the doctor strung up from the ceiling by his hands in the room beside us, the table of instruments ready. The glass wall makes it possible to see what is happening. It can be frosted to prevent it when needed too.

The walls are soundproofed down here, including the one between the two interrogation rooms. However, we have a speaker system set up so that if we want sounds to travel between the two chambers, they can.

I can hear Bernardino's heavy breathing, so I know Ronan has the sound piping from his room.

Maybe the man's screams will motivate Martina, even if her own pain doesn't. The doctor isn't a trained soldier. He went to medical school. He has a role in the cartel that protects him.

Well, *protected* him. If he hadn't been a cheating bastard, he wouldn't be here, would he?

His first scream sounds just as Martina's eyes flutter open after I give her the shot of adrenalin. She turns her head and sees her lover take a blow from Ronan's knuckle duster covered fist.

Without blinking, she looks away and glares at me. "Do your worst. I'm not saying shit."

I do and she's wrong. She has plenty to say. So does her lover.

Most importantly, I learn that there are four more biological weapons prepared and stored at a secondary site. One we do not have on our list of locations to secure.

Martina and Bernardino weren't being called back to Colombia because they failed. They were leaving the city because they planned to lay waste to its underworld with Anthrax.

I do not feel remorse for killing to protect my mob, or to further its interests. But I always consider the risk-benefit ratio. This plan? Would never have made it past the proposal phase. And I probably would have killed whoever was shortsighted enough to suggest it.

Four damn targets. Did they fucking want to take out half of Chicago?

What would have been left for them to claim? And something like that would have brought the FEDs in like snow in winter, thinking some kind of terrorism was at play.

I may be a sociopath, but I am not a megalomaniac incapable of rational analysis of cause and effect like Eduardo Gutierrez. If he had ever been a man of reason, that time is past and his daughter shares in his delusions.

They would have destroyed my city without a qualm in order to claim it, but in doing so would have created a territory not worth claiming.

Fucking fools.

It's nearly dawn when I'm done interrogating Martina.

We don't kill either her, or Bernardino, yet. I want at least one more session to make sure we've gotten everything out of them. Sometimes the second or third rounds of interrogation are more effective than the first because of the cessation of pain only to be followed by a renewed, more concentrated effort on an already weakened body and mind.

Tomorrow, I will see how she responds to electric jolts.

I want nothing more than to go home to Anna, but the secondary site has to be secured and the bioweapons destroyed. I can't trust that to anyone else.

It's dawn and six more people are dead when I'm done. All members of the Kicks Bandidos. Or maybe just the cartel. I don't give a fuck.

They are dead. Their biological weapons are incinerated and I'm ready to go home.

Since I'm covered in blood, I stop at Lucky Charm to take a shower and collect Connor.

I don't want to scare Anna.

~ ~ ~

We're in the armored SUV on the way to the Doyle building when I finally check in on Anna. She's sitting up in our bed, doing something on her phone. Her eyes are red rimmed from lack of sleep.

She jolts and stares into the camera on the phone, like she can feel my eyes on her.

I text her.

Me: **On my way home, have to drop Connor off at his parents' house first**.

Anna: **Bring him to his apartment. He has someone waiting for him**.

What the hell does that mean? But I tell my driver to take us straight to the Doyle Building.

Me: **Okay**.

Anna: Mrs. Hart and Ini are sleeping in the guest room.

Me: **?**

Anna: I wanted them safe last night.

She knew something big was going down and she didn't ask me to stay home, or for details. She's so damn perfect for me.

She also didn't sleep. I don't like that, but I understand it. We'll sleep together.

After I lose myself in her softness. I crave her. I fucking need her. And she is mine.

~ ~ ~

Tommy and Eoin are both awake when I let myself into the apartment. So is my girl. She's wearing one of my t-shirts, her pretty blond hair a messy halo around her face and her violet eyes fixed on me.

"You're okay," she breathes and launches herself at me.

Wrapping my arms around her, I lift and her legs lock on either side of my hips. Her mouth slams onto mine and I kiss her back with all the relief and passion she's showing me.

Several cleared throats, and, "Uh, Boss," comments later, I lift my head.

Connor is listing to one side, but he's still standing. "I'm going home."

"Yeah, about that. Your kid and that Elliott guy is there, so maybe be quiet going in," Tommy says.

Connor's kid? What the actual fuck?

"Lachlan stopped by to check everything was good when he got in earlier. We'll get some shuteye at his place," Eoin says.

Because a man named Elliott and a child are staying at Connor's.

I let my cousin see with my look that I want answers. Later.

He nods and then turns to go, walking a lot faster than he has since I picked him up from the infirmary.

Eoin and Tommy leave and shut the door behind them.

"Let's go to bed." Anna has her face buried in my neck and she's inhaling my scent like she does sometimes.

"Do you want to leave a note for your friends and tell them they can go home if they want to when they wake up?"

"Oh, yes. That's a good idea. Mrs. Hart gets up early and that means Ini will too."

I let Anna down, but keep a hand on her while she writes the note and leaves it next to the espresso maker. "Ini always goes for coffee first thing in the morning. She won't miss it here."

We head into my bedroom and I shut the door, locking it and closing us into our own little world. I start shucking my clothes immediately. I don't want anything between my skin and Anna's.

"Is everything okay now?" she asks.

"We lost some good men. The funerals will be this week. You'll go with me." I know she doesn't like crowds and I'll keep a buffer between her and everyone else, but my mob brothers need to know my woman is part of this family now.

"Of course."

I pull her in for a kiss, just wanting to feel her against me. She pulls her lips from mine sooner than I want. "Is it over?"

"Mostly."

"What's left?" she asks, her voice strained.

"Nothing for you to worry about." We need to finish our interrogations and share the intel we've gathered with our allies.

Only some of them want to participate in taking down the cartel, which doesn't surprise me. For most, having eradicated the problem in our city is enough.

But I want to take the head off the snake. If that means putting someone less volatile in his place, I'm open to it. I'm also prepared to destroy the whole fucking cartel.

All the gang's product and resources were confiscated by the syndicates covering their territories. They had a shitload of weapons and drugs.

We'll be testing any product before we put it into our inventory. I'm not letting our people sell crap that will kill our customers.

I think about what I just said and sigh. "I might have to go to Colombia for a while."

"Okay."

Her easy agreement surprises me.

She adds, "But I'll need to get my passport. I don't have one."

"You're not going," I tell her in no uncertain terms.

She just looks at me and I curse.

"I mean it. If you're there, I'll be too worried about keeping you safe to do what I need to. This is war, *mo chroí* and the general can't have his attention split."

"Generals don't go to the front line."

"Good ones do."

"Fine. You're a good one. Probably the best. But I'm going with you if you're leaving the country."

The idea of hiring mercs to take out the cartel's compound is sounding better and better. Maybe we can use the product we confiscated for part of their payment. Let them worry about its purity.

Before I can say anything else, Anna drops to her knees in front of me. My semi starts to grow from having her face so close.

"I want to taste you," she says.

CHAPTER 39

CIAN

Since I just showered at Lucky Charm, I have no objections. Hell, I'm not sure if I was still bloody and sweaty that I would have the strength to tell her *no*.

Anna reaches out to touch me, curving her hand around my now hard cock. Her fingers don't quite touch but she doesn't seem to mind as she jacks me.

A bead of precum forms on my slit and she leans forward to lap it up. Without any warning, she opens her mouth and takes me in as deeply as she can. I hit the back of her throat and she chokes, pulling her head back, but keeping me inside her hot mouth.

My girl likes to learn new things and right now she's learning my taste and the shape of me. Her soft tongue explores while she inhales deeply.

After a full body shudder, she pulls back and looks up at me. "I read about this. I'm going to try swallowing and taking more of you. I might choke a little. If I don't like it, I'll stop."

My knees about buckle. If she does what she says, they probably will so I tug her up and move over to the bed. I sit on the edge and spread my legs so she can kneel between them.

Which she does. Giving me one of the best images I've ever seen in my life.

This time she puts both of her hands around my dick, moving them up and down while she licks and suckles on the head. I let my hands rest in her silky hair, not pushing, just connecting.

She gives no more warning this time than the last when she decides to take me in, but when I hit the back of her throat, she swallows. She gags too.

And she's so damn right. It feels like heaven on my cock. She doesn't back off though; she keeps swallowing. Tears form in her eyes and roll down her cheeks in her body's automatic response to the gagging.

Knowing that, I still ask, "You okay?"

She nods as much as she can with my dick down her throat. The movement sends jolts of pleasure along my length.

I feel my impending climax at the base of my spine and I gently push back against her shoulders. "I want to come on your tits."

We'll both sleep better if I do. Besides I want to eat my girl to her own orgasm first. Once I come, I'm done. I know it and I'm not going into oblivion without making sure she's pleasured too.

Anna pulls back slowly, releasing my cock with a pop. Saliva drools down her face and she swipes at it. "That's messy, but I like it. Did you?"

"Can't you tell, *mo chroí*? I'm ready to come, but you first."

She doesn't understand what I mean until I pull the t-shirt off her and get her to lie down. When my head is between her thighs, she moans.

I haven't even touched her yet. But she knows what's coming.

She smells so damn good, her pink pussy lips glistening with her arousal. She liked giving me head. A lot.

It takes no time at all to bring her to a screaming orgasm and then I surge up her body and jack myself until I come like I wanted to. All over her gorgeous tits.

I rub the cum in, but this time she helps, her beautiful violet eyes hazy like they get just for me.

ANNA

I'm not sure how long Cian and I sleep, but when I wake up, I feel good. Rested. I'm wrapped tightly in his arms, the scent of our lovemaking all around me.

Content to stay as we are, I think about last night. It was scary, but Cian came home unharmed. Connor was hurt though. He had some kind of bandage on his chest and his arm was in a sling.

That only registers now. Last night my direct focus was entirely on Cian. I wonder how Elliott reacted to Connor's wound. Was Connor glad to find his boyfriend and their baby in his apartment?

I bet he was.

Not wanting to disturb Cian, I reach for my phone charging on the nightstand.

I text Connor.

Me: **Is Elliott still there?**

I text Elliott.

Me: **Are you okay? Was Connor hurt very badly? I noticed he had a bandage**.

Connor's reply comes in first.

Connor: **Yes. Thank you. You kept them safe for me. Coming home to them, I realized this is where they belong. I'll talk to Cian before I take Elliott and Dot to my parents' house for dinner**.

Elliott's answer comes in while I'm reading Connor's text. I tap into the text stream.

Elliott: **He was shot. Angry face emoji. Crying emoji. But he's okay. Smiley face emoji. At least he says he is. I mean, he was okay enough to...winky face emoji. Eggplant emoji. Grin emoji. Three heart emojis**.

I'm so happy for my friends. I text thumbs up and heart emojis back to both of them.

"Are you texting Ini?" Cian rumbles from behind me.

"Not yet. I was checking on Connor and Elliott."

Cian pulls me onto my back and kisses me before asking, "Who is Elliott?"

"Connor needs to talk to you before dinner."

It's a little after one, so there should be time.

"After."

"After what?"

But then Cian's hands start moving and I smile. "Oh, that. Yes, after." Definitely after.

CIAN

Eoin takes Anna to visit Ini before Connor arrives. She promises not to stay long, but it's still hard to let her go. I don't tell her that.

She knows anyway and sends me a selfie from the car of her smiling. Then another from the elevator in the apartment building, this one she's got her top up and she's flashing me her tits with a mischievous grin. Eoin had better be facing the other direction and no one else be on that elevator with her.

A text follows the selfie.

Anna: **Eoin faced the wall and we were alone on th elevator. Winky face emoji**.

My girl knows me well. The last selfie is from outside Ini's apartment. In this one, Anna is blowing me a kiss.

She's so fucking perfect for me.

I watch her on the spycam on her phone, but the selfies settle the beast prowling inside me in a way just watching her can't right now. They tell me we are connected. That her focus is on me like mine is on her, even when we're with other people.

I'm watching her talk to Ini when a loud knock sounds on my door before it opens.

"It's me."

Looking up from my spot on the sectional I meet my cousin's gaze. His eyes reflect both wariness and determination. He's not wearing the sling the Butcher gave him after patching him up, but he's moving stiffly.

"Sit." I indicate the other end of the sectional with my chin.

Connor sits on the edge, instead of relaxing against the back like he usually does. His body buzzes with nervous energy.

Narrowing my eyes at him, I ask, "What the fuck, Connor?"

"Anna doesn't like you saying that word."

"She's not here." I don't bother to hide my annoyance at that situation from my cousin.

He knows how far gone I am on my girl.

Connors lips tilt briefly in a smile. "You have got it bad, Boss."

I don't deny it. I just wait. Connor wants to talk to me. He'll say what he needs to say.

"I'm gay," he blurts out and his muscles tense in preparation for movement.

"Okay."

He frowns at me. "Nobody is gay in the mob."

"You are proof that's not true."

"Elliott is my boyfriend."

"Is it serious?" If it is, Elliott will have to get the training we give spouses and live-in lovers.

"He had my baby."

"He?" I ask, confused.

"Yes." Connor sighs. "He was still presenting as a she when we hooked up. I was looking for a one-night stand to prove to the guys I'm like them."

"He's more than a one-night stand if he gave birth to your baby." Even if they aren't committed to each other, Elliott is family now.

"He is. He found me after starting his transition. He was scared of how I'd react."

"He's your boyfriend now. You couldn't have fucked up too much."

Connor laughs and finally relaxes against the sofa. "I was seriously into him before I found out the baby in the stroller he was pushing was mine. He looked familiar, but I didn't realize he was my one hookup from over a year ago."

"Your ma is going to smother that kid." My aunt wants grandchildren and she's not shy about it.

Connor is her only kid. He's only twenty-two. I figured she had some years of hinting ahead of her. I was wrong.

"Yeah. Dot might be the one thing that saves me from my parents disowning me when they find out I'm gay."

"Jimmy and Lila aren't bigots."

"It's different when it's your own kid."

"You know this how?"

"Friends."

"Well, your friends don't have Jimmy and Lila for parents."

"Anna said you wouldn't care."

"She knows me."

"I've known you longer, and I wasn't sure."

"Fear clouds your judgment."

"Like you've ever been afraid of anything."

I shrug. "I never was, before I met Anna."

"Now, you're afraid of losing her. She'll never leave you."

"Not willingly, but things happen." She's out there, right now, in the City, where bad things happen all the time.

She's got her bodyguard, but she had bodyguards when Grieves and Samuels took her too. They all know now, that if they let her get taken by *anyone*, their lives are forfeit.

"You'll keep her safe. Just like I'll keep Elliott and Dot safe."

I nod.

"The mob..." Connor sighs and shakes his head. "There are a lot of traditions we uphold, not everyone is going to be okay with me having a boyfriend."

"Tell me if anyone gives you shit. I'll set them straight." Connor is family. No one messes with my own.

"I can fight my own battles."

"Sure. Tell me anyway."

He rolls his eyes, reminding me of his teen years. "You can't go around beating on everyone who has an issue with my sexuality."

"I won't."

"Then what's your plan?"

"I'll kill them. No one threatens my family."

I see the moment my cousin realizes I'm serious. I'm not a joking kind of guy, but still people, even family, mistake my words for humor when they're not.

"Do you want to meet Elliott and Dot?"

"Yes." I think of something and smile.

Connor jerks back, like I threatened him with a gun. "What is that look for?" he asks me.

"Anna is afraid to have kids because she doesn't know how to be around them, or how she will react to them. Dot will give her the chance to see she'll be a natural mom."

"You're so sure she will?" Connor asks.

"You aren't?"

"I've got no doubts," Connor says hastily. Maybe he sees how much I don't like him questioning that. "She's sweet and loyal. Elliott really likes her too."

"Elliott knows she's taken right?"

Connor laughs. "Elliott is very much taken and also, he's gay. You've got nothing to worry about on that score."

I frown, but I don't say anything. Logic would say he's right, but logic doesn't play a big role in how I react to all things Anna.

After Connor leaves, I call my Uncle Jimmy.

"Hello, Cian. What can I do for you?"

"Connor is coming over tonight."

"He is. His ma is making him all his favorites. She about ate the head off me when she found out he'd been shot. She wants him staying here, but he says no."

Why the Irish-ism *ate the head off* is more disturbing than the American equivalent of *bit my head off*, I don't know. Especially as I'm disturbed by so little. Maybe it's the added implication of cannibalism?

Doesn't matter.

I have more important things to consider right now than my uncle's Irish slang.

"There's a reason for that," I tell my uncle. "You'll learn it tonight. I want you and Aunt Lila to understand that I'm okay with what he's going to tell you. I expect you to be too."

"You talking to me as my nephew, or the mob boss?" Jimmy asks cautiously.

"Both." I'll be disappointed if any member of my family has an issue with my cousin being gay.

As the boss, that disappointment will manifest more definitively.

"I don't know what this is about, but I love my son. There isn't anything he could tell me that would change that."

My uncle claims he doesn't know what Connor is going to say, and he's half right, but I think the gay part? Jimmy suspects that.

My da raised me to a be a loyal but brutal mobster. Jimmy trained Connor to be a good man. They're closer than me and my da ever were. If da were still alive, he'd probably try to spirit Anna away like he did Helen.

I'm glad he's not here so I don't have to acknowledge what I would do to my father in that situation. But there's no question whether I would accept it like I did before. I would not.

Anna is the sun and Helen was a dimly lit star. Both make me feel something, but with Anna it's not just something, it's everything.

CHAPTER 40

CIAN

The next couple of weeks are uneventful. We finish the interrogations of the gang members and Ronan lets Carmen finish off her cousin and husband.

He seems to think it will give her closure. I'm not sure anything will get rid of that haunted look in her eyes. Her entire family deemed her expendable and betrayed her.

Through Brogan Shaughnessy, I'm contacted by a Cosa Nostra don in New York. Severu De Luca. He wants to destroy the Gutierrez Cartel for some shit they pulled in his city.

"Are we going to work with them?" Lachlan asks me after my video meeting with De Luca.

Anna is sitting at her desk with her noise cancelling headphones in, but I'm on to her tricks. She's probably listening in. I don't care as long as no one else realizes she does it.

That would put her at risk, and I won't allow that.

She's so pretty in her pink top and skirt. She doesn't wear dresses unless they're designed with easy access to her tits. She knows sometimes the only thing that calms me down is touching her beautiful body.

When she lets me, it always does something to her, sending her to that place she calls her *safe headspace*. It's safe as long as I can hold her afterward, which I never forget to take into account.

We bought her a bunch of new clothes, crop tops that give me easy access, but opaque enough she can go without a bra and no one gets to see the outline of her gorgeous areolas. Nothing can hide the way her tits sway, or when her nipples get hard though.

Not unless she wears some kind of jacket or sweater and I don't want that. So, I deal. I'm doing pretty good too, only considering gouging other men's eyes out about a dozen times a day.

Everything is made of soft, natural fibers. Denim that has been washed and worn so many times it holds no stiffness anymore. Which means buying some things second hand. Whatever makes her happy, is good with me.

"Uh, boss..." Lachlan brings my attention back to our discussion.

The little smirk on Anna's face tells me she knows my attention wandered and she guesses why. She is listening.

My girl has a mischievous streak I'm just getting to know.

"Yes," I answer Lachlan's question.

De Luca and Shaughnessy agree that taking out Eduardo and his lieutenants and replacing them with players not megalomaniac enough to try to take over major US cities is a good strategy.

We wouldn't know who those people are without Carmen and the information we got out of interrogating *El Fantasma* and Bernardino.

"You've done a lot more collaboration lately than you used to." Lachlan gives me a look I don't try to read. "Hell, you even offered to keep your alliance with the Walsh mob if Éamon stepped down as the boss."

His nephew approached me, worried we were going to target their mob next. He said his uncle hadn't made a deal with the cartel, but that he'd tried to keep the peace. Too comfortable in his life to fight for his territory, Éamon had been willing to share his streets with the interlopers rather than go to war.

The nephew is hungry with a reputation for brutal reprisal already. He'll do as their new boss.

"It's good for the mob."

"And it keeps our loved ones safe," Lachlan adds with a significant glance toward Anna.

I shrug. It's true. "Keeping them safe *is* good for the mob." A mobster with something to lose is a man willing to risk his life to protect it. He's less likely to go off halfcocked too.

That's not a bad thing.

~ ~ ~

When Anna's passport arrives, I know we need to use mercenaries for our attack on the cartel's compound and I can't be the one to oversee the mission.

My girl didn't tell me she was getting her passport, and the only reason she would do it is because she's determined to go with me if I leave the country.

For a trip to Europe to see the sights and maybe visit with my family? That's fine. But I am not taking Anna to Colombia to wage war against a demented cartel leader.

Surprisingly, or maybe not so much, Shaughnessy, De Luca, Drakos and Murphy all agree with the mercenary idea and will help fund it. Someone has to go to Colombia though, to make contact with the cartel members we plan to install as the new leadership.

Carmen insists she can help and I believe her. Just because her family doesn't value her, doesn't mean the rest of her cartel sees her as worthless. Ronan insists on going too, which works.

ANNA

After the night they decimated the street gang trying to move in on the mob and Greek mafia's territories in Chicago, Cian is super busy. He works long hours in his office running the business, but he also spends a lot of time at Lucky Charm and the apartment safehouse.

I know, because he takes me with him. He always leaves me someplace safe while he's seeing to whatever leaves him with busted knuckles and blood spatter on his clothes, but he never leaves me behind.

Tonight he tells me to get dressed up. He's taking me out to dinner. I wear a new dress he bought me. It's purple silk, the same shade as my eyes, with a plunging neckline and full skirt that hits me just below mid-thigh.

He likes the halter neckline because he can slide his hands in and cup my breasts from both the sides and the front. I like that too. Just thinking about it makes me shiver.

After we are seated at a table overlooking the river, he tosses my new passport on the table between us.

So, he knows I got it. I had to pay extra to expedite the processing and then I also asked Lachlan if he could hurry it along. And he did.

"I'm going with you if you leave the country," I inform him. I inhale deeply, reminding myself this is too important to give in on.

His eyes flick to my chest but then zero in on my face again and he just stares at me for a minute, like he does sometimes. He gets lost in me the same as I get lost in him.

"That's what I'm counting on." He winks at me.

Winks! Mr. Oh So Serious.

Desire pools deep in my belly and my ovaries start singing Taylor Swift ballads.

"What do you mean?"

"I'm flying out to Spain to see Ma and Shea next week. You're coming with me."

"Really?" Excitement zings through me.

I've never been out of the country before. And I miss Shea. We video chat, but it's not the same. There are still so many shadows in her eyes, but the longer they are in Spain, the more pieces of her old self she seems to get back.

Reality tempers my delight. "I'm not sure how I'll do on a plane filled with people I don't know. I mean if I sit by the window and you sit on my other side, I'll probably be okay."

He still calms the chaos for me; I just don't know how well I'll deal with chaos I've never experienced before. I would have forced myself to deal with it to follow him to Colombia. And I'll get through the plane ride now.

I'm just worried. A little. Maybe a lot.

I'll take Things that are Hard but Worth Doing, Alex.

He smiles, his blue eyes softening, like they only do with me. "I have a private jet, *mo chroí.*"

"Oh. That's wonderful!"

~ ~ ~

And it is. His jet looks bigger on the outside than the inside until I realize there is a bedroom in the back of the plane. "Are there seatbelts on the bed?" I ask.

"No, my sweet girl. Once we are at cruising altitude, it's perfectly safe to go without a seatbelt."

"Unless we hit bad turbulence."

"If we're in the bed, the worst that will happen is we might shift around a little."

"Huh..." I think about that and my eyes nearly cross considering what we might be doing and what might shift.

I almost want there to be turbulence.

"It's about an eight-hour flight to the private airport near where Ma and Shea are staying. We'll definitely be using the bed." He winks at me. Again.

My ovaries are swooning.

~ ~ ~

We do use the bed on the plane, but we don't sleep. Not a wink. I orgasm four times and he lets me go down on him before he coats my boobs in his ejaculate. I'm floating in a state of post orgasmic euphoria when he carries me off the plane to the waiting car.

We have eight of his men with us as guards, including Lachlan. None of them said a thing when we left the main cabin to use the plane's bedroom, although Lachlan gave me a teasing waggle of his eyebrows when we came out.

He's in the car with us now, along with the driver. There are three guards in a car ahead of us and three in a car behind us.

We drive along the coast of the freaking Mediterranean to reach the villa Mrs. Doyle and Shea are staying in. It's in a gated community and the guards check credentials before letting us through.

The villa we park in front of is more like a mansion and I'm less worried than I was before about all the new people finding accommodation within. Yes, I worry about the little details.

Mrs. Doyle is waiting for us when we come inside. I'm glad I took a shower on the plane. As much as I hate washing Cian's scent from my body, I don't want to greet his mother smelling like his semen.

She smiles warmly at us. "Oh, it's so good to see you all. I've been so worried."

"I called," Cian says pragmatically, no inflection in his tone.

"Yes, and I still had to learn about my new great-niece from my sister-in-law and not my son."

Cian doesn't reply, but turns to the men and gives them instructions.

I smile and give a little shrug to Mrs. Doyle. "Dot is really cute," I offer.

I've been spending time with her every day. Sometimes with Elliott, or him and Connor and sometimes on my own. I have a feeling Cian is behind the requests to watch the baby for short periods.

I don't mind. Spending time with her has put a lot of my fears to rest about how I would cope with motherhood. Not enough for me to get pregnant. I haven't had the baby overnight yet.

After I told Elliott I wanted to watch her overnight when she was teething, he laughed out loud. Then he realized I wasn't kidding and he nodded enthusiastically. "I am so down for that."

"I'm sure she is." Mrs. Doyle sniffs. "Not that I have had a chance to see her."

"Cian said you and Shea will be coming back to Chicago when the cartel is sorted."

Everyone around me sort of goes still, except Cian, who pulls me into his arms to rest against his body.

"He talks to you about business?" Mrs. Doyle asks, sounding shocked.

"Not specifics," I assure her. Though I'm confident he's figured out that I eavesdrop. I never mention the stuff I overhear though.

"That's more specific than his father ever was with me," Mrs. Doyle replies. "In fact, my son only told me that Shea and I would be safer here in Spain for now."

"Oh. Well, that's true too," I say.

Cian doesn't lie, even if he doesn't always share everything.

"Shea is on the terrace. Come through when you're ready." Mrs. Doyle turns to go.

"She didn't hug you," I say to Cian.

Mrs. Doyle stops walking, but she doesn't turn. It's like she wants to hear his reply.

"I'm not big on hugs."

"Neither am I, but she's your mom," I tell him.

"Hey, ma," Cian says.

Mrs. Doyle turns, a strange expression on her face.

"Do you want a hug?"

She swallows and nods. "That would be nice."

I step away from Cian and he moves forward to take his mom in a tight hug. She wraps her arms around him and holds on tight. "It's good to see you, boyo."

They step away from each other and Cian's hand comes out toward me. I rush forward to take it and smile up at him.

We go out to the terrace, four of the guards taking up positions to augment the security already there.

Lachlan joins us at the table where Shea and now Mrs. Doyle are sitting, a pitcher of some kind of fruit juice in the center.

I don't ask what it is. I just pour myself a glass of water from the carafe beside it. I'm thirsty, so I drink, but I don't sit down.

Shea grins at me, the expression almost natural. "Hi, friend. I'm glad Cian brought you to visit."

Pulling my hand from Cian's, I go around the table and give Shea a quick half hug. "I'm so glad you're doing better," I tell her.

She nods and her gaze lands on Lachlan before skittering away again. "The Spanish sun is very healing."

After we all sit down, Shea and Mrs. Doyle tell us about their time in Spain.

"The food here is amazing, but I'm glad I have a kitchen. Sometimes, you just need a good Irish stew," Cian's mom says.

"Speaking of Irish soup, could you teach me to make that seafood stew Cian pilfered from your freezer, Mrs. Doyle? It was delicious."

I've looked up recipes online and tried a couple, but none tasted exactly like hers.

"Cian raided Ma's freezer to feed you?" Shea asks, her tone surprised.

"Please call me Mona, dear. Though I think you'll be calling me Ma sooner than later. And of course I'll show you how to make it. I like to serve it with soda bread."

"Connor got some of that from his mom for us to have with the soup."

"What do you think of Elliott?" Mrs. Doy—Mona asks me.

"He's really nice. He's really into Connor and they share their baby with me. I'm learning a lot about being around children and how to care for them. Elliott and Connor are both good dads."

Mona says, "I would expect nothing less of my nephew. I'm glad his, um...boyfriend is also a good father. My great-niece deserves only the best."

Mona hesitated before saying boyfriend. I don't know if it's because she's uncomfortable learning her nephew is gay, or that his partner is a transgender male, but she doesn't misidentify and she doesn't sneer. So, I'm sure she will do her best to be accepting and loving toward the new little family.

She's clearly already fiercely protective toward Dot.

"Dot needs family that accepts her dads and their relationship. Elliott's parents don't and it has caused a lot of stress for Elliott."

Cian looks at me. "I didn't know that. I'll sort them when we get back to Chicago."

Lachlan laughs. "If you don't think Connor already has, you don't know your cousin very well."

Everyone laughs, except me. I'm thinking about how protective Connor is toward Elliott and Dot. Cian is just as protective of me.

Connor loves Elliott. He told me so. I'm not sure Cian loves me and I don't think it matters. As long as he wants to make a life with me.

CHAPTER 41

ANNA

Mona and I make the Irish Seafood Stew for dinner that night and true to her word, she shows me step by step how to prepare it and the soda bread she says Cian enjoys.

Once the bread is in the oven, Mona turns to me and gives me a searching, worried look. "I don't know if he can love you."

"My parents loved me, but I was still too much for them," I tell her. "I'm not too much for Cian. He is my person, but I'm his person too."

"Being Cian's person could become smothering," she says in a tentative tone.

I touch her shoulder briefly, wanting to comfort, but not wanting to prolong contact. "People think we're both broken, but our broken pieces lock together and make us both whole."

"That's beautiful." Mona gives me a quivering smile. "And neither of you are broken. You're just you."

I smile back, my heart light. "I like being me when I am with him."

"And you don't think that will change?"

"Do you think he'll get tired of being my touchstone?"

"No. He's obsessed with ye and I do not see that changing, lass."

"I'm obsessed with him too." To the point that I like it best when his cum is rubbed into my skin.

"You were made for each other." She shakes her head, tears trickling from her eyes that she dashes away with the side of her hand. "I didn't think my boyo would ever find someone like you."

"I needed to be found." It's nothing less than the truth.

~ ~ ~

Later that night, Cian has me wrapped in his arms after we make love and I smell like us. Just like I need to so I'll sleep deeply. It's better than my lean-to.

Or Cian's...our panic room that is now set up as my quiet space.

"I heard you and Ma talking in the kitchen."

I smile against his side, drawing a pattern over his muscled pecs with one fingertip. "I think she likes me."

"I think she loves you."

"Oh." That would be nice, to be loved by a mom again. A mom who wouldn't get tired of me because her son is my touchstone, not her.

"She was wrong about something."

I lift my head to look at him. His blue eyes blaze with emotion that everyone, including him, says he doesn't feel.

"What?" I ask.

"She said I can't love you."

My heart stutters and then starts galloping. "Are you saying you can?"

"More than can. I do. I didn't think I could feel this, but Anna, *mo chroí,* I told you that you are my beating heart and I meant it. Without you, the world is in shades of grey. I care for my family, but they are not vital to me. You are vital."

He cups my face, his expression not exactly vulnerable, but more open than I've ever seen it. "You are my earth, my moon, my sun, and my stars. I don't want to take a single breath in this world without you in it. What is that, if not love?"

"I think it's love." Tears burn at the back of my eyes and there's a lump in my throat. This man. "And I feel the same toward you. Everything is too much without you, but when I am with you, it all makes sense. I love you, Cian Doyle."

"I would destroy the world to keep you safe, to keep you with me," he says fiercely.

I do not doubt him. I offer my own promise. "I would brave a stadium full of people to be with you."

He smiles and because it's so rare for him, it is like being given diamonds. "I'll never make you do that."

"I didn't think you'd want to go to a Taylor Swift concert, but if you did, I would go."

Chuckling, he holds me tight. "Don't worry, I'm not my cousin."

"It's not Connor that's going to the concert. It's Minx. She's really excited. I get hives just thinking about it."

Because I've spent so much time at Lucky Charm with Cian, I've gotten to know the escort. I like her and she's another new friend. My life has gotten so full since meeting my mob boss.

"And you'd still go for me?"

I inhale the scent of his skin and revel in the rightness of it. "I'd do anything for you."

"Even marry me?"

I know Cian doesn't tease often, but he does sometimes. Please don't let this be one of those times. His handsome face is cast in serious lines, but I have to be sure.

"You want to get married?" I ask, my voice squeaking on the word *married*.

He kisses me, devouring my mouth with his until we are both panting and his sex is hard against my thigh. "I want to tie you to me in every way possible."

His vehemence could be frightening, if it wasn't about something I want just as much.

"I want that. I never, ever, ever want to live without you."

"You never, ever, ever will. I am yours and you are mine."

"The vows we made with our bodies."

"Yes. But I want those vows public for everyone to hear and I'm not sexing you up on the conference table. No one gets to see your delicious curves but me. That means a wedding."

"Your mom is going to be over the moon."

"We'll give her three months to plan whatever she wants, but I'm not waiting a day longer to change your name to Doyle."

"What if I want to keep my last name?"

"What if you do?" he asks right back.

And I grin. "Then I would. But I don't. I want to be a Doyle. I think I was born to be part of the Doyle & Byrne mob."

"You were born to be mine. Whatever heart there is within me loves you, Anna Lake, soon to be Doyle."

We spend the rest of the night showing that love with our bodies.

But he whispers the words again in my ear as we finally relax for sleep. And I let them burrow deeply into my heart.

He is my person and I am his and we are never going to let each other go.

EPILOGUE: RETRIBUTION

CIAN

The Colombia mission was a success and so was my plan for Grieves. He and Samuels are under investigation by Internal Affairs with more and more details of their dirty deeds being leaked out. No one is surprised when he disappears.

They think he ran. I know better.

The week after I deal with Grieves, I break into Samuels's apartment and wait for her. She's at dinner with friends who are still supporting her, but won't once all the details of her crimes come to light. She didn't just victimize people she and Grieves arrested or took in for questioning. She sold her fellow cops out for quick cash.

More than one investigation got derailed because of her, but worse, her fellow cops were injured and one died because of the information she sold.

She turns on a lamp in the living room after coming inside and jumps back with a shriek when she realizes I'm there.

Lifting my gun, I point it at her. "Hands where I can see them."

She stops grappling for her off-duty piece in the holster on her ankle and straightens up, her hands to her side, palms out and open. "Mr. Doyle. I know who you are, but I don't know why you are here."

"Your partner left you holding the bag." I know Grieves is dead after days of torture, because I killed him.

No one will ever find his body though. His ashes are dumped in the sewer drains with the rest of the shit, just where he belongs.

"He'll be back." She doesn't believe that. Her eyes tell the truth. Helpless fury at being left to face the consequences of their shared criminality.

And Samuels doesn't even know Grieves *can't* come back. Just like everyone else, she believes he ran. No honor among corrupt cops, I guess.

"It's too bad he won't be here to go to prison for his crimes, but you are. You will."

"I won't go to prison," she scoffs. "They'll fire me, but criminal charges won't be filed. It would leave the city too vulnerable to lawsuits."

"You'll go to prison. You think the assaults on your victims are the only crimes my people handed over to your IA?"

Her face leaches of color. She knows there is plenty to send her to prison for that won't risk a rash of lawsuits for the city. "What's it to you what I did? You're a goddamn mob boss. Don't tell me upholding the law means anything to you."

The law? Not so much. Honor? Yes.

Businesses pay us for protection. We protect. Clients come to us for companionship? They don't get rolled for their credit cards. Our workers trust us to keep them safe? We do.

"You let your partner molest the people in your custody. You could have stopped him, but you didn't. You got off on watching him hurt them."

"Who cares about whores and druggies?"

"I do." I'm not a compassionate man, but I live by the code my father raised me to. "But it wasn't only them, was it?"

She knows exactly what I'm talking about, but I spell it out anyway. "You took money from the Kicks Bandidos to go after my woman."

"I'm sorry about that, okay? It's not like he fucked her. He just groped her a little."

I think about how traumatized my girl was and I'm tempted to kill this bitch right now, but my plans for her will make her misery last longer. Prison is no picnic for a cop. Especially when some of the women she let her partner hurt will be fellow inmates.

"He would have done more though, wouldn't he? If the captain hadn't stepped in."

"No," she lies.

Neither of us believes her.

"Please, I can do things for you. I have connections."

"Anna asked you to help her. To make your partner stop. You ignored her."

Disgust roils in my gut. I'm a mob boss, but I don't prey on the people who are supposed to be under my protection.

"It wasn't personal. It was just business. You have to understand that. Your people kill for hire."

"Unlucky for you, what you did was personal to me." I tap my gun against my thigh. "I could get you out of trouble as easily as I got you in it, but I won't. I'm going to stand by and fucking enjoy watching you squirm."

Just like she did with Anna.

"I'll run."

"Try." She won't get two blocks. I have people on her. She'll stand trial and she *will* go to prison.

"You can't do this!"

I don't bother answering that bit of stupidity. I go to leave, but stop at the door, and say over my shoulder, "If you make it out of prison alive, you won't have long to enjoy your freedom."

No one gets away with hurting my girl.

EPILOGUE: THE WEDDING

ANNA

One, two, look at my shoe.

The white butter-soft leather ballet flats make me smile. Cian had them specially made so I would be comfortable.

Three, four, find the door.

The wedding march swells, and someone opens the door to the sanctuary. I look through the opening and see Ini waiting at the altar to the left of the priest. She is my maid of honor.

Sliding my gaze to the right, I see my groom. Cian is wearing a black silk tuxedo with a white shirt and black bowtie. Traditional like his mom wants, but so incredibly handsome.

I feel a smile creasing my face. I'm glowing inside.

Five, six, click, click, clicks.

I don't tap my fingernails together, but I do begin to walk toward the man who will always hold my heart.

The sea of faces to either side of the aisle do not register. Cian is a mob boss, but he insisted that our wedding not be attended by anyone other than close friends and family.

The reception is going to be huge, but from the raised dais for our table to our special dances not being accompanied by any of the other guests, Mona arranged each element so I would not get overwhelmed.

Seven, eight, release the weight.

There is no weight as I float forward buoyed by joy.

Nine, ten, inhale the Zen.

I inhale as the heated look in Cian's blue eyes draws me forward like a magnet.

Now start again.

But I don't need to. I'm almost there.

Cian steps away from Lachlan, his best man, and toward me, reaching out with his hand.

I'm running by the time I reach him and take it.

He pulls me in and kisses me. "You look beautiful, *mo chroí*. My heart and my queen."

"I love you, Cian."

He kisses me again. "I love you."

The priest clears his throat, and we turn to face him. Both Lachlan and Ini are grinning. The priest looks amused, even if he isn't exactly smiling.

He's been very accommodating.

Mona was not happy about planning a big Irish wedding in three months, but Cian? He refused to compromise on the timing by even a week.

Which meant finessing with the priest and event coordinator for the Irish Catholic church in order to get the wedding on the date of choice. Shea told me finessing meant bribing in the form of financing a new outreach program the priest has been wanting to implement for the last few years.

Whatever it took, I'm standing here now in a beautiful silk wedding dress with no beading or sequins to irritate my skin. The simple halter neckline and full, floor length skirt makes me feel like a princess.

Ini said I look like one. Mrs. Hart, Mona, Shea and even Máire, who I just met this week, agreed. All of them insisted on being there while I got ready. Ini did my hair. Shea did my makeup. Mona and Mrs. Hart gave lots of advice.

They all understood that I didn't want strangers touching me. Even with Ini and Shea, I was glad both opted for a simplified, elegant approach so they fussed with me the least amount of time necessary.

It was all worth it though, to be here, ready to speak the vows aloud Cian and I have already made with our bodies. The service is long, but when it comes time to speak our promises, the only person who registers is Cian.

I look directly into his beautiful blue eyes. "You will always be my person. I will love you every day of my life and try to be the best person I can for our family. When we have children, I promise to be a loving and involved mom even if I can't do the big group things."

His gaze flares with joy when I mention children. Yes, his plan to practice with Dot worked and I'm not so afraid now. Elliott and Connor have shown me that being a good parent doesn't look the same for everyone. And Mona thinks I'll be a fantastic mom. She said so. The woman can't wait to be a grandmother.

But most importantly, I want to bring a person into this world that is a little part of Cian and a little part of me and a lot themself.

Cian kisses both of my hands before saying, "I promise to always love you, to always be your person and to be grateful every day that you are mine. I will keep you..." He swallows like he's overcome with emotion. "And our children safe. I am who and what I am, but I will be the best version of that man for you."

I hear a sob and know Mona is crying. She's so happy Cian loves me and that I love him. She told me she was scared at first of his obsessiveness, but that now she knows I was made exactly to fit with him.

She's going to be an amazing mother-in-law. Maybe raising Cian gave her special insight, but she never pushes me to be like everyone else.

The word *normal* is not allowed in her home.

She and Mrs. Hart sit in the front row together. Since Ini, Mrs. Hart and Minx are the only people I put on the guest list, the church is not separated in *his* and *her* sides.

All of them cheer when Cian and I kiss for the first time as a married couple. Then he sweeps me up into his arms and carries me out of the church to his armored SUV.

He asked if I wanted a limo, but I said no. I'm used to the SUV. It feels familiar and there's enough going on today that doesn't.

When we get inside, I'm happy to see that Tommy is driving and Eoin is in the front passenger seat. Arlo is part of the detail behind us. And there are three guards I got to know in Spain in the detail in front.

Cian will always make sure I am safe. Even on our Wedding Day.

He takes my hand as the cavalcade starts forward. "Hello, Mrs. Doyle."

I grin. "Hello, Mr. Doyle."

"So, kids?"

I nod. "I want to wait a year, but then, yes. Until then, we'll have to rely on my IUD."

I wasn't sure about having something in my body and my research revealed that some women find the devices painful, but I wanted to try. Because I want to go without condoms, and I know Cian does too.

I don't feel it at all though.

"You are on birth control?" he asks in a voice that makes me shiver.

"I wanted our Wedding Night to be special."

"It would have been special regardless."

"You always say the right thing."

"Only for you."

"I wish we could skip the reception."

"So do I," he says with sensual promise.

We can't though and it turns out much better than I expect. Cian forgoes the reception line and Mona supports him in doing it. No one, except our closest family and friends, are allowed to get within two feet of me. Which makes the big crowd much more tolerable.

We leave after our dance. There is no cake cutting because we opted to have petit fours rather than a multi-tiered cake.

The trip back to our apartment is rife with sexual tension. Neither of us so much as brushes a fingertip against the other's hand. We vibrate with anticipation.

Our first time together without a condom.

Oh, gosh, I want it.

Tomorrow, we will fly on Cian's private jet to a private island in the Mediterranean owned by his friend Mr. Drakos. We'll spend a week by ourselves, celebrating our marriage.

But tonight?

We are going to make love without any barriers between us.

CIAN

I want to fuck my wife so bad. I can't even touch her on the drive back to the apartment. Or I will end up throwing up her skirts and taking her on the back seat.

I crave her all the time, but knowing I can put my bare cock into her tight pussy has me rock hard and aching. Damn it.

When we get to the parking garage, Tommy parks by the elevators and I force myself to wait for the security detail to clear the area before throwing open my door. I practically run around the car to yank open Anna's. She's already got her seatbelt off. I lift her out and rush to the elevator.

She leans into me and inhales like she does and it sends need zinging straight to my dick.

We're barely inside the apartment before I drop her to her feet, spin her to face away from me and slide my hands inside the halter bodice of her dress, cupping her luscious tits.

"This is how we started," she gasps. "You touching me here."

"No, *mo chroí*, we started with me seeing you sitting in a chair in human resources. I knew you were mine the minute your pretty violet eyes met mine."

"Love at first sight?" she teases even as her breathing goes choppy.

I'm playing with her nipples and she loves that. I've brought her to climax just by playing with them, but not tonight. Tonight, she's coming on my cock.

"Love? I didn't think so, but possession? Yes. I knew you belonged to me."

And I show her what that means, like I have a hundred times before. But this time, she's my wife and I'm her husband.

Fuck.

We undress as we make our way to the bedroom. We're both naked when I throw her onto the bed and jump after her.

She laughs and the sound fills me with something I've only ever known with her. Joy.

I taste her body, like it's the first time. She moans and writhes under me, touching whatever part of me she can reach as I shift around for the best angle to get my mouth on her.

When she's gasping and begging for me to come inside her, I move down her body so I can put my mouth where she wants it most. On her delicious, wet pussy.

She tastes like everything I've ever wanted and what I never thought I would have. Home. Love. Sweet submission.

As soon as I suckle her clit through her first orgasm, I surge up her body and press my cock against her soaked entrance. Silky and wet, I slide inside easily.

Our eyes meet and hers are dark with emotion. Love. Lust. Happiness. Anticipation.

"You are mine," I shout as I take her body with one long, hard thrust.

"Yours," she cries back to me and then she grabs my arms, her nails digging in. "And you are mine."

"Yours," I vow.

I'm not going to last long. Her soft channel squeezes me too tight. So, I rub her sensitized and swollen clit with my thumb.

We come together, my cum pulsing inside her for the first time. It's fucking profound.

I never come in her mouth because when she sucks me I come on her tits. This? It's the claiming I've needed every fucking day since the first time.

She is mine. And in a year, her belly is going to swell with my baby.

Our baby. Our family.

Born of a love I didn't think I was capable of feeling.

But with Anna? Anything is possible.

"It feels special," she says, tears tracking down her temples.

"Every time with you is special, but now your pussy is marked inside by me just like I've marked you with my cum on your beautiful, perfect tits so many times."

"Yes," she breathes and just like that, her eyes go unfocused and my sweet, sweet girl's mind is off.

But she's still here with me and her body responds when I start moving again.

It's going to be a long night, starting forever.

THE END

ABOUT THE AUTHOR

With more than 10 million copies of her books in print worldwide, award winning and internationally bestselling author, Lucy Monroe, has published over 85 books and had her stories translated for sale all over the world. While her latest series is mafia romance, written as an indie author, all of Lucy's books are passionate, deeply emotional and adhere to the concept that love wins. Even if that victory isn't an easy one.

Want to talk about the characters, read snippets of Lucy's WIPs before anyone else, and chat with other readers who love Lucy's books? Join her FB Group .

FOLLOW LUCY ON SOCIAL MEDIA
BookBub: Lucy Monroe
goodreads: Lucy Monroe
Facebook: LucyMonroe.Romance
TikTok: lucymonroeauthor
Instagram: lucymonroeromance
Pinterest: lucymonroebooks
YouTube: @LucyMonroeBooks
Threads: lucymonroeromance
Lucy's website: www.lucymonroe.com

ALSO BY LUCY MONROE

THE REAL DEAL
WILD HEAT (Connected to Hot Alaska Nights - Not a Billionaire)
HOT ALASKA NIGHTS
3 Brides for 3 Bad Boys Trilogy
RAND, COLTON & CARTER

Harlequin Presents
THE GREEK'S ULTIMATUM
THE ITALIAN'S SUITABLE WIFE
THE BILLIONAIRE'S PREGNANT MISTRESS
THE SHEIKH'S BARTERED BRIDE
THE GREEK'S INNOCENT VIRGIN
BLACKMAILED INTO MARRIAGE
THE GREEK'S CHRISTMAS BABY
WEDDING VOW OF REVENGE
THE PRINCE'S VIRGIN WIFE
HIS ROYAL LOVE-CHILD
THE SCORSOLINI MARRIAGE BARGAIN
THE PLAYBOY'S SEDUCTION
PREGNANCY OF PASSION
THE SICILIAN'S MARRIAGE ARRANGEMENT
BOUGHT: THE GREEK'S BRIDE
TAKEN: THE SPANIARD'S VIRGIN
HOT DESERT NIGHTS
THE RANCHER'S RULES
FORBIDDEN: THE BILLIONAIRE'S VIRGIN PRINCESS
HOUSEKEEPER TO THE MILLIONAIRE
HIRED: THE SHEIKH'S SECRETARY MISTRESS
VALENTINO'S LOVE-CHILD
THE LATIN LOVER 2-IN-1 HARLEQUIN PRESENTS
(WITH THE GREEK TYCOON'S INHERITED BRIDE)
THE SHY BRIDE
THE GREEK'S PREGNANT LOVER
FOR DUTY'S SAKE

HEART OF A DESERT WARRIOR
NOT JUST THE GREEK'S WIFE
SCORSOLINI BABY SCANDAL
ONE NIGHT HEIR
PRINCE OF SECRETS
MILLION DOLLAR CHRISTMAS PROPOSAL
SHEIKH'S SCANDAL
AN HEIRESS FOR HIS EMPIRE
A VIRGIN FOR HIS PRIZE
2017 CHRISTMAS CODA: The Greek Tycoons
KOSTA'S CONVENIENT BRIDE
THE SPANIARD'S PLEASURABLE VENGEANCE
AFTER THE BILLIONAIRE'S WEDDING VOWS
QUEEN BY ROYAL APPOINTMENT
HIS MAJESTY'S HIDDEN HEIR
THE COST OF THEIR ROYAL FLING

Anthologies & Novellas
SILVER BELLA
DELICIOUS: Moon Magnetism
by Lori Foster, et. al.
HE'S THE ONE: Seducing Tabby
by Linda Lael Miller, et. al.
THE POWER OF LOVE: No Angel
by Lori Foster, et. al.
BODYGUARDS IN BED:
Who's Been Sleeping in my Brother's Bed?
by Lucy Monroe et. al.

Historical Romance
ANNABELLE'S COURTSHIP
The Langley Family Trilogy
TOUCH ME, TEMPT ME & TAKE ME
MASQUERADE IN EGYPT

Paranormal Romance
Children of the Moon Novels
MOON AWAKENING
MOON CRAVING
MOON BURNING
DRAGON'S MOON
ENTHRALLED anthology: Ecstasy Under the Moon
WARRIOR'S MOON
VIKING'S MOON
DESERT MOON
HIGHLANDER'S MOON
Montana Wolves
COME MOONRISE
MONTANA MOON

Made in the USA
Monee, IL
04 December 2024

72347272R00173